Praise for Florida Straits:

'... as crisp and posturing as a fresh hundred-dollar bill. Sooner or later you gotta do yourself a favour. You gotta read this book.'

MIAMI HERALD

'Sharp and funny ... a comic suspense novel where the comic and suspenseful are beautifully merged ... funky, funny characters that will have you hooked on the whole ride.'

WASHINGTON POST

'Funny, elegantly written, and hip ... a nifty new crime novel.'

LOS ANGELES TIMES

'Packed with bad guys in shiny blue suits and good guys in pink bikini briefs ... *Florida Straits* is too wondafull fa woids.'

PEOPLE MAGAZINE

Laurence Shames divides his time between homes in Key West, Florida, and Shelter Island, New York

LAURENCE SHAMES

SCAVENGER REEF

PAN BOOKS

First published 1994 by Simon & Schuster Inc.

First published in Great Britain 1995 by Pan Books
an imprint of Macmillan General Books
25 Eccleston Place, London SW1W 9NF
and Basingstoke

Associated companies throughout the world

ISBN 0 330 33150 7

1 3 5 7 9 8 6 4 2

A CIP catalogue record for this book is available from
the British Library

Typeset by CentraCet Limited, Cambridge
Printed and bound in Great Britain by
Cox & Wyman Ltd, Reading, Berkshire

ACKNOWLEDGMENTS

Hearty thanks to my editor, Chuck Adams, and my agent, Stuart Krichevsky, for doing much of the thinking and most of the worrying, while telling me just to keep writing and having fun. With them on my side, I did.

And a hug to Edie, who knows what it's really all about.

For Marilyn with love.
KNOCK WOOD – HOW DID I GET SO LUCKY?

PART ONE

CHAPTER ONE

'FUNERALS WORK BEST in the rain,' said Robert Natchez.

'It isn't a funeral,' said Ray Yates. 'It's a memorial service.' Yates licked another swath of salt from the rim of his glass and sucked on his tequila. He was slightly drunk, and increasingly fascinated by the wet circles his iced glass left on the varnished table at Raul's. Natchez ignored him.

'The gray sky, the black umbrellas – humble separate shelters against the damp—'

'You're a pompous pain in the ass,' said Yates.

'Separate shelters,' Natchez murmured. 'I like that.'

'It stinks,' Yates told him. He wiped his moist hand on the front of his shirt. The shirt had a pattern of washed-out palm fronds and small flamingoes with the pink faded from their plumage.

'Then too,' Natchez went on, 'there's the way the rain softens the ground, the way the earth yields, squishes underfoot. Gentle or horrifying? Embracing the dead body, or pulling it down like—'

'There is no body.' Yates slurped the last of his drink and gestured for another round. 'And it isn't gonna rain.

3

And people don't get buried here. They get filed, like in drawers. And you're a morbid sonofabitch.'

They waited for their cocktails. It was mid-April in Key West, the night air was thick and smelled of old seaweed and dry shells. On the open roof of the old cafe, the trellised bougainvillea had darkened to a lewd and tired brownish pink, the petals were thin and brittle as crepe paper. Robert Natchez was tall, lean, and totally dressed in black. It was not a token of mourning, it was just the way he dressed.

'I'm sad,' he suddenly announced. He sounded confused by an emotion that could be simply told.

'Augie shouldn't have died,' said Ray Yates. 'He was better than any of us, less full of shit, and he shouldn't have died.'

The drinks arrived, the waiter wiped away the last round's rings of dampness. Overhead, a landing plane clattered past, bringing more of Augie Silver's many friends to say goodbye.

'He should never have stopped painting,' said Claire Steiger, towel-drying her curly hair. 'I pleaded with him not to stop.'

Her husband nestled deeper into the hotel bathrobe and sipped champagne. 'Because some mysterious intuition told you something terrible would happen three years after?' He fingered the fruit plate provided with the suite at the Flagler House, and briefly wondered why hotel mangoes were never ripe, hotel strawberries never red. 'Or because his work was keeping the gallery afloat?'

4

Claire Steiger had soft brown eyes that kept their tender look no matter what she said. 'The gallery's doing just fine, Kip. You're the one who's bankrupt, remember?'

It had been a lousy trip down from New York. A chilly yellow mist kept them on the La Guardia runway for forty minutes, which made them miss their connection in Miami, and they'd sat in the cramped and porous commuter terminal for two hours, eating jet exhaust and nursing grievances. Claire had spent a long time in the bath, and her skin still felt like an airport.

'Of course,' said Kip Cunningham, 'the canvases are worth a great deal more now that—'

'Kip, shut up. Don't be hateful.'

'Hateful?' he echoed. It was a word that seemed to crop up often in the months since his overextended real estate company had collapsed under the weight of its debts, its velvety stationery, and its pretensions to empire. Lawyers were hateful. Judges were hateful. It was hateful that he could no longer pay his University Club dues out of company funds, hateful that creditors held liens against his horses. 'Since when is it hateful to be candid?' he said. 'You're in a business like any other, kiddo. Supply and demand. Artist dies, no more supply. Ever. Prices—'

'You're gonna lecture me about capitalism, Kip? Lecture me about Chapter Eleven.'

He poured more champagne and went to the window. Below, the coconut palms were dead still and threw heavy moonshadows across the sand. The calm water of the Florida Straits gleamed with just a hint of goldish green. 'Of course,' the husband went on, his back to his wife, 'how can you be rational about art if you're in love with the artist?'

'Everyone was in love with Augie. That was Augie.'

Kip turned. He was a blandly handsome man, smooth-skinned and even-featured, and he now pulled back his thin lips to show a set of perfect teeth. 'Strange, though, that he could have had the gallery owner – all it would have taken was a wink, the raise of an eyebrow – and he ran off instead with the assistant . . . Of course, she was younger. Slimmer. Better-bred, some might say.'

Claire Steiger kept right on toweling her hair. 'Darling,' she said, 'you're pathetic enough to be jealous of a dead man. Am I supposed to be jealous of a live widow?'

'Lemme tell ya somethin' about Augie Silver,' said Jimmy Gibbs.

He was sitting at the Clove Hitch bar, dockside at City Marina, and tucked between his spread-out elbows was a shot of Jack Daniel's and a bottle of Bud. He was speaking in the general direction of Hogfish Mike Curran, the proprietor, but he wanted to talk and he didn't much care who if anyone was listening.

'Augie Silver was the best damn sailor I ever saw. Always calm. A natural. The wind talked to him. The seas like made a road to let him through. Currents, he always managed it so they helped him. That boat a his – thirty-seven feet, singlehanded he sailed it nimble as a dinghy . . . What happened t'Augie, it coulda happened t'anyone. It was a freak. Fuckin' world is all fucked up. Fuckin' weather, ya can't count on it no more. Waterspout in January. Who ever heard of a fuckin' waterspout in January?'

'Happens,' said Hogfish Mike. 'Not often, but it happens.'

Gibbs snorted disapproval, then nipped into his shot and his beer. He wore his salt-and-pepper hair pulled tightly back in a little pony-tail, and after several boilermakers his scalp felt pinched. He reached up and loosened the elastic band. A pelican jumped clumsily from a nearby piling and splashed into the shallow water of Garrison Bight.

'Vicious, those waterspouts,' Hogfish Mike went on. He crossed his ropy forearms and almost smiled. The ready violence of the natural world was for him a kind of confirmation. 'Funnel comes down. Black as sin, you can almost see it spinning. Holy shit – do ya zig or zag? If it catches ya, you're fucked. Spout digs a hole innee ocean, makes a whirlpool that churns like a goddamn Maytag. Sucks fish right outta the water, twirls boats around till they rip apart or crash up onna reef. Breaks off masts like fuckin' bread-sticks. I hate to think what would happen to a man in one of those. He'd get yanked to pieces, busted up like the dummy without the seat belt on.'

Hogfish paused and finally noticed that his description was causing pain. He leaned across the bar toward Jimmy Gibbs and dropped his voice to a conspiratorial whisper. 'Jimmy, hey, it's not like the guy was your bubba. He was a Yankee. Nice house. Big boat. OK, he paid you fair to do the grunt work. Maybe he bought you a drink now and then. But come on—'

'Augie wasn't like the others,' said Jimmy Gibbs, and there was something in his tone that made Hogfish Mike back off. 'He treated a person like a person. Lemme get another round.'

'Got cash, Jimmy? No tabs here, you know the rules.'

Gibbs looked sadly down at his shot glass with nothing at the bottom but an amber stain. Then he considered his beer and sloshed around the last lukewarm pull. A seagull screamed nearby. 'Come on, Hogfish, we known each other a lotta years.'

'That's the problem, Jimmy,' said Hogfish Mike. 'That's the problem.'

'You like'a heah?' said Reuben the Cuban, suspending a huge vase of lilies and orchids above the center of a long split-willow table.

Nina Alonzo-Silver stood hands on hips in the middle of her living room and weighed the arrangement with her eyes. 'Too heavy there,' she said. 'Try it over by the lamp.'

The housekeeper moved the flowers. He was a slight, wiry young man with the surprising yellowish pallor of certain Key West Cubans; he moved in a low-slung whisper like a cat or a Japanese woman, and he nearly disappeared behind the thick stems of the lilies. 'Oba heah?' he said.

The widow nodded. Then she cast an appraising glance at the buffet dishes and glasses already arrayed on the sideboard, and at her dead husband's paintings beautifully hung and immaculately lit on every wall. Through the French doors at the rear of the house, a soft blue gleam wafted up from the lights in the pool. In a big enameled cage near the door, a twitchy green parrot looked on. The widow squared a picture frame that had been perhaps a quarter-inch off-true. Then she tried to smile.

'You see, Reuben,' she said. 'It's just like getting ready for an opening.'

'Art sucks,' said the parrot. 'Johnnie Walker.' The sound was metallic and wildly abrupt, scratchy as the sand in the bird's idiot throat.

'*Tranquillo*, Fred,' said Reuben the Cuban.

'Cutty Sark. Where's Augie?' the parrot responded, and the widow started to cry. She made no sound. Her shoulders hunched slightly and flat streaks of wet almost instantly appeared under her slate-gray eyes.

'Noon tomorrow,' she said.

Reuben didn't understand exactly what she meant. He stood there silent, hoping to be able to help.

'Service at ten,' she said, her voice soft but without a quaver. 'No rabbi. No minister. No God. No heaven. The way Augie would have wanted. Just some stories, some laughing, some crying, some wine. A lot of wine. Then noon.'

'Noon what?' asked Reuben.

The widow tried to smile again and the tear streaks took a sudden turn around the changed contours of her face. 'Noon tomorrow. The official unofficial time to give up hope.'

CHAPTER TWO

'AUGIE SILVER,' intoned his best friend, Clayton Phipps, once a promising playwright, now for many years the publisher, editor, and sole contributor to a quaint little newsletter called *Best Revenge*. 'Augie Silver.'

Phipps paused, leaning against a makeshift lectern set up at the deep end of the dead man's pool. He let the syllables hang in the bright, clear morning air, hoping to evoke the entire miracle and tragedy of a human being through the thin yet potent fact of his name. Much underrated, the magic of a name. It was the ultimate container, the profoundest and most elegant summing-up of the passions, capacities, follies, likes and dislikes, the fears, quests, and eccentricities that made one person distinguishable from all others.

'Augie Silver.' Phipps chanted it a third time, and under a poinciana tree, very near the table with the liquor, Ray Yates elbowed Robert Natchez in the ribs.

'Only guy I know who's a more pompous asshole than you are.'

Natchez frowned his disapproval and tugged at the cuffs of another black shirt. Reuben the Cuban slunk silently among the guests, content in the belief that in pouring coffee and delivering mimosas he was paying homage to the dead husband and bringing comfort to the widow.

Perhaps a hundred fifty people had come together to honor Augie Silver's memory, and they reflected the breadth and oddness of the painter's personal democracy. The art establishment, of course, was represented. There was an editor from *Picture Plane*, a publication that had once dubbed the deceased 'a minor yet searing talent, achingly pure and infuriatingly unambitious.' There was the famously snide yet annoyingly accurate critic Peter Brandenburg, who years before had described Silver as 'a lavishly gifted under-achiever who is gaining renown less for the canvases he paints than for those we hope he'll paint.' There were reviewers from the newsmagazines and from papers in New York, Chicago, and Washington. There was even a gallery owner from Paris who happened to be vacationing in South Beach.

But when, ten years before, Augie Silver had moved to Key West from Manhattan, it was with the clear intention of escaping the hothouse atmosphere of the art capitals, broadening his circle beyond the clutch of those who could do favors and those who wanted favors done. To be sure, the Key West artsy set had gravitated to him: the writers who didn't write, the sculptors who didn't sculpt, the trust-funders kept just shy of suicidal self-loathing by the mercifully untested belief that they were in some sense creative. They could be quite amusing, these constipated, deluded bohemians and hangers-on: Their vision had nowhere to go except into what

11

they said and how they lived, and their frustrations often gave rise to piquant comments on human nature and the state of the world.

Still, it was not the Ray Yateses and Bob Natchezes who had given the greatest zest to Augie Silver's last years. It was the people who were strangers to poetry, innocent of art. It was the wharf rats like Jimmy Gibbs, half of whom had done jail time. It was the fishing captains who at first took Augie out as one more pain-in-the-ass know-nothing client, then later invited him as a soothing companion. It was the old Cubans who poled out in the back country and showed him how to dig a sponge. They too were represented at Augie's corpseless send-off. They milled shyly along the periphery, these outsiders, bashful of the canapes, made nervous by the thinness of the glassware. They wanted to pay their respects and get the hell out of this elegant backyard, but Clayton Phipps was not about to race through his moment of high praise for his friend and spotlight for himself.

'Augie Silver was the most generous man I ever knew,' said the eulogist. 'Ya know, some people *decide* to be generous. It *occurs* to them to give you something. Augie wasn't like that. He didn't decide. It just happened. It was his nature. Gifts flowed from him. He was a source, a well. Life burned in him, and he could not help but give back warmth.'

Phipps looked toward the shady place where Nina Silver was sitting, all alone. A hundred people had greeted her, many had embraced her, and yet there had remained a dread and stubborn space around her, a cuticle of passionate blankness that she would not allow to be moved aside or filled.

'Who among us,' he went on, 'does not have something of Augie's? Some remembered story, some flash of insight or shred of his wise-ass wisdom. Some taste or preference we learned from him. A sweater he gave you because you said you liked the color. A jacket he put around your shoulders because you were cold and he was not. A tool he lent and promptly forgot about, a book he thought you might like . . .'

Around the dead man's yard and through the open doors of his house, the mourners shifted from foot to foot, remembered, smiled privately, and glanced at each other, secretly wondering who'd gotten the sweaters, the jackets . . .

'And the paintings,' Clayton Phipps resumed. 'My God, the paintings! The man gave them away like they were so much scratch paper. His life's work, his livelihood, his legacy. Where did he find the strength and the humor that enabled him to take it all so lightly? "Here," he'd say, about a canvas that had taken him a month. "You like it? Put it in your house." "Here," he'd say with this amazing casualness. "This little one? Sell it if you can – get your boat fixed." "Here, put this over your desk for luck." "Here, put this in your kid's room." How many beautiful and precious paintings did Augie Silver give away? Does anybody even know?'

The question rose up over the swimming pool and hovered there. Claire Steiger, the dead man's agent, read her bankrupt husband's face and despised him for the bloodless calculations she knew were going on behind it.

And she wondered if it showed in her own expression that she could not help but do some calculating too.

By 1 P.M. the speeches were over, the ice cubes were melted, the crowd had thinned, and Nina Silver had barely noticed that her promised deadline of hope had come and gone and nothing whatever had changed in her heart. She bid farewell to the dispersing guests, accepted their sincere and irrelevant sympathies, nodded to all the well-meant pledges to stay close, to see more of one another. She yearned for everyone to be gone and dreaded the moment when the house would once again be empty. Emptier than before, with no event to plan, no exquisitely small details – irises or lilies? Champagne or Chardonnay? – to rivet her attention. She straightened a picture frame that a departing friend had shouldered awry, then stared at the level edge to steady herself, the way a seasick man searches for sanity in a clear horizon.

Out in the garden, a few men whose nature it was to be the last to leave were honoring Augie the way the men of Athens honored the martyred Socrates, by talking and drinking, drinking and arguing.

'Here's the part I still don't get,' Ray Yates said, slipping into the mock-ingenuous interviewer's tone he used in his radio show. He was sitting on a white wrought-iron chair and his inappropriately cheery shirt was darkened here and there with moisture. Yates was thickly built, squat and hairy, the type that's always sweaty. It didn't help that there was no ice left for his rum. 'Guy's got this great career. A New York gallery

14

that loves him. He can sell whatever he paints, prices are better all the time . . . Then he just stops working. Why?'

Clayton Phipps sipped his warmish Sancerre and noted how the flinty taste turned cactusy as the wine approached body temperature. He hooked a thumb through one of his suspenders and slid it to a fresh place on his shoulder. 'Ray,' he said, 'this might be tough for you to grasp, but it had to do with standards. I remember a dinner I had with Augie, about five years ago. We were drinking a Lynch Bages 'seventy-eight, rather young but very concen—'

'Who gives a shit what you were drinking?' interjected Robert Natchez.

Phipps glared at him from under his heavy brows. 'It speaks of the quality of the moment, Natch. Isn't that what you poets supposedly care about? Anyway, we were talking about standards. About the difference between talent and genius. Between skilled painting and great painting. Augie had no fake modesty – we all know that. He knew he had talent. He knew he had skill. He doubted he had genius. And he was coming to feel that if he didn't have genius, then what was the point—'

'The point,' said Ray Yates, 'was that there were all these people who would buy his stuff.'

Phipps shook his head, glanced upward through the feathery leaves of the poinciana tree. 'No offense, Ray. You're a slut.'

'Just because I think if a guy's making a good living—'

'Where's your judgment?' Phipps interrupted. 'Where's your imagination? You believe something's good just because there's some schmuck out there who'll pay for it?'

'Usually it's just the opposite,' put in Robert Natchez. 'If something's commercial—'

Phipps wheeled toward him with a vehemence that surprised all three of them. 'And that's bullshit too. Ray's a slut, you're an undergraduate. You're both children, for chrissake. Augie was a realist. He used his skill to buy himself the life he wanted. Period. No high-flown crap about art, no sucking up to the marketplace. He had a skill, he used it.'

Phipps paused, and noticed rather suddenly that he was smashed. Grief, heat, alcohol, and candor: The blend was making him dizzy, and the shade of the poinciana offered no coolness but seemed rather to hold congealed sunshine that pressed directly on his bald and throbbing head. He glanced with a queasy blend of affection and despising at Natchez and Yates; he dimly wondered if they realized that when he compared people unfavorably to Augie, he was talking first and foremost of himself. It was probably for the best that he was prevented from rambling on by the sudden appearance of Nina Silver.

She'd come through the French doors, silently skirted the pool, and stood before them; in her drained look there was something very touching but uncomfortably intimate, an exposure like the sudden scrubbing off of makeup, like a privileged glimpse of a sleeping face on a pillow. Her gray eyes were weary, the slight smile she managed held no joy but only a tired tenderness. The widow had decided against wearing black, and her sea-green linen suit was slightly wilted. Only her hair

16

remained perfect. Short, thick, raven, it framed her face and tucked under her jawline the way an acorn top hugs the smooth curve of the acorn. She put one hand on Ray Yates's shoulder, the other on Bob Natchez's.

'Gents,' she said, 'I have to go lie down. You'll help yourselves to whatever you want?'

It was an innocent offer but perhaps an injudicious one from a woman newly alone. Nina managed something like a smile, then turned, and had any of the men been watching the others' eyes instead of her retreating form, he might perhaps have noticed a glimmer of something beyond mere disinterested concern for the widow of their fallen friend.

CHAPTER THREE

'THAT ISN'T HOW it's done,' Claire Steiger said.

'How many paintings do we still have?' pressed her husband.

'We?' She spit out the word as if it were a rotten piece of fruit and went back to her magazine. The northbound plane was somewhere off Cape Hatteras, and in the first-class cabin coffee was being offered with petit fours, little pink squares whose icing stuck to the ribbed paper of their nests.

'Look, there's a psychological moment to these things,' said Kip Cunningham. 'How long does a dead artist stay fashionable? A few months maybe? While he's still news, while he's still being talked about at dinner parties. After that he's just one more dead painter. Last year's tragedy. Who cares?'

Exasperated, Claire Steiger grabbed a petit four and ate half of it before she realized what she was doing. More annoyed than before, she put the other half back into its paper cup and squashed it past all temptation. Raspberry jam oozed out on her thumb. 'Kip,' she said, 'now you're explaining to me the mental quirks of art buyers?'

'I'm only saying—'

'You're only saying things you would have heard a hundred times if you listened when I talked.'

'This again, Claire?'

'Yeah, Kip, this again. Because now you can't afford to ignore me. Now you can't act like your business is the be-all end-all, and mine's a little hobby, good for some social cachet, nice for getting us invited . . .'

The husband rolled his head against the back of the leather seat and entertained the unholy wish that the wings would fall off the airplane, that the naked fuselage, aerodynamic as a cucumber, would plummet into the sea, settling everything with a gruesome splash no one would hear. At that moment, no price seemed too high to pay to get another human being to shut up, and without actually deciding to, Kip played a card he'd been saving for some time, one of the few cards he had left.

'Claire, we're going to lose the Sagaponack house. Are you aware of that?'

There are two best ways to hurt someone. One is through what is most feared, the other through what is most loved. Claire Steiger's mouth stayed open but sound stopped coming out. Something had slammed shut at the back of her throat, and her eyes had started instantly to burn. She loved that house, took delight from every colorless weatherbeaten board of it. It was half a block from the beach, always swollen and ripe with moisture and salt. The first porch step gave a welcoming squeak when she arrived on summer Fridays. The shutters were the most wonderful shade of grayed-out blue, and the wet light that filtered through the bedroom curtains reminded her of the radiance that came through angels' wings in seventeenth-century murals.

'There's a huge payment due the first of July,' Kip went on. 'The house is collateral against it.' His tone had become weirdly threatening, as if he had willed himself back to the good old days when he was the one foreclosing and not the one foreclosed. 'We've gotta turn some cash, Claire. A lot of cash.'

She turned away and looked out the window. It was an unrewarding view: flat tops of featureless clouds gapping here and there to reveal a blank gray ocean. 'Kip,' she said, 'you don't understand. I've spent a lot of years building a clientele, making a reputation for doing business a certain way. A dignified, discreet way, Kip. I don't do fire sales. I don't cash in on drowned artists. I don't slap paintings on the walls with price tags dangling from them. The Ars Longa Gallery has a certain image—'

'Fuck the image,' said Kip Cunningham without parting his small and perfect teeth. 'We're broke.'

Claire Steiger reached for another petit four, then regarded her outstretched hand as if it belonged to someone else, some piggish guest, and yanked it back before it had snatched the pastry. Claire was not fat, just round, put together out of circles. Her coarse curly hair haloed her head in a spherical do. Her face was round, her hips were round, her breasts were round. When she lost weight, certain dimensions flattened out and became disklike but never angular.

'It wouldn't work,' she told her husband. 'Even if I said the hell with being classy, let's go for the quick score

20

– it wouldn't work. Serious collectors don't buy that way, Kip. They're not impulsive. They wait for assurance from the critics. They're going to spend six, maybe seven figures for a canvas, they want the big auction houses' stamp of approval—'

'So why don't we sell through an auction house?'

'Then why do we have a gallery?'

'Sotheby's,' Kip Cunningham said. It sounded like a prayer. 'Don't they do a big painting sale in June?'

'The Solstice Show. Biggest of the year. But Kip, what'll it accomplish? Say we're the only ones unloading Augie Silvers. If anything, it'll drive the prices down. It'll look like we're dumping. Like we're desperate.'

'We are desperate.'

The flight attendant came by to refresh their coffee, and had the tact not to ask if everything was all right. The speaker system switched on and a voice from the flight deck informed them that those seated on the left side of the airplane could look down and see Washington, DC.

'Who gives a good goddamn?' grumbled Kip. He pushed his coffee aside and asked for a brandy. He was sipping it sullenly when his wife spoke again.

'How much we need for the July payment?' she asked.

'Two million four,' said Kip.

'And the total indebtedness?'

'Personal or corporate?'

'Corporate's not my problem.' Claire fixed her husband with her tender brown eyes. 'I'm asking how much you're in hock on things that are half mine.'

Kip blinked down at his tray table. It befuddled him

that he couldn't figure exactly when or how this toy called debt was transfigured into money he actually had to pay. 'Eight million,' he mumbled. 'A little less.'

His wife considered. 'I've got an idea. I think I can raise enough for July at least, maybe the whole nut. But it comes with a price tag, Kip. I bail you out, the Sagaponack house goes into my name and my name alone.'

Kip Cunningham had the kind of fragile handsomeness that one moment seemed polished, cocksure, and composed, and with the smallest shift could collapse into the sniveling pout of a spoiled child, a defeated brat snufflng outside a squash-court door. He glanced sideways at his wife, his mouth flat as snake lips, his eyes hard with the furtive meanness of the weak. He gave a brief laugh that was meant to be sardonic. 'So what are you saying, Claire? Are you saying you're going to divorce me?'

She flashed her tender eyes at him. 'I might.'

She reached again for a petit four and didn't stop herself this time. She bit into it, luxuriating in the rasp of grainy sugar against her teeth, the squish of yellow cake and apricot preserve against her tongue. 'It seems more possible every day.'

CHAPTER FOUR

'CLAY, DON'T,' said Nina Silver.

She gently but firmly grasped the family friend's thick wrist before his hand could slide down onto her breast, and pushed his large warm face away from her neck.

Phipps, a gentleman more or less, didn't wait for the attempted embrace to become a grovel, a grope, some unseemly echo of adolescence. He sat up straight on the settee alongside Augie Silver's blue-lit swimming pool, partly disappointed, part contrite, maybe even part relieved. 'Nina,' he said, 'I'm sorry.' In a move to recapture his dignity, he smoothed the placket of his linen shirt the way a riled bird resettles its feathers. 'Loss does strange things to people. I'm a mess.'

Augie's widow gave him a soft smile and patted him on the knee. It was a gesture of caring and acceptance, but it somehow made Phipps feel worse. Was he so ridiculous a suitor that the woman he'd just been trying to seduce would feel not the slightest threat in touching his leg? He took stock. He was fifty-eight years old. OK, not young, but only one year older than Augie. He was bald, yes, but had always been told he had a well-shaped head. He wasn't rich, but managed to live as though he was. He wasn't famous, but enjoyed many of the perks thereof. His little newsletter was highly respected by those who knew and cherished the finer things; his endorsement was coveted around the world. Clayton Phipps was acknowledged as a formidable judge of wine, a gourmet of nice discernment and enviable experience, a canny traveler who had filled ten passports with visa stamps.

All those hotel rooms, he reflected wryly, sitting next to Augie Silver's lovely widow. Overlooking the Bay of Naples, Sydney Harbour, the Tyrolean Alps. All those beautiful, romantic, complimentary suites – brass beds, marble bathtubs – he'd occupied alone. All those marvelous dinners taken at small tables in the sycophantic company of proprietors. All those tastings of legendary Bordeaux, sipped elbow to elbow with a bunch of crotchety old men in caves. Nearing the age of sixty, Clayton Phipps admitted to himself what a damnably clever job he'd done of living life for free, keeping himself unfettered, independent, sought after, and alone.

'Nina, Nina, you know what it is?' Emerging from his thoughts, Phipps didn't notice the abruptness of his voice in the night air that was perfumed with frangipani and chlorine. 'What it is I really want? I want what you and Augie had.'

'Of course you do,' the widow said softly. Loss, for her, had made everything seem simple, obvious, reduced to its essentials. People wanted love, intimacy, the sense of being mated. They wanted to feel the profound familiarity that made another person's nearness as basic as the taste of water. 'Everyone wants what Augie and I had. I want it. I want it back.'

Clayton Phipps was not an unfeeling man, not usually, but in the grip of his newly acknowledged loneliness he failed to see that the widow's pain was infinitely sharper than his own because she knew exactly what she was missing while he had only the vague awareness that something precious had eluded him all his life. 'With someone else . . .' he began. It wasn't quite a question, not quite a statement. It was off the beat and had the awkwardness of doomed pleading.

'There is no one else, Clay,' said the widow, and there was defiance in her voice. The defiance was not aimed at Clayton Phipps, but still it stung him, made him feel a flash of shaming envy and even bitterness, even spite, toward his dead friend. Why should Augie Silver be so loved?

'Come now, Nina,' he said. Phipps felt as if he'd slipped into a chasm of longing that had little to do with Nina Silver, a slippery pit in which his isolation was the only fact, and he tried to climb out of it with handholds of cynicism couched as worldliness. 'Aren't we a little old to believe in this *one right person* nonsense?'

'I don't believe in that,' said Nina. 'I think there are any number of people right for each other—'

'Well then,' Phipps cut in. His tone had turned professorial. If charm couldn't rescue the moment, maybe logic would save him. 'If there are any number—'

The widow interrupted in turn, soft but unstoppable as a train. 'Until you really fall in love with one. Then the others dim out, fade away, come to seem – I don't mean this personally, Clay – a little bit absurd.'

They sat. A scrap of breeze sent tiny ripples across the pool and lifted a wet green smell from the hedge. Inside the house, soft yellow lights gleamed against the dark wood walls. Augie's paintings loomed, unmoved in the week since the memorial. The parrot cage stood near the door; Fred was covered for the night, dreaming what visions of jungle, berries, feathers, and flight might come to a bird in sleep.

And Nina Alonzo saw Augie Silver for the first time.

It was twelve years ago. She was twenty-nine. She was sitting at her desk at the gallery on 57th Street. She heard a strange scuffing sound on the marble floor and looked up to see her future husband strolling in his meandering way, looking over first one shoulder, then the other, halfway twirling, wearing boat shoes. Boat shoes in midtown Manhattan in March. He approached her. He had on a black cashmere turtleneck, the collar askew but tucked high under the chin, and over the sweater was a light jacket of fawn-colored pigskin suede. It vaguely occurred to her that these were tiger colors, black and tan, and it registered only very dimly that everything the painter wore would feel good. His hair was thick, wavy, and almost perfect white, tinged here and there with an oddly pinkish bronze, but his skin was youthful, smooth and ruddy as an Indian's. His eyes were an electric blue, and they rested far back in sockets so deep that they suggested lighthouse beams, piercing, narrow-focused lenses that swept across his range of vision and shone with unsettling concentration on one thing at a time. And now they were fixed on Nina Alonzo. 'Hello,' he said. 'I'm Augie Silver.' Then he did something that quietly amazed her when she thought about it afterward, amazed her because it could only have been carried off with perfect confidence, perfect ease, with a manner as comfortable as his clothes. He half-sat on her desk, stretched a leg alongside the phone, the files, the exhibition catalogues. His trousers were of beefy corduroy, and some of the wales were rubbed almost smooth . . .

'Nina, are you all right?'

She flinched just slightly at the sound of Phipps's voice, and felt not gratitude but resentment for the intrusive concern that had pulled her back to the here and now. 'No,' she said after a moment, 'I'm not all right. My husband has been gone – what is it, Clay, three months now? – and he's more alive to me than anybody living. I'm not all right.'

Phipps took her hand, and neither of them could help glancing down at the suspect twining of their fingers. Twenty minutes ago, before his bizarre and meager attempt at lust, the contact would have been clean. 'Nina, is there anything I can do for you? Anything at all?'

Even in his own ears, the question sounded a shade unwholesome, and Clay Phipps understood that he had forever forfeited the privilege of being totally trusted, of being mistaken for unselfish.

The widow took her hand away. 'Don't try to be Augie, Clay. That's what you can do for me. Don't try to be the man I love.'

Later, asleep, Nina again saw Augie Silver.

She saw him often in dreams, and savored these

meetings as if they were deliciously forbidden trysts. They were always different and always the same, these dreams, full of the sore joy of reunion which then melted into a growing but never serene acceptance that the reunion was unreal.

This time Nina saw Augie while she was sitting in the kitchen drinking a mug of coffee. The front door opened and there he was. He hadn't shaved, his face gleamed with a steely stubble, and his throat was very tan beneath the collar of his shirt. 'Augie,' she said. She held her mug in front of her, smelling the fragrant steam and embracing the miracle of her husband coming back.

'Coffee?' he said, and walked through the living room toward the counter. She glanced at the coffee maker and noticed that the red brew light was flickering, blinking like a buoy at sea. She watched Augie walk, and though his walk was casual, shuffling as always, he became more insubstantial with each step, his form flattening, his feet in less secure contact with the floor, and the sleeping Nina felt him slipping away yet again. With the dreamer's comforting illusion that she could choose, she wrestled with the choice of waking up to dream-capture him before he had vanished, or staying asleep and willing him not to fade, willing him to explain but most of all to keep existing. 'Just a cup of coffee,' she said in the dream, and in her empty bedroom the words came out only as a soft mumble that woke her up. She opened her eyes, lifted onto her elbows for just a moment, and tried to memorize this most recent visit with her husband. He'd looked so handsome coming through the door.

CHAPTER FIVE

JIMMY GIBBS pushed the point of his knife into the anus of a six-pound mutton snapper and slit its belly to the arc of bone beneath its jaw. Absently, he felt the fish deflate, then reached into the body cavity and plucked out the guts. Tubes and membranes, red nodes and green sacs came away in his hand, and he flung them into the shallow water shimmering with fish oil. It was a measure of Jimmy Gibbs's mood, where he flung the guts. When he was happy, feeling benign, he tossed them in the air so the wheeling gulls could snag the unspeakable morsels from the sky. When he was feeling foul, he threw the slimy viscera into Garrison Bight and made the squawking, miserable scavengers dunk for them.

Today Jimmy Gibbs was feeling especially foul. His back hurt. His hands were stiff, his fingers crosshatched with tiny cuts from spiny fish fins, edges of scales, other people's hooks. He had complaining knees, a swollen liver, a weakening bladder, and he was too damn old to be a mate on someone else's boat. Fifty-two, and a beat-up fifty-two at that. Living in a trailer; driving an ancient pickup that sifted rust every time he closed the door; and having something under nine hundred dollars of cash

29

money in the bank. He yanked the innards out of another fish and swept them disgustedly off his cleaning table. They left behind a bloody and slightly iridescent smear.

'Whole or fillet?' Gibbs said to the tourist who, with a great deal of help and plenty of coaching, had managed to catch some fish. The tourist just stood there blankly. Was it too fucking difficult a question? Was it unthinkable that the tourist, God forbid, might sometime have to eat something with a bone in it? It was five o'clock, the sun was still hot, and Jimmy Gibbs had two more buckets of dead fish to clean.

'Fillet,' the tourist said at last; and with more force than was required, Gibbs slashed the glistening flesh away from the pliant backbones. The tourist reached a clean hand into a clean pocket and came up with a dollar. He took his fish fillets in a plastic bag and dropped the bill onto the cleaning table, where it soaked up some slime. It was breezy on the dock but the dollar didn't blow away because fish stuff was gluing it to the plywood.

Gibbs looked down at the bill. What the fuck was a dollar? Two-thirds of a beer. Three quarts of gas. One three-hundredth of his rent. Nothing that would last the evening. Gibbs's hairline itched. He raked his forearm across it, then took a moment to look up and down the dock at the Key West charter fleet. There were maybe thirty boats that cost an average, say, of eighty thousand bucks apiece. Fuck had all that money come from? Some of it, Gibbs knew, was drug money. Well, OK, people would do what they had to do, and anyone who thought otherwise was an idiot. Some of it had come from land that the old families, the real Conchs, sold off to developers for what seemed at first vast sums then always turned out to be a lousy deal, a deal that ate the soul. Then of course there were the guys who acted like big shots but were really hired help, the paid captains with the silent partners in Dallas, Atlanta, or New York. They'd use the boat a week or two, these money guys, and take most of the profits the rest of the time. They liked the idea of being able to say they had a fishing boat in Key West. *My* boat. *My* captain. *My* crew. It gave them a hard-on, they could run around all thinking they were little Hemingways.

Gibbs reached into a bucket, grabbed a grouper by the tail, slapped it onto the cleaning table, and stabbed and slashed it open. He'd almost bought a boat once, Jimmy had. It was during the recession that most people hardly remembered, '81-'82, when business stank, no one was making money, and the market was flooded with bargains. There was an old Bertram, thirty-one feet, twin gas inboards, worth a good forty grand and going begging at twenty-seven. Back then, Jimmy Gibbs had five thousand dollars put away, the proceeds of some discreet transporting of bales of marijuana. He'd put on a fresh blue shirt and jeans with a crease and gone to the bank to borrow the rest.

The banker was a realist. 'Lotta guys, Jimmy, they think a charter boat's a money machine, think once ya got the boat, everything is easy. Not true. Things go wrong. There's a lousy season. Ya get sick. Someone breaks a leg and sues. A lotta guys can't cut it. And we take the boats back, Jimmy. Don't think for a second we don't. It's embarrassing, it makes you crazy mad, and you can't ever borrow money again. You sure ya wanna try?'

Gibbs yanked the guts out of the grouper, flicked off a loop of purplish intestine that was clinging to his finger. He had been sure he wanted the loan, until he came to the part of the application that asked if he'd ever been convicted of a felony. 'I gotta answer this?' he'd asked.

The banker had folded his hands, dropped his voice, and put on an expression that was a mixture of concern and grisly curiosity. 'Jimmy, we're a local bank. You're a local guy from a local family. Up to a point, we're very understanding . . . What you did, how bad was it?'

Gibbs slid the hollowed grouper to the edge of the cleaning table and plunged into the bucket for a yellowtail. It had already begun to curl and grow rigid, he had to flatten it with one hand while puncturing its belly. Jimmy Gibbs didn't go around telling people what he'd done as a younger man with a vicious temper and a stock of grievances close-packed as a seaman's trunk. He'd told the banker he'd finish the application at home. Then he'd left, crumpled up the paper in the parking lot, dropped it in the trash, gone out and gotten shitface drunk, and that was as close as he'd come to owning a boat. Now he reached into the yellowtail and felt its gelatinous organs turn to a warm paste between his fingers.

'Whole or fillet?' he said to the tourist who owned the gutted fish.

The tourist was short and sunburned and had white cream on his lips. 'Lemme ask the wife,' he said, and he turned away to find her.

Jimmy Gibbs stood there, the hot sun on the back of his neck, his nicked fingers smarting from the salt and the drying fish blood, and the hand that held the filleting knife was twitching as he waited.

'How 'bout you, cap'n?' he asked the next know-nothing fisherman down the line. It seemed that Jimmy Gibbs couldn't wait to plunge his blade back into something. 'How you want them snappers?'

CHAPTER SIX

'IT'S AS GOOD A SYSTEM as any other,' said Ray Yates, stepping gingerly through the kennel area at the Stock Island dog track between the evening's sixth and seventh races.

'It's asinine,' said Robert Natchez. Natchez, a fastidious man, picked his footfalls even more carefully than his friend. He was wearing black sneakers, black jeans, black T-shirt, and black blazer.

Around the two men, nervous greyhounds, their limbs taut as frogs' legs, their gleaming fur given a hellish orange cast by the strange stadium lights, were being led out of their pens. Handlers stroked their lean flanks and petted their bony heads while fitting on their numbers. The dogs pranced, high-stepping as carousel horses frozen in the glory of full gait. Now and then one of the animals would pause, sniff the ground, lower its elegantly rippling haunches, fix the nearest human with a gaze of sympathetic candor, and take a dump.

When that happened, Ray Yates would reach for his program and check the dog's name against its number. 'There's your winner,' he'd confidently say to Natchez. 'A lighter dog is a faster dog.'

'That hasn't proven true so far,' Natchez pointed out. The information wafted gently over the radio host without putting the slightest dent in his certainty.

Back in the grandstand, the audience of hard-core bettors, bored locals, and ragtag tourists waited for the next grim pursuit of Swifty the mechanical rabbit. Beauty parlor blondes, their lobes stretched tribal-style by weighty jangling earrings, sucked powdery whiskey sours through straws. Fat men in the inevitable plaids smoked Cuban cigars that had been bought with a wink in Miami. The night sky was reduced to a hazy black bowl above the pink glare of the floods.

'Gimme two dollars on number seven,' said Robert Natchez. He didn't quite know why he'd agreed to accompany Ray Yates to the track, this place of shit and greed. He'd told himself the artist should see everything, however tawdry. But Key West offered abundant seaminess, squalor, pathos, and depravity without the need of going to the dogs.

Yates glanced at his annotated program. 'Number seven didn't go,' he advised.

'Maybe he runs better constipated,' Natchez said. 'I'll take my chances.'

The more systematic bettor shrugged. 'My two simoleons are going on the lighter number four.'

Yates took Natchez's money and went to place the bets. Low to the ground and purposeful, he bulled through the milling crowd, his palm-tree shirt just slightly damp with sweat. A queasy and familiar excitement overtook him as he neared the barred, illicit cashier's window. The excitement started as a tickle at the backs of his knees, then became a not unpleasant burning in his stomach. The burning transformed itself to a twinge in his loins followed by a pulsing in the veins of his neck. Now he stood directly in front of the dead-faced woman who punched the pari-mutuel machine and his mouth was dry. He took a quick look over his shoulder to make sure that Robert Natchez, his closest friend, had not for some reason followed him. Then, with fingers that were not quite steady, he reached across and placed a two-dollar bet on number seven and bought another hundred dollars' worth of losing tickets for himself.

Later, after nine dull races and a nightcap under the bougainvillea at Raul's, Robert Natchez returned to his small apartment to do some work. He had a grant application to complete. And maybe, he admitted to himself, that was the real reason he'd agreed to waste the evening at the track: to avoid yet another confrontation with the inane, insulting, subtly humiliating questions on yet another grant form. He'd applied for them all at one time or another. National Endowment. Florida Arts Council. Southeastern Poetry Foundation. They all asked, in their polite and neutered institutional prose, why he wanted the grant. Morons! How about to *eat*? They all wanted to know what he would bring to the program. On this question, Natchez's colossal arrogance contended with his fragile sense of decorum. When decorum lost out, he'd submit answers like 'a bracingly fresh approach to language coupled with a masterful grasp of poetic form and an emotional intensity reminiscent of Pound.' To go on record with a self-evaluation like that and still not get the grant was a distressing experience.

Even on those rare occasions when the funding came through, the result was generally depressing. Three thousand dollars to drag himself around the flat and endless state of Florida giving poetry workshops to baffled, nose-picking, germ-carrying first-graders in the public schools. Two thousand to read soothing verses to frothing schizophrenics in county nuthouses, to dozing oldsters in their rubber-sheeted beds. So worthy, these foundation projects, and so futile and bad-paying. Though Robert Natchez could never have brought himself to acknowledge it, they made him feel like a runt kitten still burrowing blindly toward some grudging public tit while his more robust and savvy peers had opened their eyes, stretched their legs, and set out to stalk their destinies in the wider world.

The poet picked up his pen, angled the application in the pool of yellow lamplight in front of him, and stared at the wall.

The wall was of dark wood, old Dade County pine. Dade County pine was purportedly termite-proof, but Natchez's walls were riddled with tiny holes, out of which, on windy days or when a plane went over especially low, flew termite droppings slightly smaller than poppy seeds. It had become second nature to Natchez to begin work by shaking the pellets off his papers and into the trash.

He'd had the apartment eighteen years, an astonishing

tenure in transient Key West. At first it had seemed the perfect writer's garret. Not the classical northern garret of Dostoyevsky or *La Bohème*: no snow climbing up the windowpanes, no burning of timeless manuscripts for a few moments' warmth. This was a tropical garret. It had a moist, rank, generative smell from the rotting leaves in the vacant lot next door; from that lot, as well, came feral sounds of rutting cats and the brainless clucking of runaway chickens that led unimaginable lives and some-times laid eggs in the undergrowth. As the setting was funky, so was the furniture – rickety wicker, cracked and squeaky rattan, end tables found by chance, thrift-shop lamps of cheap archaic charm.

Women loved the place – or used to. Lank-haired and blithe, they came to him easily in the early years, drawn by the aura of the pure and struggling artist. They were won over by the chipped coffee cups, content to get politely plastered on syrupy Liebfraumilch or vinegary Bardolino swigged from glasses that had formerly held grated supermarket parmesan. And when Natchez had a poem accepted at one of the little magazines and a check for fifteen or twenty-five dollars arrived, there was cause for pride and celebration.

Then the eighties descended and the honor went out of being poor. Women no longer seemed titillated at the thought of sleeping in Robert Natchez's platform bed that one had to crawl across to reach the john. Incon-veniently, the poet passed the age of forty, and season by season his image slipped from that of someone very intriguing to that of someone not quite suitable. His apartment underwent a similarly discouraging change. It was no longer cozy; it was cramped. It was no longer quaint; it was dark, musty, and held a perennial and unromantic whiff of mildew.

'My God, man,' Augie Silver had said to him the very first time he visited, 'you need a window.'

So Augie went home and painted him one. It was a canvas full of light and air, with suggestions of brilliant sky, hints of spring-green lawn, a calm movement running through it as of wind-tossed fronds. It was the cheeriest object by far in Natchez's apartment and had recently become by a vast margin the most valuable.

The poet looked over at it now, dropped his pen, and turned his thoughts to the dead painter. There is an awe spiked with envy and verging on hatred that those for whom life is difficult feel for those to whom life comes easily. And life, or so it seemed, had come easily to Augie Silver. He didn't agonize about painting; he painted. He didn't agonize about quitting; he quit. He had with his wife the sort of apparently effortless contentment that is the steadiest form of affection and regard, and that remains an utter mystery to those outside of it. He made enough money and, perversely, seemed to make more the less he worked.

And he wasn't, even by his own assessment, a major artist. That was the part that nettled Natchez, or that justified his pique. To the great artist, much was allowed, maybe everything; that was basic. But why should Augie Silver – a gifted dauber, a freakishly facile lightweight – have been admired, fawned on, taken seriously, while Natchez, who knew beyond a doubt that he was an important poet, a major voice, was still filling out applications like a goddamn high school senior? Where was the justice in it? he burned to know.

Disgusted, feeling wronged and righteous, Natchez pushed aside the grant forms, switched off his desk light, and walked the one step to the kitchenette to pour a glass of rum. Justice. It mattered deeply to Robert Natchez, as it matters to all profoundly frustrated people. As long as they themselves are the ones defining what is just and, in fantasy at least, the ones with the awful power to see that every person ends up as he deserves.

CHAPTER SEVEN

'DARLING, how are you?' asked Claire Steiger.

Nina Silver briefly hesitated at her end of the phone line. How was she? Only lately had the widow noticed how often and offhandedly this bedeviling little question was asked. Take it seriously, and it was intimate as a bath. 'I'm as well as I can be, Claire. How are you?'

'Me?' She sounded faintly surprised at the inquiry, but that, Nina reflected, was Claire. It was axiomatic that she was fine. The self-made woman who'd opened a dinky exhibition space in a side-street storefront, given it the grand name Ars Longa, and in less than a decade turned it into one of New York's most formidable tastemaking galleries. Who'd snagged herself a square-jawed husband from among the East Side's thin crop of croquet-playing, equestrian bluebloods. Who'd done all this, moreover, without independent wealth or the cheap currency of great beauty or any particular genius except a genius for reaching the end point of her wishes. 'Very busy. Hectic ... It was a lovely memorial the other week.'

What did one say to this? *Thank you for approving of my taste in mourning?* Nina had years ago stopped competing with her former boss on issues of style and refinement, had stopped competing with anyone about anything. She kept silent and looked around her own modest premises, the Vita Brevis Gallery. Augie had suggested the name over a bottle of champagne, and it had proven irresistible. It was a sweet space, the Vita Brevis, pine-floored and washed in north light, and its overhead was low enough that Nina Silver could turn a profit while showing exactly what she pleased. With modesty of aims came freedom. That was something Nina's former colleagues in New York found it difficult to understand.

'Nina,' Claire Steiger resumed, 'let me tell you why I'm calling. I'm mounting a show of Augie's work. A retrospective.'

The news should hardly have shocked the widow. This was how it happened: A painter died, and after a brief interval came a show, a look back, a reconsideration of the work, now that the work was finished. But usually when a painter died it was clearer he was dead. There was a body. There was a chance to look down at the dead face and confirm that it was lifeless, an opportunity to lay one's cheek against the still chest and convince oneself that it was void of breath. There was the final sound of tossed dirt crunching down on a lowered coffin. Nina Silver felt a moment of bewilderment and mistrust. It seemed to her that people were conspiring in some sadistic hoax to persuade her that her husband wasn't coming back – when in her heart, against all evidence and all rules of the natural world, she yet believed he was. She saw him, after all, nearly every night, his ruddy face flush with life, his meandering step as full of curiosity as ever . . . The widow groped for something to say, something that would reconnect her with the ordinary waking world in which plans were made, things decided.

'But Claire,' she managed. 'Nothing's settled. The estate—'

'Nothing will be for sale,' said Augie Silver's agent. 'Nina, the show is meant as an homage, a tribute.'

Again the widow was stopped short. Claire Steiger was a merchant, not a curator; she showed paintings to sell paintings, and it had not occurred to Nina that the precious square footage of Ars Longa might be given over simply to the admiration of canvases. The widow felt remorse. Was she already slipping into bitterness, beginning to assume that everything was a sham, a cheat, just because her own life had been cheated? 'Claire,' she said, 'I suppose I should be grateful. It's just that—'

'Just what, darling?'

'I don't know. It seems so soon.' Even as Nina was saying the words, she knew they were beside the point. Twenty years from now it would still seem soon.

'Nina, listen, I understand that everything feels very new right now, very raw. But this show will be a celebration – the kind of big overview that Augie would have wanted.'

'I don't think Augie wanted that,' said Nina, and a flash of suspicion again arced through her brain. Living artists had a lot to say about when, where, and how they were shown; dead artists were not consulted. Someone had to step in and tell the world what the painter *would have wanted*. That someone was usually a dealer, and

43

mysteriously, what the painter *would have wanted* fit in very neatly with a marketing plan. 'Claire,' the widow said, 'I don't think I like this.'

The proprietor of the Ars Longa Gallery looked out her office window at the springtime bustle of 57th Street, the veering taxis and recession-proof limos. Over the years, she'd developed a very versatile and effective stratagem for avoiding arguments. When a disagreement loomed, she simply ignored it and went on to announce her intentions. 'The gallery has seventeen major works on hand,' she told Nina Silver. 'Collectors have so far agreed to lend another dozen. If you'd consent to lend the canvases you have, we'd of course pay shipping and insur—'

'Claire, this is all just business, isn't it? This is no homage, no tribute.'

'Nina, your husband's reputation—'

'My husband doesn't – didn't – particularly give a damn about his reputation. I think we agree that was part of his charm.'

'We can't all afford to be quite so cavalier about it, Nina. Let's be professional here, shall we? As Augie's agent, I'm asking you to lend the paintings. Will you?'

'No.'

'I'll ask another time, when you're less upset.'

'Don't bother, Claire.'

'And one more thing, Nina. Did Augie in fact make no pictures at all the last three years? Was he perhaps working quietly—'

Nina Silver hung up the phone. She didn't slam it down, didn't even drop it with particular suddenness.

She placed it gently in its cradle, crossed her arms against her midriff, and blew out a long slow breath.

On 57th Street, Claire Steiger stared blankly at the dead receiver in her hand and wondered for just a moment if her unaccustomed desperation had led her to a rare strategic blunder. But she allowed herself little time to linger on the question. She had other calls to make.

Nina Silver, like most Key Westers, went most places by bicycle.

Her bike was an old fat-tire one-speed, powder blue, with a corroded wire basket and a rusted bell whose clapper stuck after three weak and unresounding taps against its casing. She'd had the bike eight years and found it a perennial source of mind-easing delight. It wasn't that the bike reminded her of childhood; rather, it leavened her notion of what it was to be a grownup. It was impossible to take oneself too seriously while astride an old fat-tire bike. The world, and the sense of one's place in it, came back to scale and flooded in as one pedaled by at eight miles an hour, with a vantage point some four feet off the ground.

As the widow cruised slowly up Olivia Street, the sun's last low rays were slanting in from the Gulf side of the island, and the light was so soft yet compelling that the pink and red oleanders seemed not shined upon but fired from within. Confident dogs sprawled in the street, serenely nestled against the tires of parked cars. Stray cats missing patches of fur and pieces of ears mixed democratically with brushed pets in the shady places under porch stairs. Amorous doves puffed up on wires and hopefully sang out: ta-*kee*-ya, ta-*kee*-ya. And with a sometimes audible creaking and squeaking, the old wooden houses of Key West began to recover from the daytime baking that had swelled their window frames and bowed their door-jambs, made their beams and joists as painfully taut as a fat man's ankles.

Nina chained her bike and climbed the three front stairs, took a last look across her porch rail at the splendid light, and slipped her key into the lock. She was a half-step into her living room, looking down as she replaced her key ring in her bag, when out of the corner of her eye she glimpsed a male form in the kitchen. Her feet froze, her throat clamped shut as if squeezed by a cold hand, her heart stalled and then began to hammer.

It was Reuben the Cuban.

He was standing at the counter, a dish towel in his hand, drying glasses. 'Hello, Meesus Silber,' he said. 'I run berry late today.'

This was a lie. Reuben never ran late. But on Tuesdays, the day he cleaned the Silvers' house, he often stayed overtime because he thought it might be a comfort to the widow to have someone there when she arrived. She might need something moved. She might need an errand run. There might be any number of things that needed doing, and Reuben wanted to be the person to do them if he could.

Nina moved slowly into the house, still waiting for her pulse to slow.

Fred the parrot greeted her. 'Awk. Jack Daniel's. Where's Augie?'

The widow sat on the edge of the sofa. Her legs were warm from biking, and the upholstery felt good. 'Someday,' she said, 'I'm going to strangle that bird.'

Reuben the Cuban reached up and put a glass on a high shelf. Then he moved gracefully to Fred's cage and offered the parrot a knuckle to peck. 'Thees bird, he love you and Meester Silber too. He not try to make you feel bad.'

Nina kicked off her shoes and reflected that there are people who think the worst and people who think the best. Even about parrots. 'You're a very kind person, Reuben.'

The young man absorbed the compliment with great solemnity. He'd glided back to the kitchen and was now buffing flatware and putting it away. He took care not to mar the moment by jangling forks and knives.

The widow leaned back on the sofa and let her head fall against the top of the cushion. The light in the living room was so soft it had turned grainy; the brighter glow from the kitchen made the house seem cozy and safe, inviolable. Nina was ready to think about the day just ending. 'Reuben,' she said softly, 'what's a friend? What do you think a friend is, Reuben?'

The young Cuban dropped his cloth, pondered a moment, then absently began polishing the countertop with slow round movements. He hadn't known a lot of friendship in his life. He had a father who was so ashamed of him that Reuben couldn't remember the last time he'd seen the old man's eyes, and a mother who claimed to love him but was always praying on her swollen knees for a miracle that would make him other than he was. He had a brother who'd promised to kill him if he showed his faggot face in certain places, and he'd had lovers who had promised him romance and devotion, then easily cast him aside. He was too bashful and unfinished to be at ease among the smart, theatric Old Town gays, too tender and too dignified to seek solace in the shadowy places where lonely young men collided. In Key West, a town that prides itself on having room for everyone, there didn't seem to be a spot for him.

But there is as much wisdom in pure yearning as in flawed experience, and on the subject of friendship Reuben had strongly held beliefs. 'A friend,' he said, 'is when you cry, the tears fall in his heart. When he laughs, it is bread and wine, it is like food, enough for happiness. A friend, you would do anything, you would look for more that you could do, you would watch the world like a fisherman watches the sky to see if there is danger, to keep your friend safe by watching closely—'

The housekeeper suddenly broke off. He was unaccustomed to talking so much; he was still making slow circles with the dishcloth. In the dark living room, Nina Silver had become a silhouette, a still dim outline against the furniture. 'You ask a lot,' she said. 'Of yourself.'

'Yes,' said Reuben.

'You should,' said the widow. Then she thought of certain people with whom her life had been very much involved and whose goodwill she was each day less sure that she could trust. 'Only ... only, if you ask so much of a friend, I'm not sure anyone really has one. I don't feel that I do.'

Reuben the Cuban fretted with his dish towel, closed the drawer that held the flatware. He pressed his teeth together to keep his face composed but his heart was wild with a secret, modest pride, the knightly ecstasy of one who stands ready to do all and asks nothing in return. 'You do,' he said, leaning just slightly across the kitchen counter. 'You do, Meesus Silber.'

CHAPTER EIGHT

'So this Steiger woman,' said Ray Yates. 'She call you?'

Clayton Phipps took a small sip of extremely nasty white wine and silently cursed himself for being talked into slumming at the Clove Hitch bar. It was well and good for Yates to play out this man-of-the-people routine; he *had* to, being a radio host, a local personality. But why should Phipps have to subject himself to this resinous, oxidized fluid out of a green gallon screw-top jug with an ear? 'Yes,' the connoisseur said reluctantly. 'She called.'

'She want your paintings?' Yates pressed.

'She wants to *show* my paintings,' Phipps corrected. 'There's an understanding that it's strictly NFS.'

'NFS,' muttered Robert Natchez, who was sitting on Phipps's other side. Like most pretentious people, the poet was uncannily sensitive to pretension in others, it irritated him like sand in the mesh cup of a bathing suit. 'Goddamnit, Clay, can't you just say "not for sale" like a normal human being?'

Phipps shrugged. The whole subject of the paintings made him highly uncomfortable, and his discomfort made him feel as nasty as the wine. 'OK, Natch,' he said. 'Not for sale. Like your journals.'

There was a pause. The three friends blinked across the glare of Garrison Bight and watched the charter boats straggle in, their practiced captains working shifters and throttles to back them into their slips with swagger. Red and seasick tourists gathered at the sterns, jockeying for position to be the first ones back on land. Pelicans sat in the water, still as bathtub toys, cormorants stood on pilings and spread their prehistoric wings to dry.

'How many paintings ya got?' asked Ray Yates.

The question fell just as Clay Phipps had let himself imagine that the topic of Augie's canvases was closed, and for all Yates's efforts to sound offhanded, there was something inherently rude, salacious even, about the inquiry, like casually asking someone the length of his dick or the amount of money in his Keogh plan.

There had always been a certain competitiveness among Augie Silver's friends. It stemmed from the fact that they all admired Augie more than they did each other, and more than they did themselves. There was something about the man that made it seem crucial to be liked by him. He was a natural arbiter, he conferred esteem the way a king grants titles of nobility, and his favor suggested not just personal preference but fundamental worth. In the matter of gift paintings, his favor could also confer large amounts of cold cash, but that was something no one wanted to be crude enough to be the first to mention.

'Six,' said Clayton Phipps. He said it softly, shyly even, looking down at his cheap scratched wineglass, yet could not quite squelch a nervous smile, a hint of bragging.

'Six!' said Ray Yates. His voice was also soft, but an octave above its usual smooth range.

'Three large, three small,' Phipps went on. It seemed he'd decided to make a full disclosure of his holdings and have it over with. 'Three oils, one acrylic, two water-colors. Done over a span of twenty years.'

'You sound like a fucking exhibition catalogue,' groused Robert Natchez.

Phipps did not immediately answer. He glanced across the pier, saw fishermen hanging grouper on scales and nailing angry-eyed barracuda onto posts. Jealousy. He knew he was dealing with Natchez's scattershot corrosive jealousy and that the higher course would be to let it slide. But lately Phipps's higher impulses had been consistently losing out. Augie's death, his rebuff at the gentle but definite hands of Augie's widow – things like that made him weary of the vigilance it took to be dignified. 'How many d'you have?' he taunted Natchez.

'Just the one. You know that.'

'Ah. It's one of the nicer of the small ones.'

'I have two,' Ray Yates volunteered. 'A good-size oil on the boat and a little watercolor I hung at the studio.'

'Take it home, Ray,' said Natchez bitterly. 'It's gonna be worth money.'

Money. So there it was. The unholy word was dropped like a plateful of soup and was as hard to ignore as a food stain on a tie, but the other two men strove gamely to ignore it. They sipped their drinks, glanced around them at the bar beginning to fill up now with boat crews and returning sailors. The sun was low enough that there were hems of pink on the bottoms of the puffy clouds.

'So Clay,' said Yates, 'you gonna send your paintings?'

'I haven't decided,' said Phipps, though in fact he had. 'I just wish I was surer what Augie would want.'

'What Augie would want,' Yates said, 'is not to be dead.'

To this, the two men clinked their smudged and murky glasses. It was the sort of comradely gesture they used to do more of, generally with Augie taking the lead. Now it had less the feel of something done in the present than of something re-enacted, an old routine trotted out without great conviction, and Robert Natchez made no effort to join the toast.

'Clay,' he said, 'you know you want those paintings in the show. Make you look like a big collector. And what the hell – it's only NFS.'

Some time later, Jimmy Gibbs parked his sore legs and aching back on a stool at the Clove Hitch bar and ordered up a double Wild Turkey, rocks, chased by a longneck Bud. His captain, Matty Barnett, had offered to buy him a drink, and Gibbs was not one to short-change himself in matters of the cocktail. He tipped his beer in thanks and sucked the neck of the bottle dry while it was good and cold. Matty Barnett sipped tomato juice livened up with horse-radish. He'd been sober fifteen years, ever since he drove his 1970 Bonneville convertible off the bridge and into the Cow Key Channel. It wasn't sinking the car that had scared Barnett onto the wagon; it was that a lot of time went by before he'd noticed he was in the water. Now he watched his first mate sponging up alcohol with the kindly disapproval of a Hindu watching someone wolf a burger.

'Jimmy,' he began, 'you got any idea why I wanna talk to you?'

'Nope,' said Gibbs, although several possibilities had crossed his mind. He'd been late, hung over, a couple times in the last week or so – but hey, no one expected a mate on a charter boat to be a model of promptness and propriety. He'd been, well, a little sarcastic to clients now and again – but it had seemed to him the clients were too nauseous, nervous, and ignorant to pick it up. Besides, Jimmy wasn't there to be anybody's best buddy; he was there to rig the lines, keep them clear, land the fish despite the customers' endless talent for losing them – and he defied Matty Barnett or anybody else to question the quality of his skill.

'I'm thinking of retiring, Jimmy.'

This Gibbs had not expected, and it made him take a hard look at his boss. Barnett was barely older than he was, maybe fifty-five, fifty-seven tops. That did not seem like retirement age to Gibbs. He had a tough time imagining someone being far enough ahead of himself, moneywise. Besides, it didn't look to him that the captain really worked that hard. True, he had a constant weight of responsibility on him, but that wasn't work like hauling lines and scaling fish was work. It didn't make your back hurt, didn't ding up your hands.

'I useta love getting out on the water,' Barnett went on. 'Now it's just a job. Fishing's not what it was. Or maybe it's just me. Anyway, I'm over it. I got a little place up the Keys. Own it free and clear. The wife's got five, six years to go with the Aqueduct. So the way I'm figuring . . .'

Gibbs knew by now how Matty Barnett was figuring, and the knowledge put a knot in his gut. Barnett was going to offer him a good deal on the boat that Gibbs ached to have and could not possibly buy. The impossibility of it made him furious with everything and persuaded him that there could be no pure motive, no generous impulse, no fairness in all the world. 'The way you're figuring is business is lousy anyway so you may as well sell the *Fin Finder* to me.'

Barnett backed off. He seemed truly miffed and Gibbs felt ashamed. He punished and soothed himself with a swig of bourbon, then stared off toward the western sky. There was a band of yellow near the horizon, and above that a lot of green.

'I'm offering it to you first,' Barnett said mildly. 'It'd please me to have you be the next skipper. If you're not interested, that's fine.'

Gibbs glanced sideways at his captain. Decades of scanning the glaring water for fish had bleached out Matty's eyes and made their sockets pink and crinkly like the eyes of Santa Claus. Gibbs could almost find it in himself to apologize and to tell the other man of course he was interested, but he suddenly had the ridiculous feeling that if he tried to speak he would start to cry.

'Here's the situation,' Barnett resumed. 'Boat's worth sixty-five, seventy. I'll let it go for fifty. I still owe eleven on it myself, so I need that much up front. The rest, I'd work with you, you could pay it off as—'

'Matty,' said Jimmy Gibbs in a raspy, strangled whisper, 'where in fucking hell am I supposed to get the first eleven thousand?'

Barnett blinked his pink eyes, sipped his tomato juice. 'I dunno, Jimmy. I thought you might have something put away.'

Gibbs looked down at the bar as if he wanted to gnaw it to splinters. Only logical, he told himself, to imagine that a gray-haired man who'd worked thirty-eight years might have a measly eleven thousand dollars put away. Who wouldn't? 'Thanks for thinkin' a me, Matty,' he said, but his tone made it clear that Barnett had done him no favor.

'Sure,' said the captain. He put down his tomato-stained glass, dropped ten dollars on the bar, and got up to leave. 'Have another round, Jimmy. And if anything changes, lemme know.'

'Wha'd Matty want?' asked Hogfish Mike Curran.

The sky was full dark now, and the Clove Hitch bar had emptied out. It was an early place, a two-pops-after-work kind of place. By 9 P.M. there wasn't much left for the proprietor to do but throw ice in the urinals and hang the beer steins on their pegs.

'Nothin',' said Jimmy Gibbs. 'He wanted nothin' and he got it.'

Curran looked at Gibbs with gruff admiration; the man was a moody sonofabitch, give him that. He'd polished off Barnett's second double and was now nursing the dregs of one he'd purchased for himself. Hogfish Mike jerked some glasses up and down the bottle brush and tried a different conversational approach.

'Some guys were in before, Ray Yates and a couple others, talkin' about your buddy Augie Silver.'

Gibbs was in that state of deep sulk where it becomes a sort of sick victory to remain utterly uninterested, but he could not help giving in to curiosity. 'What about 'im?'

'Didn't hear that much. Something about paintings. Selling 'em. Supposedly they're worth some money.'

Jimmy Gibbs looked down and shook his glass. He was trying to look indifferent and trying to rattle his ice cubes, but it was a hot night and the pieces left were in weightless crescent slivers that made no noise.

Hogfish Mike flicked dishwater off his hands in an oddly dainty manner. 'You got a painting a his, don'tcha?' he asked.

Gibbs had known the question was coming and vaguely wondered why he'd felt reluctant in advance to answer it. He nodded. Then he couldn't swallow a cockeyed smile. 'He gimme this painting, said he hoped it wouldn't remind me too much a work. It's kind of a spooky picture, ya want the truth. Like a fish-eye view of gutted fish.'

'Like cannibals?' said Curran.

Gibbs shrugged. He hadn't thought of it exactly that way. 'More like Who's next?'

The proprietor of the Clove Hitch was wiping his bar with a rag. 'Worth money, though.'

'Hogfish, hey, it was a gift.'

Jimmy Gibbs hefted his beer bottle and reminded himself for the fourth time it was empty. He thought of ordering another, then remembered he needed all the cash he had to pay the overdue electric bill. He pictured the line of dirtbags at the City Electric office, their crusty feet and filthy sandals, everyone ready with their red-bordered shut-off notices and their bullshit excuses, and he was weary to death of always being broke. 'Besides,' he mumbled, 'fuck could it be worth? Couple hundred?'

Curran shrugged, moved down the long teak slab, mopping up water and emptying ashtrays as he went. Gibbs tossed back the last of his bourbon. It left a satisfying burn where his teeth poked out of his gums. He thought about the *Fin Finder*. It had twin big-ass Yamahas, outriggers arched and graceful like something off a bridge, and a man really looked like someone standing at the steering station, with the radar slowly spinning and the tuna tower gleaming in the sun. Jimmy Gibbs coughed softly in his fist and made his voice sound casual. 'Few hundred, right, Hogfish? I mean, ain't likely to be more'n that.'

CHAPTER NINE

ON A WEDNESDAY EVENING in early May, Kip Cunningham sipped champagne, poked a silver stud through the placket of his dress shirt, then responded with a tired sense of duty to his wife's request for assistance in doing up her dress. He cinched its panels together, tucked the zipper tab down neatly in its groove, finessed the hook through its little loop of thread, and vaguely noticed the way the top of the silk bodice bit softly into the flesh of Claire Steiger's back. He used to find her back very beautiful, that much Kip Cunningham remembered. Her back wasn't freckled, exactly, but there were light mottlings below the surface; the effect was of looking not at her skin but into it, it was like peering through sunshot water in a trout stream and seeing pebbles at the bottom. Was her back still beautiful? Her husband could not really have said. He was losing her, though the loss that was happening now had mainly to do with money and social ease. The deeper loss he was oddly numb to because he'd inflicted it on himself, subtly, gradually murdering his chance for happiness with the slow poison of inattention.

'What if someone tries to buy—' he began.

The zip job completed, his wife slid away from his

touch and cut him off. 'At an opening, Kip? None of my clients would be so tacky.'

Cunningham flipped his collar up and began the painstaking process of tying his tie. 'There might be discreet inquiries, hints as to price.'

Claire leaned forward and examined her eyes. What on earth, she wondered, had been on her mind eight years ago when she and the decorator designed this grand double bathroom with its his-and-hers mirrors, its twin dressing alcoves, its side-by-side scallop-shell sinks? She knew damn well what had been on her mind, and the recalling of it mocked her. What had been on her mind was a Hepburn–Tracy romance. Scintillating chit-chat and intimate, brainy repartee while quaffing bubbly and grooming each other for some gala evening where they would take great pleasure and pride from being mates. Parts of the fantasy had come true, Claire Steiger reflected. If anything, there'd been too damn many black-tie evenings, an exhausting excess of verbal spar-ring, and perhaps too much fine wine. The only thing missing had been the marriage.

'Kip,' said the gallery owner, 'you used to be a businessman. You can't talk about price until there's some basis for a price.'

'But—'

'Ink, Kip. The show is about ink. Publicity. Reviews. You wanna help, do what you do best. Play squash.'

'What's that supposed to mean?'

'Smile, Kip. Be your blithe preppy self. Don't talk about money and for Christ's sake don't talk about art.

60

Talk horses, talk sports. Invite some critics to the club. They like that.'

Cunningham smoothed his collar and lifted his glass. With more champagne in him it was easier to imagine that his wife's contempt was only a form of affectionate banter. 'Anybody in particular?'

'You know who's who. Find someone susceptible to your boyish charm.'

The husband secured his cummerbund around his still-flat tummy. 'So we get the ink. Then what?'

Claire blotted her lipstick before she answered. 'If the reviews are good, we've got six weeks' buildup before the auction. Enough time for the momentum to build, not enough time for the bubble to burst.'

The bankrupt examined himself in profile. 'And if the reviews are bad?'

'If they're bad?' said his wife. 'If they're bad, I'm stuck with a bunch of damaged goods. Augie Silver goes down in history as one more second-rater. We'll lose the beach house and whatever else you've pawned.'

She moved to the small bathroom window that over-looked Fifth Avenue and stared down at Central Park. The spring foliage already looked sooty, the cherry blossoms were going brown and rank, they had the sodden look of yesterday's salad. 'But there's a bright side, I suppose.'

Kip Cunningham did not ask what the bright side was. He knew it wouldn't really be bright, and he knew his wife would tell him anyway. He drained his glass.

'The more we lose up front,' she said, 'the less to give up when I get free of you.'

In the dim living room of the house on Olivia Street, Nina Silver nestled into her soft-pillowed sofa and talked to her dead husband. She hadn't begun by speaking to him; she'd begun by looking at his paintings and thinking. But as the light had faded, as the windows stopped framing colors and patterns and just passed along a uniform gray, there seemed less and less reason to deprive herself of the company of speech. 'Augie,' she said. 'Up in New York, they're making you a star right now. D'you know that, Augie? A big fancy opening. Caviar. Canapes. Limos all up and down the street . . . Just the sort of thing you always hated. Men looking ridiculous in patent-leather shoes. Young jealous colleagues wearing capes, dying to know what the critics are scrawling in their notebooks. The inevitable two women in the same expensive dress . . . "What's it got to do with the work?" you'd say. "What's it got to do with anything?"'

She paused, and it seemed that Fred the parrot felt compelled to fill the silence. The big green bird riffled through its limited vocabulary and picked some sounds at random. 'Incha Pinch. Alla joke.'

'What's it got to do with anything?' the widow said again.

*

'What's it got to do with anything?' asked Kip Cunningham, leaning against the marble counter at the entrance of Ars Longa. His voice was thick with wine, his tie was crooked, his shave no longer fresh, and in all he was about as trashed as the gallery itself. Champagne corks swollen up like tumors littered the tables and the countertops. Lipstick-stained glasses lay on their sides like toy soldiers killed by kisses. Here and there the marble floor had been scorched by cigarettes. The ladies' toilet needed plunging, and someone, it seemed, had walked off with the crystal paperweight that held down the stack of catalogues.

'I just can't believe that someone would steal a paperweight,' said Claire Steiger. 'That's all.'

It was 11 P.M. The hostess looked fresh as an anchorwoman, but she was in the grip of the sort of brain fatigue that makes little things like stolen paperweights into large distractions that call forth a draining and useless indignation. She'd been up since six that morning. She'd overseen the hanging of the show, the catering, dealt with the last-minute RSVPs. She'd strutted through the evening in high-heel shoes and greeted perhaps two hundred people by name. Used to be, she cruised through days like this on waves of glad ambition; the grasping joy of reaching her next goal would keep her primed with adrenaline. Now the ambition was mainly habit; it kept its form just as her hair and makeup kept their form, but the joy had dried up inside it the way a stranded clam bakes away to a gooey nothing. 'I mean,' she went on, 'who would be so small—'

'Claire, fuck the paperweight,' slurred her husband. 'How'd we do?'

The gallery owner paused, then fluttered her soft brown eyes as if waking from a nap. She was ready to go one more mile. 'The right people showed up,' she said. 'Some big-money no-nerve collectors – the kind who wait for the Grade A stamp. Couple of agents for Japanese investors. The heavy critics.'

'I talked to a few,' said Cunningham. He was pleased with himself, gave a drunk smile. 'Joe Rudman from the *Times*. Talked ponies. What's-his-name, the *Newsweek* guy. Likes croquet. And Peter Brandenburg – I'm playing squash with him tomorrow.'

It had been a long time since Claire Steiger approved of anything her husband had done, but she could not now prevent an impressed look from stealing across her tired face. 'He counts, Kip. He counts a lot.'

Cunningham nodded. Then he grabbed an end of his tie and pulled out the knot. When he'd been younger, less embittered, when his shallowness could pass for finesse and his essential dullness for aristocratic restraint, he'd looked especially debonair with his tie undone and hanging on his chest. Now he just looked dissolute, hollowed out, ready for three aspirin and an icepack. Absently, with no great interest, he jerked a thumb toward the softly spotlighted paintings on the gallery walls. 'For what it's worth,' he said, 'you think this stuff is any good?'

'Everything I show is good,' Claire Steiger said. Outside, on 57th Street, someone honked a horn. A crosstown bus whined loudly as it pulled away from a stop, and the gallery owner somewhat guiltily indulged herself in an unchecked yawn. 'You've got to believe in the product, Kip. That's rule number one.'

CHAPTER TEN

RAY YATES had always wanted to be a local character.

He'd tried on towns like some people try on hats, telling himself he needed one that fit his image, but in fact looking for the image in the hat. What he was searching for was a place that would embrace him as a perfect type, adopt him as a kind of mascot.

He'd had false starts in several careers, and these had been custom-fitted to various cities. In Boston, all in tweeds and baggy corduroys, he'd edited a small and unprofitable magazine of poetry and opinion. In Los Angeles, he'd managed to make seven payments on a leased Porsche before realizing that no one was going to hire him to doctor scripts. In Chicago, the last newspaper town, he'd worn real suits and the ugly ties reporters wear, but quit when he realized it might be twenty frigid winters before he was recognized on Michigan Avenue.

When he arrived in Key West six years ago, he'd immediately begun trying to out-local the locals. His wardrobe turned abruptly turquoise, he bought a stack of palm-tree and flamingo shirts, which he laundered repeatedly to fade. He bought sandals and denied himself the use of Band-Aids, hoping to speed the process by which blisters turned to calluses. He rented a houseboat, and felt extremely Floridian having a teensy toilet with a hand pump and a gangplank for a driveway.

As for a job, Yates hadn't known exactly what he'd do. He didn't want to work very hard. He didn't want to start early in the morning. And he wanted the kind of position that would help him insinuate himself, that would give him the kind of access, insiderness, small renown even, that had eluded him in bigger, more important places.

So it had seemed providential when, at a cocktail party, he'd met Rich Florio, manager of radio station WKEY. KEY was nothing if not local. It broadcast from an ancient cottage in a downtown alley and had a transmitter slightly more powerful than an undercounter microwave; in perfect atmospheric conditions, its signal could be detected as far away as mile marker twenty. The format was eclectic: pop in the morning, jazz at night, some classical on Sundays, and lots of local news and notices. School-board meetings. Church outings. Benefits to save the reef, the manatee, the embossed tin roofs of Old Town.

But the station lacked a talk show, and Ray Yates, drinking tequila on the strength of a third-hand invitation, found himself pitching one to the station manager. 'In a town with so much going on,' he'd said. 'So many writers, artists, so many famous people . . . An interview show. Early evenings. Call it . . . call it Culture Cocktail.'

They'd agreed to talk further, and when Florio hired Yates, the new Key Wester thought he'd done a masterful sell job, though the truth was that the station manager had been having the damnedest time recruiting anyone remotely qualified who would work for what KEY could pay. But Yates was in it for the entrée, not the money. His rent was cheap, he had some savings from Chicago, and if he kept his gambling under control, he could get by.

The problem, as he discovered early on, was that Key West was not nearly as sophisticated or culturally vibrant as its reputation – the reputation that Yates had whole-heartedly bought into, and which he now had both to exploit and to perpetuate. Writers' haven. Ha! Maybe two dozen writers, most of them bad sober and worse drunk, perhaps four of whom were actually working at a given time. Artists? Well, if you granted the premise that painting on T-shirts was a major art form, then, yes, Key West abounded in artists. Theater, you could take your pick between drag shows downtown and road companies doing recycled musicals out at the college. True, there were the street performers from Mallory Dock – but juggling was not ideally suited to radio and nothing was surer to make dials turn than a guy playing bagpipes. Faced with the unremitting task of filling air time, Ray Yates had grown every year more grateful for the exist-ence of the Gay Men's Chorus, the Lesbian Political Verse Initiative, the annual Tattoo Show.

Still, every now and then Yates had the pleasure of reporting a real piece of culture news, an item that did not need to be qualified by the diminutive term *local*, something of interest north of mile marker twenty. On an evening toward the middle of May, he had such a story, and he devoted the last segment of his show to it. He swept off his headset and spread a yellow-highlighted magazine in front of him. He glanced at the big clock above the engineer's booth window. Then he laid his forearms against the cheap veneers of the studio table and leaned in toward his microphone.

'Back live on Culture Cocktail,' he said as the producer gave the signal that the hair-salon and dive-shop ads were over. 'Friends, it's always been my belief that all of us who love Key West should root for each other, should take pride whenever the accomplishments of one of our own are recognized by the outside world. So I'd like to share with you an art review from this week's *Manhattan* magazine. The review is by Peter Brandenburg. Some of you might know of him. He's got a reputation as the hardest marker around, someone with such exquisite taste that he doesn't like anything. Except he loves our former Key West neighbor Augie Silver.

'Probably a lot of you knew Augie – knew him as a wonderful companion who loved his food and drink, a man interested and generous toward local causes, a man who celebrated the beauty and uniqueness of the Keys. But I wonder how many of us realized we had a truly major painter in our midst? Honestly, I'm not sure I did – and Augie Silver was one of my dearest friends.

'"Some painters are badly served by retrospectives." I'm quoting Brandenburg now. "Comprehensive shows reveal less of their talent than their limitations. We see the place they stopped growing, ran dry of ideas, almost as clearly as if a black line were painted on the wall, separating the discoveries from the walk-throughs. Such was not the case with Augie Silver. He never reached a plateau and never coasted. He reinvented his vision with every canvas, and in this regard the inevitable comparisons are with Picasso and Matisse – tireless talents who kept exploring and refining till the day they died."

'Picasso and Matisse!' editorialized Ray Yates. He could not help glancing at the small painting Augie had given him and which hung now, crooked on a rusty nail, on the smudged wall of the studio.

'Farther on, here's what Brandenburg says: "He belonged to no school, subscribed to no trends. At a time when many painters appeared to care less about craft than about theory, Silver cared only for the quality of what was on the canvas. In an era when artists seemed to feel that, to be taken seriously, their work had to be ugly, jarring, or pointlessly original, Silver clung to a riper, braver, more classic kind of wisdom: His work depicts a world almost unbearably lush, tender, beautiful, and temporary. In his love of color, his unabashed sensuality, he is a pure romantic; yet even in his most gorgeous pictures there is an awareness of death, of decay – the calm, sad resignation of the tropics. And what more poignant and honest reflection of that resignation than that Augie Silver, as if in humble acceptance of the paltriness of human effort, should have stopped working altogether in his final years? This passionate inactivity seems the final proof of his sincerity, his miraculous freedom from ambition. And while his premature death was certainly a tragedy, the current show at Ars Longa will assure him a place in the top rank of contemporary painters. Long after the dreary canvases by this season's art-journal darlings have come to seem dated and dull, Augie Silver's work – eccentric, indifferent to fashion, happily outside the mainstream – will speak to us of the power of untrammeled temperament wedded to talent, possibly to genius."'

Yates stopped reading and looked up at the clock. It was twenty seconds before 7 P.M., and behind the engineer's booth window his producer was flashing him the OK sign. The host searched for some final comment, a capper, and when none came he decided that the most effective way to end the show was to let the Brandenburg review hang in the air through a rare moment of radio silence. He paused a double beat, then said, 'This is Ray Yates, and this is WKEY, the voice of the lower Keys. See you tomorrow on Culture Cocktail.'

He gave a nod and a point, and the producer played his theme music. It was a tune that always made Yates thirsty. Most evenings he bolted immediately from the padded womb of the studio and went directly to Raul's for several drinks. Tonight he broke the pattern. He looked at the painting on the wall. It was an impression of wind-lashed trees against a green sky full of reverence and menace. More important, it was a signed original Augie Silver. Picasso, thought Ray Yates. Matisse. You didn't leave such things around a public place where anyone could grab them. He decided to bring the picture to the houseboat, and reminded himself to install the dead bolt he'd meant to put on months ago. He owned two works by someone in the top rank of contemporary painters, and he felt a twinge as at a betting window when he let himself imagine how much they might be worth.

CHAPTER ELEVEN

NINA SILVER switched off the radio, walked softly through the French doors at the back of the living room, and sat down near the pool. Strange, she thought, what happens to a person when he's dead. He becomes the property of others, part of some ghastly common pot from which anyone may feed, a shared blurred memory that can be put to many uses. He can be talked about, written about, set up as a yardstick to measure or to shame the living. A person, dead, becomes a topic, a silent, neutral thing about which others have opinions. Chatter that would be called mere gossip in regard to the living passes for serious appraisal, something right and fitting, when applied to someone dead.

But it was still gossip, reflected Nina Silver. Gossip and presumption by people trying to lay claim to a ghost. What did any of the chatter have to do with the flesh and blood man who had been her husband? What did it say about the smell of coffee on his morning breath, the glad gleam in his open eyes when their faces were close and they were making love? What did it say about the particular warp of his wit, the gruff charm that was indescribably different from the charm of other charming men, as ticklish, comforting, and sometimes prickly as an unshaved cheek?

The widow sat and smelled the evening. Salt and iodine flavored the air, a slippery odor as of earthworms in wet dirt wafted up from the cooling ground. The poinciana was just coming into flower, and Nina noticed for the thousandth time what tiny, feathery leaves it had for such a big and spreading tree; it always made her think of a great fat man with the palest, daintiest fingers.

Time passed. She knew this because the mosquitoes had come and gone, the western sky had phased from pink to lavender to jewel-box blue, and higher up Castor and Pollux, the tall spring twins, were nearly at the zenith. Nina Silver was wondering if she too was trying to lay claim to a ghost. Her claim, she told herself, at least was lawful – lawful in that vague portentous sense of *lawful wedded wife*. But what did that really mean? Did it set her up beyond dispute as the keeper of the true memory, the vestal standing guard against the vandals? She had built, was still building, a shrine of remembrance; other people – friends, colleagues, self-appointed judges – were building other shrines. Nina told herself her own temple was the grandest because it was built with the greatest love. But what it had in common with all the others was that it was meant to house, contain, hold captive the ghost of Augie Silver – and maybe Augie's ghost did not wish to be held.

This was a terrible thought, a thought to turn grief guilty. Perhaps, of all the rudenesses and well-meaning indignities that the living heaped upon the longed-for and admired dead, the worst was simply that they wouldn't let them go. Perhaps the dead were like tired guests who truly wanted nothing more than to leave the party and have some peace. Why did the noisy, selfish, stubborn living try to bully them into staying?

'Augie,' Nina Silver said aloud, 'do you really want to go?'

That night, as usual, she dreamed of her dead husband.

In the first dream he was walking with her down a New York street. It was winter, night, big halos of icy blue surrounded all the streetlights. The parked cars were so black they gleamed like schist, and the brownstones all had stately stoops that exactly paralleled each other, like something out of Egypt. It was cold, with a gritty wind, but Nina didn't mind because she had her warmest jacket on and she was holding Augie's arm. He wore a camel topcoat, carelessly buttoned, and though she couldn't see his hands she knew they were balled lightly into fists at the bottom of his pockets. She was looking at the sidewalk; it had small shiny stones embedded in it. Then something went wrong. Nina had the sudden certainty that she was holding not her husband's arm but an empty sleeve. When she looked up they were standing at a broad intersection. Many traffic lights were flashing and the wind was blowing from everywhere at once. Augie was now standing outside his coat. He was naked, pale as egg, and skin was blowing off of him, his face was distorted and flesh was being stretched and torn away like leaves from a tree in the first November storm.

Nina sat up groaning, then leaned back on her elbows. She brought a hand to her throat and felt her racing pulse. She poured some water from her nightstand carafe. A late moon had risen and a dim ivory light was spilling through the thin curtains. It put a soft gleam on the pine-cone bedposts, and the gleam reminded Nina of the delicious and secure fatigue of childhood. After a while she went back to sleep.

When she dreamed again, the dream was gentler. She was on a beach, sitting at the water's edge, letting wet sand sift through her fingers. The sun was hot on her shoulders, the water so flat she could see the place where the earth curved underneath it. Augie was behind her, lying in a hammock. At least she trusted that he was: She could only see his leg, pegged in the sand like a bird's leg, his toes faintly wiggling just below the surface. She was happy. She looked down the beach and saw a black man selling coconuts. He was wearing a big hat of woven palm. She wanted to buy a coconut for her husband. She wanted to surprise him, to see him drink the rich milk through a straw. But there was a dilemma. She was happy as she was, knowing Augie's toes were wiggling. She would be happier sitting next to him and giving him a coconut, but she feared that if she reached for greater happiness she might lose the happiness she had. She glanced up the beach, then back at the hammock. She gestured toward the man with the coconuts. Then her nerve failed and she woke up just enough to break the dream, to finish it without an ending.

She rolled over and smoothed an imagined crease in

her pillowcase. Her leg twitched once, she cleared her throat, and some time later her husband appeared to her once more.

He stood before her looking very old and thin, as if he'd been dead for many years. His hair was pure white and hung down past his shoulders. He had a beard dry as tinsel on his sunken cheeks, and his cheeks were not ashen but burned the color of rosewood. He wore a threadbare shirt, a pauper's shirt, and on his shoulder perched a parrot.

'Nina,' said her husband. 'I've come home.'

The widow smiled sadly on her pillow. Augie had never before appeared in such a ghostlike way, never seemed so old, so low, so fragile. Yet his deep eyes in the moonlight seemed at peace. 'Augie,' she murmured. She froze his image for a moment, nestled it into her shrine of recollection, then blinked herself awake.

Or thought she did. The apparition did not vanish. The widow tried to shake herself out of a sleep that was stubborn as memory, stubborn as love, struggled upward as from a dive where one has gone too deep, but still her husband's image loomed before her. She was dreaming now that she was sitting up, looking past the dead man's tinsel hair at the familiar curtains moving with the breeze, though she knew this could not be.

'Whiskey sour,' squawked Fred the parrot. 'Pretty Nina.'

'Augie?' said his wife.

He sat down on the bed. He'd grown so light he barely made a dent. His wife reached out a trembling hand to touch him. The parrot fluttered in protest and moved to its master's other shoulder. 'I'm very tired,' said the painter. 'Very tired.'

He swiveled slowly on his shrunken hips, let himself fall backward, and was sleeping in an instant. The bird jumped onto its bedside perch and sat there preening in the moonlight.

PART TWO

PART TWO

CHAPTER TWELVE

NINA SILVER lay awake the rest of the night, afraid that if she blinked, her husband would again be gone. She held back from touching him, terrified her hand would slip right through his outline, that his shirt would be vacant, would prove to be nothing more than a twisted piece of bedsheet, errant cloth throwing the shadow of a man. She lay on her side and breathed deeply. She thought she smelled the ocean, and now and then a sweet chalky smell that made her remember the taste of her husband's mouth.

Dawn came, and with it came growing belief: The private madnesses allowed in the dark cannot, for the sane, cross the border into day. The bedroom windows began just barely to lighten, and still Augie Silver was there in his bed. His wife dared to put her face against his arm. It was shrunken but it was warm. She cried silently and she dozed.

When she awoke, the room was bright. Augie was gone, and in some awful way Nina Silver was not surprised, only confused to see Fred the parrot on his bedside perch.

Then she heard the sound of tinkling, and a moment later her husband was standing in the bathroom doorway.

Seeing his wife awake, he flashed her a tired smile that was full of the reverent screwball miracle of finding himself alive. The smile banished doubt forever. Nothing but a living person could have an expression so wry, beat up, and full of zest.

'Augie.'

'Nina.'

'Cutty Sark. Awk, awk.'

The painter, still in his clothes, came back to bed and took his wife in his wizened arms. The movement and the embrace seemed to drain him. 'I'm so weak,' he said. It was not a complaint, just an observation, made with the sort of detached amusement that comes to grownups when they watch a baby try to walk.

'Can you tell me?' asked his wife. 'Can you tell me what happened?'

Augie settled in flat on his back and stared up past the still fan at the ceiling. 'I can try,' he said, as if he was being asked to relate a story of something that happened long ago, to someone else. 'But there's a lot I don't remember even now.'

He shifted just slightly, and his crinkly white hair spread around him on the pillow, his tinsel beard folded down onto his chest. 'It was a beautiful January afternoon. Bright sun. Not too much humidity—'

'I remember the day,' she gently interrupted.

'Yes, of course,' he said. 'Well, I was out past Scavenger Reef. I'd just come through it, I could see the line of the Gulf Stream maybe two miles up ahead. It was gorgeous. Pointy little whitecaps in the shallow water – nervous whitecaps, high-pitched, like kids' voices. Then the slow, thick purple swells in the deep. Off to the west there were huge tall clouds – not anvil tops exactly, but mountain clouds, whole ranges of them. I watched them. I wasn't the least bit worried, not even about getting rained on – the weather was from the east. The boat was heeled but steady, I just watched the clouds, sketched the shapes in my mind.

'Then it was like the clouds were melting, like there was a table across the sky and the clouds were pouring down across it, perfectly flat, much heavier, denser than before. They started rolling toward me; it was like a domed stadium slamming shut. The sky got very confused, low clouds going one way, high clouds going another, this odd sensation that the earth had started spinning faster. Half the sky was black, the other half an acid green. There was a wash of white over the shallow water and a dull gleam like wet lead over the Gulf Stream. The wind picked up – but not too much. I was enjoying it.'

His wife looked at him strangely, but Augie didn't notice. He took a deep and labored breath that moved the white bristles of his mustache. Outside, the morning's first breeze set the palm fronds scratching at the tin roofs of Olivia Street.

'Then I saw the spouts starting to drop,' the painter resumed. 'I'd never actually seen that before, and it's not the way I would have imagined. I would have pictured great dark funnels thrusting fully formed down from the clouds. But in fact they slip out almost shyly, like a man sticking a toe in cold water. Wisps and scraps, little rags of cloud. They hesitate, sometimes they crawl back up.

Then they venture down a little farther, and then they start to spin. Once they start turning, they digest the whole huge cloud they came from, suck it all down through their writhing hollow bodies.

'I saw three spouts touch down, and they all were moving toward me. I had to make a choice: drop sail and take my chances or try to outrun the storm. You know me, I made a race of it. I sailed away. The funnels followed. I headed farther out to sea – away from the reef, away from the shallows. The wind started really ripping, and then in an instant it totally changed direction. I wasn't ready for that. I got slammed around, I couldn't even hold the wheel, there was no way I could keep my course.

'I looked up and a spout was dancing straight toward me, shimmying, swaying like a genie, homing in like it had radar. I tried to dodge it. But it was too close now, the swirling wind kept pulling the ocean out from under me like a rug. I thought it was starting to hail, then I realized what was hitting me was little fish, snappers and ballyhoo, that had gotten sucked into the spout and now were raining down, bouncing off the deck, slapping into the cockpit. The shrouds were twanging and groaning. I think the mainsail tore but I can't be sure; the jib came loose and was whipping around like a flag in a battle.

'And I really don't know what happened next,' the painter said. He was still staring at the ceiling and speaking in a quiet monotone. His parrot shifted on its perch and scratched its chest with its beak. 'I might've been carried back to the coral, I really can't be sure. Either I was pulled out of the boat or the boat broke up around me. I think something hit me in the head – maybe the boom, maybe just something flying. I suppose I was knocked out. Then suddenly I was in the water, awake enough to thrash through the foam like a madman. I looked around for the boat. It was gone. I thought I saw the top of the mast disappearing, but I may have imagined it. My arms were getting exhausted, I was sucking too much water. Then the dinghy – half the dinghy – came bobbing by. I managed to grab it and nestle in; it was like a leaky clamshell. I must've passed out again.'

Nina Silver put her hand on her husband's. His skin was so thin it felt powdery and she thought she could distinguish the small bones in his fingers. 'Augie,' she said, 'if this is too painful . . .'

The painter seemed surprised at the word. He smiled, and his wife noticed how deep were the fissures in his burned lips. They seemed to divide his mouth almost into tiles of flesh. 'Painful? I wasn't aware of it being painful. Beautiful and terrifying. Painful, no.'

He looked at his wife and realized he had been misunderstood, and that the misunderstanding had hurt her. 'Missing you,' he said. 'That was painful. The thought of leaving you by dying – that was painful. But those things I didn't feel till later – till I remembered. For a long time I knew nothing except what I imagine an animal knows: I knew I was alive. I knew I was in danger. And that was all.'

He paused and closed his eyes. His wife nestled closer and waited for him to continue. But he didn't continue. His breathing fell back into the rhythm of sleep, his foot kicked weakly under the sheet and half awakened him. 'I love you, Nina,' he mumbled, and then his breath began to whistle softly through his nose. His wife stayed in bed a few minutes more, then went, as on any ordinary morning, to put up coffee.

CHAPTER THIRTEEN

'NO,' SAID CLAIRE STEIGER, 'there won't be any sales before the auction.'

She hugged the phone against her shoulder and looked down at her fingernails. It was a muggy morning in springtime New York, a May day on the lam from August. Viscous, dirty light spilled in through the windows of the gallery office. Below, on 57th Street, people looked stylishly limp in the season's first wilting linens.

'Yes, Avi,' the dealer was saying, 'I know you've been a terrific client. I appreciate it. But this time I can't make any special deals. The situation's too volatile, you know that as well as I do.'

The would-be buyer paused, then there was a soft popping sound as of heavy lips reluctantly letting go of a damp cigar. Avi Klein resumed his wheedling, and Claire Steiger reflected with gamy zest on the perverse and malleable machinery of human wants. What was so especially delicious about the phantom cookie at the bottom of the empty bag? What was so particularly beautiful about the painting that could not be had? Why was Avi Klein, a generally shrewd and cool-headed collector, suddenly prostrating himself for the privilege of paying more by far than had ever been paid for an Augie Silver canvas?

'Half a million is a lot of money,' Claire Steiger purred. She gave an impressed curl to her lips, as though the client were in the room, looking to be stroked. 'Are you sure it's worth that much?'

Klein was the fourth big customer to call that morning, and Claire Steiger was having a better time than she could easily remember having. She was dusting off some of her favorite moves, the feints and tactics she had refined in the years when the building of her business had seemed each day an adventure. There was flattery, of course; nothing so crude as compliments, but the passive flattery of sitting tight and letting someone show off the size of his wallet. There was the pre-empting of doubt, the sly reversal that forced the buyer to defend his judgment and so sell the painting to himself.

Though in the present instance the idea was *not* to sell the painting – and this offered an impish satisfaction all its own. Withholding. There was a power in it that was like the power of sex. The power to entice and frustrate, to beckon and dismiss. When its exercise was temporary, playful, that power could be delicious, could stoke appetites and make the nerve synapses incandescent. But when withholding became one's normal stance, a habit of the heart . . .

Claire Steiger did not ask to be visited by this thought. It simply descended in the midst of her negotiations and spoiled her mood the way a swarm of gnats spoils a walk in the garden. She fell out of her professional trance and remembered her life. She was married to a man she no longer loved. She was no longer on the glad ascent of making her reputation and her fortune, but was locked now in the squalid scramble of trying to hold on to those very few things she still cared about. A wave of bitterness squeezed up from her belly and brought an evil taste to her throat. Avi Klein was still talking moistly in her ear, still trying to persuade her, and his voice had become maddening, appalling, a devil voice that spoke glozingly of wanting and paying, selling and haggling, a wet salacious voice that made all transactions seem inherently shameful, fundamentally corrupt, and somehow humiliating. For an instant the dealer envied Augie Silver, serenely dead and beyond the fray. When she spoke again, her voice was sour and abrupt, the charm had dried up like a lemon forgotten at the back of the fridge.

'Avi, I'm leaving this to the open market. I hope to see you at Sotheby's.'

'What the fuck is Sotheby's?' asked Jimmy Gibbs.

Ray Yates, his apricot and turquoise shirt sticking to his broad and furry back, sucked an ice cube and reminded himself where he was and who he was talking to. Key West. A piece of limestone crust barely poking out of the ocean a hundred fifty miles from anywhere, the very tip of the very long tail of keys tucked under the sandy ass of the American dog. Difficult of access, bathed in sun and myth, splendidly uninterested in the high dry world outside, it was one of the last places where a person could truly be provincial. Had Jimmy Gibbs ever read a newspaper other than the Key West *Sentinel*? Did he read that for any farther-afield intelligence than the hopeful fibs of the fishing report and to see which of his bubbas had made the police blotter? *What the fuck is Sotheby's?* This was in its way a glorious question, a question full of archaic purity.

'It's an auction house, Jimmy,' Yates told him. 'Ya know, a place where people bid on things. Art, antiques, famous people's autographs.'

Gibbs took a pull of his beer, clattered the dripping bottle back onto the bar, and belched demurely into his nicked-up fist. 'What kinda asshole would pay good money just for someone's autograph?'

'Lotta people do, Jimmy. They keep 'em awhile, then sell 'em at a profit.'

'To a bigger asshole.'

Yates shrugged, and Gibbs tried to picture what this Sotheby's must be like. He'd been to an auction once. It was up on Big Pine, mile marker thirty-one. It was held in a church parking lot under sheets of corrugated tin nailed down on four-by-fours. The auctioneer was a cranelike man in a string tie, and he'd had a voice as loud and irritating as an outboard with the cowling off. Jimmy Gibbs didn't like to talk in front of a lot of people, but he'd bid on a couple of things by raising his hand. He went three dollars on a tackle box of someone who had died, but the gear ended up fetching five fifty. Feeling thwarted, he bid eight bucks on a slightly used dinette set for the trailer, but the auctioneer had hawked his way into double figures before Jimmy Gibbs knew what hit him.

'It's indoors, this Sotheby's place?' he asked.

'Jimmy,' said Ray Yates, 'this is like a very fancy operation. Big room. Crystal chandeliers. Women in designer suits. Men with hundred-dollar ties. You get the picture?'

Gibbs sucked beer and burped.

'People fly in from London, Paris, just to go to these auctions. People phone in bids from Tokyo, Germany – '

'They don't even see what they're buying?'

'They have advisers.'

'They need other people to tell 'em what they want?'

Yates ran a hand through his damp hair. The humidity and Jimmy Gibbs's logic were making him confused and sleepy. He sipped his tequila and glanced around the Clove Hitch bar. If you kept your eyes under the pseudo-thatch roof of the open structure, the light was soft and easy, but as soon as your glance strayed onto the water or over to the charter-boat docks, the late sunshine was sharp and scalding. The earth was tilting each day a little farther toward full summer, the ever-fiercer sun made the whole world seem to creak the way swollen wood complains at an overtightened screw. Ray Yates was getting irritable, wondering why he'd bothered to try doing the impossible Gibbs a favor.

'Jimmy,' he said, 'you do what you like. But I'm telling you, you wanna pull some money out of that painting, that's the way to do it.'

Gibbs considered. The first thing he considered was whether, if he signaled for another drink, it would still be on Ray Yates. The radio host had paid for the first round with a twenty. Fourteen bucks in soggy bills and some silver was sitting on the bar, and Jimmy Gibbs decided to take a chance. He caught the eye of Hogfish Mike Curran, wagged his empty bottle, then, as the proprietor approached, gave the slightest and most discreet nod in the direction of Yates's cash. Curran bounced this signal over to the talk-show host in the form of a subtly lifted eyebrow, and Yates answered with a no less minimal tilt of his chin: The deal was done, a successful transaction among men who drink.

Gibbs then turned his attention to the question of Augie Silver's painting. The fact was he, Gibbs, was vaguely terrified at the thought of picking up the phone, calling New York, and having to explain to someone who talked fast and had a brisk and snooty Yankee accent who he was and what he wanted. He was afraid he'd be asked to describe the picture, and his description would sound stupid. He'd have to ask all sorts of dumb questions about how to wrap the painting, how to send it. 'Seems like a lotta trouble,' he said at last. 'I mean, what could the thing be worth – three, four hundred dollars?'

Ray Yates hadn't wanted another drink, or at least he hadn't until one was put in front of him. Then he couldn't help noticing that the fresh ice and lime tasted great and the alcohol wasn't too bad either. He smacked his lips, put his glass down slowly, and made a grand sweeping gesture past the unwalled Clove Hitch bar, across the cloudy water of Garrison Bight, up the Keys to the whole snaking coastline and continent beyond. 'Jimmy,' he said, 'there's a whole 'nother world out there. We're not talking hundreds. We're talking thousands, Jimmy. Probably tens of thousands. Maybe more.'

'You're shitting me,' said Gibbs, but he looked hard at the talk-show host and realized that he wasn't. He sucked beer, swallowed it, and worked at holding his face together.

Yates studied him in turn. Gibbs's scalp had started to crawl, the gray hair pulled tightly back began to wriggle like worms so that the small ponytail bobbed up and down. It seemed to Yates that this restless writhing scalp was the birth of greed made visible, and it occurred to him to wonder whether he'd ever really intended to do Jimmy Gibbs a favor or whether his real purpose had been to observe the corrupting of a local. Corrupting not in the sense of the innocent turning bad, because there was nothing remotely innocent about Jimmy Gibbs. Corrupting, rather, in the sense of someone being pulled away from what he was and pushed toward what he could never be, tempted into a fantasy of change that could only end in bafflement and failure.

A cormorant flapped its jointed wings and took off from a post. A spray of tiny fish roiled the water as they fled some large thing feeding on them from below. Jimmy Gibbs pictured himself at the wheel of the *Fin Finder*, alone in Ray-Bans at the steering station just below the tuna tower. Captain Jimmy. He'd hire a couple young guys to haul the lines, clean the fish; his hands would heal. Maybe he'd buy himself a new truck too. Captains didn't show up at the charter docks in dinged-up old heaps that sifted rust.

Yates watched him, felt a quick pang of remorse, and raised a cautionary finger. 'No such thing as a sure thing, Jimmy. Don't spend that fortune before you have it.'

It was sound advice and it was too bad the talk-show host was not following it himself. It was five o'clock, the sun was still throwing heat as heavy as bricks tossed off a building, and Ray Yates reminded himself that he had to meet a guy to discuss a small matter of some gambling debts. He took a final swig of his tequila and got up with all the gusto of a man on his way to a root canal. He waved goodbye to Hogfish Mike, put a hand on Jimmy Gibbs's shoulder, then trudged the length of the pier. At the foot of it, right up against the seawall, the remains of a filleted fish were floating. The affronted eye stared heavenward, some opal meat still clung to the backbone, and Ray Yates didn't like the look of it at all.

CHAPTER FOURTEEN

AUGIE SILVER SLEPT FITFULLY for most of the day. It was brutally hot, the palm fronds hung limp and silent outside the bedroom window, yet the painter never lowered the cotton quilt from under his chin. He was too thin, too dry, too tired to sweat, he lay there papery and brittle, his breathing shallow, the dream movements of his eyeballs clear and disconcerting through the veiny translucent skin of their lids.

Around six o'clock he struggled out of bed, slipped out of his clothes, and went slowly to the closet for his favorite robe. It never occurred to him that the robe perhaps had been moved from its accustomed peg during his four-month absence – and it hadn't been. It hung there patient and welcoming, the loops of yellow terry-cloth worn flat and shiny at the elbows, the big soft collar suggesting a certain pomp, like the entrance of a champion boxer. Directly under the robe, as if held in place by an invisible mannequin, were the backless slippers that so perfectly suited his shuffling, meandering walk. He stepped into them with the reverent confidence of the prodigal who knows in his bones that his wanderings have made him more profoundly, more legitimately the possessor of his home, his comforts, his life.

Silently he strolled into the living room. His former widow was lying on a sofa reading, and she did not hear him approach. He took a moment to gaze around the house. His paintings hung on almost every wall, they rang in his brain with a glad but overwhelming clamor that had less to do with sight than sound, as though he were a composer and ten orchestras were simultaneously playing every tune he'd ever written.

'Looks like a goddamn museum in here,' he said.

Nina looked up. Her reading glasses stretched her eyes, made them huge and liquid, and the lifting of her head made the sinews rise and quiver from her collarbone to her jaw. She had at that moment an unposed loveliness that made Augie's knees go even weaker in appreciation of what he had come home to.

'I hung the paintings for the memorial service,' said his wife.

'Memorial service,' mused the painter. 'I keep forgetting I was dead.' He mused further. 'Guess I'm still dead, far as anybody knows. It's kind of relaxing ... Was I lavishly and excessively praised?'

'Your ears must have been on fire.'

'Who gave the eulogy?'

'Clay.'

'Ah. Elegant and flowery, I bet. I owe him one.'

Nina said nothing and Augie shuffled to the sofa. He leaned over to kiss his wife and tried not to let her see what an effort it was to straighten up again. She tried not to let him know that she had noticed.

'Hungry?'

The word sounded somehow foreign to him and he

took a moment to respond. 'I should be. But my body seems to have forgotten what to do with food.' He sat.

Nina hesitated. It seemed too soon to speak of doctors, of worries, of the fresh fear of recurring death. She draped herself across her husband's shoulders.

'I blew to Cuba,' he suddenly said, being pulled back into his story as into a fever dream. 'Funny, huh? A place I'd always wanted to go.'

'Cuba?' said his wife.

Outside, soft evening light filtered through the oleanders and the crotons. A faint smell of jasmine and mango slipped past the louvered shutters and through the unscreened windows. Augie half leaned, half fell against the back of the sofa. His robe splayed open to reveal a white thigh that had grown thinner than his knee.

'Eventually,' he said. 'I guess I passed out after hauling myself into the broken dinghy. When I came awake, I was still having trouble breathing, my arms and chest ached horribly. But the storm was over and a fresh cool norther had blown up behind it. From the color of the sea I figured I was in the Gulf Stream. It was just before sunset. I watched awhile and conked out again.

'Night came. It got cold. In the morning I was shivering and parched but alert enough to remind myself not to go crazy. I needed something to concentrate on; but when I tried to pick something, I noticed I couldn't remember my name. Or what I did. Or where I lived. Or you. For a while I was panicked, then a weird acceptance kicked in: I was in the ocean and as blank as the ocean. I drifted. I curled up this way and that way, trying to hide from the sun. Now and then I peered around, imagining

I would see a boat, an island. I tried to sleep but my head was pounding, surging like waves were trapped inside it.

'By the next day I think I was getting delirious. I shook. I tasted blood in my throat. I was no longer sure whether I was asleep or awake, wet or dry, cold or hot. The glare on the water was blinding me, I kept seeing green streamers like when you press on your eyeballs. Then I saw the fins, circling, approaching, retreating, approaching.'

Nina whimpered. It was an involuntary sound, a tiny shriek from an ancient nightmare. Augie reached out and put a hand on her head. The sleeve of his robe hung down from his bony arm. 'Sharks?' she whispered.

'Dolphins,' said her husband. 'They were swimming with me. Or at least I think they were. I was pretty out of it by then. My sense of time was all screwed up, I expect I was yammering to myself. But I had the definite impression that a pod of dolphins, four or five, was surrounding me, protecting me, guiding me to wherever it was I was floundering. I watched those beautiful arched backs, the spume flying up from their blowholes and exploding into rainbows in the sun.

'More time passed. Another day, maybe two. I could feel myself shriveling up like a leaf. My skin was cracking open. Then, when I was asleep or raving, I felt and heard the dinghy being rammed, nudged, pushed. It was the first time I was afraid of capsizing. I grabbed the gunwale and looked over the side. Coconut palms. The dolphins were shepherding me to land.

'I have a very dim recollection of crawling to shore. Pebbles and shells cutting my hands. Saltwater searing deep into my flesh. I remember cool sand against my cheek. And the next thing I knew, I was waking up in an old fisherman's hut.

'I heard voices before I could open my eyes. Spanish voices. I couldn't understand much, but I guess I wasn't in very good shape, because one of them kept saying *muerto, muerto*. That made me nervous. I felt I had to do something impressive to show them I was alive, or they might do the decent thing and bury me. So I tried to move. I couldn't. I tried to speak, to groan. Nothing. I used to think failure was relative, but this was failure in the absolute. I couldn't even blink.

'But they must've found a pulse or something,' the painter continued. 'Maybe they just didn't feel like digging right then. Anyway, they told me afterward I was unconscious for around ten days.'

'Who told you, Augie?' asked his wife.

He slowly shifted on the sofa and managed a skeletal smile. 'This old man who spoke pretty decent English. Used to work at a casino in the Batista days. Told me I almost cashed in all my *cheeps*.'

Nina tried to smile in return but found that she could not. The person to whom something terrible has happened is usually the first to be able to laugh about it; those who love him are always the last. 'But Augie,' she said, 'why did it take you so long to get home?'

'Amnesia, paranoia, and politics,' he said. 'I didn't know who I was. It wasn't till much later that I remembered the waterspouts, the wreck. I had no ID. As soon as I could speak, the fishermen realized I was American, and they didn't know what to do with me. Where I landed was very remote – an isolated little peninsula called Boca de Congrejo. What these people knew of the outside world was what the government radio told them. They were savvy enough to see I was no Yanqui imperialist devil, but they were afraid of what might happen if they turned me in.'

'Afraid for themselves?'

'For themselves. For me. Afraid. Who knows of what exactly? So they kept me under wraps. Tried to feed me fish broth. As I got a little stronger, they helped me to the beach to watch the boats. They were very kind.'

He paused, and Nina rubbed his shoulders. It was almost dark outside, the windows were soft gray pauses in the painting-covered walls. A block away a dog was barking, palm fronds scratched softly against the tin shingles of the roof.

'Only problem was, these little strands of memory started tugging at me, more and more each day. It didn't bother me especially that I didn't have a name. So what? But I was getting to ache about other things. Yearn. Yearning. I'd used those words, everybody does, but now I knew what they meant. I knew I had a home somewhere and I yearned to get back to it. I believed I had a mate, someone it was my proper destiny to be with. And I had this nagging and, if this doesn't sound too crazy, religious sense that I had work, some kind of work, to do.'

'It doesn't sound crazy,' said Nina Silver, but her husband continued as though he hadn't heard. Even through his weakness, it seemed a kind of frenzy was upon him now, and he hurtled through the rest of his story as if the meaning of it existed not in the details but in the sheer momentum.

'Day to day,' he said, 'I felt that I was getting stronger, but the strength wasn't going to my body, it was being siphoned off into this groping quest for memory, this blank struggle to recall or invent who I was and what I was put on earth to do. Everything had to be relearned; it was exhausting as childhood. Little bits of things triggered recollections that, maddeningly, went nowhere. A color. A smell. I knew them. But how? From where? I asked for a paper and pencil and I started to draw. I didn't know I knew how, I just drew. I looked for hints in the pictures. And that's what I saw: hints, nothing more. A couple of months went by. I doodled and racked my brain. Meanwhile, my body was languishing, this need to remember was like a tumor, was like a sucker on a plant, it just took all the nourishment for itself.

'Then one day it clicked. By chance. That's always how it happens, isn't it? Some screwball fact that becomes the anchor of a new universe. There was a big sportfishing tournament – marlin, sailfish – international. Big beautiful boats flocked by, the whole village stood on the beach and cheered and waved. Boats from Venezuela, Mexico, boats from Argentina, Panama. Americans weren't supposed to participate – part of the economic embargo, you understand. So if the US government says don't do something, who's the most likely person to do it? A Key Wester, right? So sure enough a Key West boat goes by. *Lip Smacker*, *Key West*. I'm standing on the beach, taking turns looking through this ancient spyglass someone had, and I see it on the transom.

'Suddenly it was as if I had a fever. I had to be carried to my cot. I spent a couple days in bed, totally immobile. I was conscious and I had the weirdest sensation I've ever had in my life: a kind of itching, clicking, sparking inside my brain, like the whole computer was being reprogrammed and it was draining every last volt from the battery. I came out of the stupor, and I remembered.

'The tournament headquarters was about thirty miles up the coast, at a small resort called Puerto Dorado. The old croupier went there and made discreet contact with the Key West captain, a real crazy man named Wahoo Mateer. For the two of them, I imagine, the whole thing was pretty titillating, both sides feeling pleasantly subversive. A couple of evenings later, Mateer came and fetched me, and here I am. In and out of Cuba without a passport.'

The painter paused and settled in further against the back of the settee. He ran the sleeve of his bathrobe across his forehead as though mopping perspiration, but there was no moisture there, only a brick-red sheeny flush through the burned and crinkly skin. He pulled a slow deep breath into his ravaged lungs, and when he spoke again his voice was even and serene.

'I'm home with my mate. And I've remembered the work I have to do. I'm going to paint again, Nina. As soon as I'm a little stronger. I'm going to paint every day. I don't have to be great. That was arrogant nonsense: genius or nothing. I'll do what I can. I'm going to fill the world with paintings.'

It was full dark beyond the windows now, and the only brightness was a yellow oval thrown by the lamp where Nina Silver had been reading. Her husband looked closely at her face and saw a catch at the corners of her mouth as she stretched her lips to smile.

'You don't think that's a good idea?' he asked.

CHAPTER FIFTEEN

CLAYTON PHIPPS EXPERTLY SLICED the lead foil from the top of a bottle of Gruaud-Larose 1975 and centered his corkscrew in the spongy wood of the stopper. He wasn't quite sure why he was squandering such a venerable wine on the unschooled palate of Robert Natchez; part of him, moreover, disapproved of the whole notion of quaffing a serious red on such a thick and sticky evening, a night that called for talcum powder, fumé blanc, and a cool washcloth on the brow. But goddamnit, there were times in a man's life when he wanted Bordeaux and nothing but Bordeaux, and Clay Phipps saw less and less the virtue of denying himself what he wanted at the moment that he wanted it. He pulled the cork. The festive pop carried with it instant scents of black currants, pepper, forest floor, and violets. Thank God there were some things, some few things, that a man could count on and that did not lose their savor.

He poured two glasses and carried them into the living room, where Robert Natchez was sitting, dressed all in black. Phipps wore tan linen, and the two of them might have been the only people in the Florida Keys, not counting maître d's and cops, in long pants just then. Clay Phipps was self-conscious about his pale and hairless calves; Robert Natchez keenly felt that shorts did not befit his dignity. So they sweated behind the knees and felt well dressed.

'Cheers,' said Phipps, handing the poet a glass. 'It's too good for you, but what the hell.'

'Ever the gracious host,' said Natchez, and he nosed into the wine.

They settled into their chairs. Clay Phipps had bought his Old Town house around a dozen years before, in the wake of the infamous Mariel boat lift. Fidel Castro, in a gesture of great magnanimity, slyness, and spite, had thrown open the gates of his country's loony bins and prisons and allowed anyone who wished to escape to America. Most of the fruitcakes, murderers, catatonics, child molesters, mental defectives, and petty thieves had made landfall in Key West, which did the local real estate market no good at all. Those who, like Clay Phipps, believed that the island outpost was a tough town to kill, scarfed up historic houses at a small fraction of their worth, and found themselves gentry when the Marielitos, not surprisingly, were absorbed into the population with barely an uptick in the crime rate and no discernible effect on the community's overall level of weirdness and delusion. So Phipps now owned a sweet dwelling on a prime block. It was one more instance of his traveling first class without paying for it, living well but without the resonance of believing that living well was an earned reward.

The walls of his house were made of horizontal slats of white-painted pine, and here and there were brighter rectangles where Augie Silver's paintings had formerly been hung. There was something naked, naughty about those paler patches, they grabbed the eye like an unexpected flash of a woman's panties. Robert Natchez looked up from his glass of ruby wine and peeked rather lewdly at the empty places.

'Show's been over a week or more,' he said. 'When're the pictures coming back?'

This was a taunt, and no mistake. Phipps took it in stride. Taunting was what he expected and in some perverse way what he needed from Robert Natchez. 'They're not,' he said.

The poet smirked in his Bordeaux. A glad cynicism opened up his sinuses and he suddenly smelled cedar and mint in the wine. 'Don't tell me you've decided to sell them? I thought everything was strictly NFS.'

'They're being offered at auction,' said the allegedly dead artist's alleged best friend. In an effort to appear casual, he swung a leg over the opposite knee. The dampness on his thigh made the nubbly linen itch. 'Sotheby's. Next month.'

'Ah,' said Natchez. He leered from under his black eyebrows at the nude rectangles, and managed to work into his expression both disapproval and nasty enjoyment. The look maneuvered his host into an abject stance of self-defense.

'You think it matters to Augie?' Phipps heard himself saying.

'I have no opinion on what matters to the dead,' said the poet. This was just the sort of pronouncement, portentous yet inane, that delighted Natchez, and he was tickled with himself for mouthing it. He paused, sipped some wine, then added, 'But they *were* gifts.'

106

At this, Clay Phipps could not hold back a nervous snorting laugh, a laugh that rasped his throat. 'A sentimentalist! You of all people a sentimentalist!'

The swarthy Natchez almost blushed at the charge, which was nearly the most debasing accusation he could imagine. 'It has nothing to do with sentiment. It has to do with what's dignified and fitting. Those paintings were given in friendship.'

'Friendship is complicated,' said Clay Phipps.

'So is envy,' said Robert Natchez. 'So is old stale jealousy. So is hate.' He swirled his wine the way he'd seen Phipps do it, drained his glass, and licked his lips. 'Any more of this?' he asked.

Phipps somewhat grudgingly got up to fetch the bottle.

Augie Silver nestled the thin smock between his skinny thighs and slowly, cautiously settled back onto the examination table. 'I feel like Mahatma Gandhi in this thing,' he said.

'You look like an anorectic Father Time,' said Manny Rucker, his doctor for the past ten years. 'Now lie still and let me goose you.'

Rucker put his soft hands on Augie's belly, pressed under his ribs to palpate the liver, felt for enlarged spleen, for hernia, for strangled loops of intestine. Augie blinked at the ceiling and was almost lulled asleep by the visceral massage. He'd spent the morning with electrodes taped onto his head and glued across his chest. He'd given blood, produced urine samples, labored mightily but without success to deliver a stool. He was exhausted.

'You are one hell of a case study,' said his doctor, and the voice pulled Augie back to the waking present: the hum of the air conditioning, hot light being sliced by narrow blinds, the waxy paper of the exam table crinkling under him, the smell of alcohol masking but not effacing the intimate aromas of sundry sorts of human goo. 'Rest awhile if you like. I'll come back for you later.'

Nina Silver was waiting in the consultation room. She sat on the edge of a green leather chair and stifled an urge to straighten the frames of the gold-sealed diplomas and purple-bordered certificates: paraphernalia of reassurance, fetishes of hope, pompous promises that things would probably turn out OK, and if they didn't, well, at least everything humanly possible had been done. A silver pen stood next to a tortoiseshell box that held prescription slips. Behind the doctor's imposing chair was a pen-and-ink caricature of a fat woman bending over to receive a shot in the behind: No Norman Rockwell prints for Manny Rucker.

He bustled in, hands buried wrist-deep in his lab-coat pockets, and started talking before he'd even reached his desk. 'Nina,' he said, 'your husband is an extremely stubborn man. He really should be dead about five different ways.'

She swallowed and slid backward in her seat. Her spine went soft and it took tremendous concentration, a gymnast's concentration, to hold herself erect. The doctor bounded around his desk, tossed a manila folder onto his green blotter, then dropped so heavily into his swiveling, rolling chair that the entire office seemed to quake around him. 'I'm not saying this to frighten you,' he resumed. 'I'm saying it because I'm impressed as hell. I'm amazed.

'Listen. We don't yet know everything that went on with him – we won't know that till the lab work is done, and even then a lot of it will be surmising, reconstructing. But here's the minimum we're up against.'

Rucker bore down on the arms of his throne until the springs creaked and the casters chattered against their plexiglass platform. He exhaled noisily, then leaned forward, opened the folder, and spread his thick and hairy elbows on either side of it.

'Last time Augie was in here, he weighed a hundred seventy-four pounds, and he wasn't fat. He now weighs one sixteen. That kind of weight loss, the dehydration, the metabolic craziness, is very debilitating. His kidneys shut down for a while – the function seems to be returning, but we can't tell how badly they've been compromised. His stomach has shrunk up smaller than a fist, which means it's going to be a long, slow process getting the weight back on him. His spleen is enlarged, who knows why. That's another obstacle to recovery.'

The doctor paused for breath, and Nina felt herself starting to cry. She struggled not to, because doctors' offices make everyone feel like children being spoken to sternly but well-meaningly by a grownup, and, absurdly, pathetically, it seems important to be brave and well behaved. Still, she thought she could feel her own stomach shrinking up like a puddle in the sun, her own spleen swelling like a sodden sponge, her kidneys growing parched and brittle, tubes and passageways caving in like long-abandoned tunnels.

Manny Rucker noticed that her face was collapsing and decided not to acknowledge it. She was not the patient and there was nothing to be gained by coddling.

'He's had a concussion,' the doctor resumed. 'That's rather a vague concept, concussion is. It basically means he's been clunked on the head and something went kerblooey. We don't yet know if he's fully recovered his memory or where the gaps might be. We don't know if the loss might recur. Probably he's now at somewhat higher risk of Parkinson's and of stroke.'

Manny Rucker flipped shut the manila folder, and Nina Silver allowed herself to exhale. She thought she'd heard all she had to listen to. She was wrong.

'There's one other thing,' the doctor told her. 'He's had a heart attack.'

Nina's eyes went out of focus and settled vaguely on the buttocks of the fat woman awaiting her injection. 'Heart attack?'

'There's a pronounced irregularity in the EKG that wasn't there before,' said Rucker. 'It's clear evidence. Too much time has passed to gauge the severity from the blood enzymes. But there's no doubt that something happened.'

The room was falling away from Nina Silver, the angles between walls and floor and ceiling becoming jarring, oblique, and insane. Her other reunions with Augie, the ones in dreams, had never been so complicated, so fraught. 'He told me his chest ached, his arms, when he crawled into the dinghy.'

Rucker nodded. 'Very possibly he was having the attack while he was in the water. Truly amazing he didn't drown.'

There was a long silence. In the examination room, Augie Silver, all alone, was rousing himself from a catnap; his bony fingers clutched the edges of the table and he gamely strained to sit himself up without assistance. His wife was trying equally hard to ask a simple question. She opened her mouth three times before the words squeezed past her clenched throat.

'Will he die?'

Rucker folded his hands and skidded his huge chair a little closer to the desk. 'Eventually,' he said. 'But he hasn't died yet, and I'm not going to bet against him now. I think he'll recover, I think he's got a good shot at a normal life span. But he needs a very long and very total rest. He's got to get the weight back. If he can't do it at home, he's got to go to the hospital—'

'He doesn't want to do that.'

'He's made that clear,' said Rucker. 'That's why I'm making it a threat. He has to eat. He has to drink. And he has to be totally shielded from stress.'

Nina Silver straightened up, willed her mind to clear, and looked at Manny Rucker with a kind of defiance. She loved her husband. She would protect him, care for him, heal him. For this she didn't need diplomas, certificates, prescription pads. 'He'll be best off at home,' she said. Then her expression softened and she almost smiled. 'Besides, this is Key West. What kind of stress could there possibly be?'

CHAPTER SIXTEEN

WHAT KIND OF STRESS?

For starters, the subtle subliminal stress of finding oneself the subject of rumors, whispers, the sort of breathless gossip that attends such odd occurrences as a slightly famous neighbor's return from the dead.

Nothing could be clearer than that Augie Silver was not yet ready for company, much less a full-scale re-emergence into society. When Nina bundled her husband into their seldom-used old Saab and drove him to Manny Rucker's Fleming Street office, it was with the intention of getting him there and back again unseen.

But Key West is a small place, a sparse place, and little that belongs to it goes unnoticed. Politics, economics, world events go largely unnoticed, being the province of the chill, drear world north of mile marker five. Tourists go unnoticed, because they are not of the town and no one cares what happens to them or what they do; they pass through as undifferentiated parcels of sunburn and noise.

It is a very different thing among the few thousand people who are truly of the place, who are the place. Unconsciously and unfailingly, they recognize each other against the backdrop of faceless transients, they pick each other out as though by some invisible genetic marking. And the Silvers, husband and wife, were very much of the place, distinctive and familiar by dozens of small details: her square-cut jet-black hair; his archaic penchant for corduroy. His meandering Socratic walk; the French net shopping bag she used for groceries. Her gallery; his death. They were known.

So it was inevitable they'd be seen as they passed, even briefly, on such a busy sidewalk as that of Fleming one block up from Duval.

The first person to see them was Lindy Barnes, a checker at Fausto's market. She did a quick and bashful double take, and later told her colleagues across the cashiers' aisles that it had to be the husband, the painter you know, I mean he looked like an old dirtbag, stooped and sick, but really who else could it be?

The second person to see them was Claire Davidson, the head teller at the downtown branch of Keys Marine. She was not a chatterbox, but it was part of her job to recognize faces and remember names, and the real or apparent return of Augie Silver was not something she could quite keep to herself.

By the end of the business day, perhaps a hundred people had heard the rumor, and one of them was Freddy McClintock, an eager young reporter for the Key West *Sentinel*. With a newsman's fine and fitting lack of decency, he decided to call the Silver home.

When the phone rang, Nina was sitting on the edge of the bed urging Augie to drink some broth. He'd managed two sips. Fred the parrot was on his perch, nuzzling his wing pit with his beak and adding a new sound to his idiot vocabulary. 'Eat,' squawked the bird. 'Jack Daniel's. Eat, eat.'

Nina went to the living room and picked up the receiver. 'Hello?'

'Mrs Silvers?'

'Silver.'

'Yes. This is Freddy McClintock, Key West *Sentinel*—'

'Thank you, we don't want a subscription.'

'We? Did you say we?'

Nina pulled the phone a few inches from her ear. Caution was not a habit with her, not since she'd left New York, nor was the feeling that she had anything to hide. 'What is it you want?' she asked.

The reporter cleared his throat. 'I've heard from a couple of sources that your husband has been seen. Alive.'

Nina said nothing.

'And I thought it'd make a terrific story,' McClintock went on. '"Key West's Own Lazarus." Or Jonah. Maybe Jonah would be better. He was lost at sea, wasn't he?'

'What if your rumor's wrong, Mr McClintock? What if you're talking to a widow?'

'Am I?' the reporter countered. 'Is your husband alive, Mrs Silver?'

'I never for a moment believed that he was dead.'

'So you're saying he's alive?'

'What I'm saying is goodbye.'

For a second she stared at the telephone as if she'd never seen one before. Then she went back to the bedroom and checked on her husband's heroic progress through half a cupful of soup.

'Who was it?' he asked.

'Hm?' she said. 'Wrong number.' A quick wave of nausea rippled through her stomach. It was an innocent fib, a protective fib, but she could not remember ever being untruthful with her husband before, and the words left a sick taste in her mouth. Stress. She had vowed to shield him from stress, to spread a calm place around him the way a tree throws a pool of shade. And it was just beginning to dawn on her that a tree casts shade only by suffering the heat itself.

As it stood, it was not much of a story. But then, the *Sentinel* was not much of a paper.

'No interview. No real confirmation. Do we go with it?' McClintock asked Arty Magnus, his editor, idol, and reluctant mentor.

'Ya got anything better?' Magnus, a wildly impractical man in all other aspects of his life, took an extremely pragmatic approach to the newspaper business. This was mainly because he didn't care about it very much. Facts bored him. Actual quotes from actual sources were always deathly dull. The best parts of a story were always the parts that somebody made up, but Magnus couldn't bring himself to tell that to the sincere, impressionable, and slightly stupid Freddy McClintock.

The young reporter riffled through his notebook. It seemed the professional thing to do, though he knew damn well he had nothing better or even anything else. 'No,' he said at last.

'Well then,' Magnus said with a shrug. He shrugged

a lot, it was a symptom of his stifled zest. He was forty and he didn't want to be sitting at a newspaper desk in front of an ancient air conditioner that managed to dribble condensation without cooling any air; he wanted to be writing novels in front of a huge window with an ocean view. Oceans of narrative truth, that's what he wanted, not flat and stagnant little pools of information. One of these days he'd find something to say, and he would say it wisely and well.

McClintock pressed the eraser end of his pencil against his lower lip. 'Boss,' he meekly said, 'what if I say he's alive and he isn't? Is that libel?'

Magnus locked his hands behind his head and pushed back in his squeaky chair. 'Freddy, do you bear malice in your heart toward Augie Silver?'

'I don't even know the man.'

'No malice, no libel.'

'I know, I know,' McClintock said. 'But what about for dead people?'

His editor considered. Facts bored him, yes, but occasionally they pretzeled up into paradoxes he found amusing. 'The only other criterion is demonstrable economic damage to someone's reputation ... But if someone's dead, how can you damage his reputation just by claiming he's alive?'

Arty Magnus was a savvy fellow, but he didn't understand the market for fine art.

CHAPTER SEVENTEEN

'SONOFABITCH,' said Kip Cunningham. 'Sonofabitch. That bastard is going to spoil everything.'

He wriggled in the stately leather chair in the locker room of the University Club, then adjusted the thick towel that had gotten tangled between his thighs as he twisted. Not far away, his squash racquet lay on top of a pile of dirty sweaty clothes that a flunky would pick up, launder, and neatly fold. He sipped his club soda and lime and cradled the phone against an ear that was still damp from the shower.

'It's only a rumor, darling,' said his wife. She'd taken to calling him darling again, and Cunningham was too oblivious to notice that she called him that the way some people call a Lhasa apso Killer or a knocked-out fighter Champ.

'Rumor? You just said it was in the paper.'

'Not a real paper,' she said. 'Only the *Sentinel*. And the *Sentinel* always gets things wrong.'

Cunningham sipped his soda and looked for the comfort in this. A couple of club colleagues strolled by, splotched with sweat and red as beef, and the bankrupt tried to look like he was doing business, real business, rather than helplessly hoping his wife would finesse him out of hock. Importantly, with great acumen, he moved the phone to his other ear.

'What if it isn't wrong?' he said at last.

Claire Steiger looked out her office window onto 57th Street. It was just after six. People were darting home from work, out for drinks, to early movies, to the park for a stroll. She tried to remember, and vaguely could, the romance, the dim still perfection of warm late-May dusks in Manhattan. Going to the theater while at the western verge of 45th Street the sky was red above the river. The cafe off Madison where darkness would slip in soft as Margaux while her handsome husband told laconic but exciting tales of business and she tried to think past his immaculate shirts to his skin. Was that this same city in this same season?

'Awkward,' she said. 'It would be very awkward.'

'Muck up the auction,' said Kip Cunningham. It wasn't a question, wasn't a statement, just a mumble. Absently he glanced toward his dressing cubicle where a white-haired black man was stooping slowly to gather his dirty clothes. 'Maybe people won't find out,' he added. The sneak's last hope.

'Kip, don't be an ass. True, not true, anybody who might conceivably be interested is going to hear about this by tomorrow.'

There was a silence. The squash player looked across the locker room at a calendar near the pro shop window. It was a pin-up calendar of sorts, but instead of women as the objects of desire, each month had a different yacht. May had an elegant Concordia with tanbark sails, but Kip Cunningham wasn't looking at the boat. He was counting days until the Solstice Show, gauging how much time it would take for things to fall apart. 'So how'll it play?'

His wife had turned her back on the window, on its mocking promise. 'Depends,' she said. 'Best-case scenario, the rumor is false. Nothing has really changed, and this buzz about the artist's return just adds interest.'

Oddly, disconnectedly, Kip Cunningham began to chuckle.

Claire Steiger could find nothing remotely humorous in what she'd said, and she imagined her husband must be party to some clownishness in the locker room. 'Kip, if you can't even pay attention to what I say—'

'Oh,' he interrupted, 'I'm paying very close attention. You just said you hope that Augie Silver's dead.'

The artist's dealer underwent a hellish moment of knowing she'd been caught, a moment as unsettling and humiliating as being discovered naked in a dream. She squirmed in her chair as though dodging thrown rocks, scrambled in her mind for some avenue of excuse, some route of escape. 'I didn't say anything about Augie Silver,' she protested, and her voice was thin and shrill. 'I was only talking about the situation.'

Kip Cunningham had not won much lately, not in business, not in squash, not in his marriage. He savored the event, let it fill his senses like wine, and when he answered, it was in the sweetly condescending tone of the victor. 'But, my dear,' he said, 'Augie Silver *is* the situation.'

*

The next day was a Tuesday, and just after ten o'clock in the morning Reuben the Cuban climbed the three porch steps of the widow Silver's house. The key he'd been given many months before was in his hand, but even though he knew that Mrs Silver would not be home, would be working at her gallery, he knocked. It was the proper thing to do, not only for a housekeeper but for anyone approaching another's place. He knocked, he waited, and was just moving the key toward the lock when the door swung open.

Nina Silver stood before him, and even though she was smiling, Reuben was concerned that she was ill or freighted with that sadness that weighed people down like the muck around the mangroves, that made it so hard for them to move that they stayed in their houses, then in their rooms, and finally in their beds. With his eyes, he asked if she was all right.

By way of answer she grabbed him by his slender wrist and coaxed him across the threshold into the living room. 'Reuben,' she said, 'something wonderful has happened. Mr Silver has come back.'

He looked at her, then past her shoulder at the blues and greens, the curves and edges of her husband's paintings. She did not seem crazy, but Reuben was afraid for her. Hadn't he served at the dead painter's memorial? Hadn't he heard the bald man with the deep voice give the eulogy?

'Come,' the former widow said, and again she took his wrist. 'I'll show you.'

Reuben's feet did not want to move, it was as if they'd been replaced by wooden skids that scraped hotly across the floor. He dreaded the moment when he would stand in the bedroom doorway and see nothing, and would know that he had lost a second friend, not to the ocean this time but to that other bottomless sea called madness. He struggled for the courage not to close his eyes.

He let himself be dragged down the hallway, and when he saw Augie Silver propped on pillows, his white beard billowing forth like foam, he did the pure and necessary thing. He fell to his knees with his chest across the returned man's bed and wept against the back of his bony hand. His tears left dark streaks on the sunscorched skin that was white-coated with a powdery dryness. The parrot looked on and did a slow dance on its perch.

'I pray for you,' Reuben said through his weeping. 'I don't like to pray, I don't believe, but I pray for you, then I feel like I believe enough to feel bad I don't believe, so I shouldn't pray. But I pray for you, Meester Silber. I do.'

Augie put his hand on the young man's dark hair. 'You're a pal, Reuben. You're really a pal.'

He received the words like an anointment and answered with a knightly modesty. 'Yes,' he said. 'A pal for you. And for Meesus Silber too. A pal.' He stood up, wiped his eyes.

'The Cubans saved my life, you know.'

'Yes?' said Reuben. There was confusion in his heart. The Cubans were his people, and if they were kind to Mister Silver he was proud. But the Cubans were also the ones who called him *maricón* and made him feel cast out, who scoffed and threatened and mimicked his walk. Why was he outside the circle of their kindness?

121

'I'll tell you about it sometime,' Augie said, and then Nina caught Reuben's eye and gestured him out of the convalescent's room.

They went to the kitchen. Morning light was pouring in through the French doors at the back of the house. Hibiscus flowers were stretching fully open, their pistils brassy with pollen and thrust forth like silent trumpets. The dark leaves of the oleanders looked almost blue.

'Reuben,' Nina said, 'Mr Silver has been very sick.'

The young man breathed deeply, taking the weight of his friend's illness into himself. He nodded solemnly.

'He needs a long rest, a perfect rest. And he needs someone to spend the days with him, to make sure he isn't bothered. Someone whose company he finds soothing. So I was wondering—'

'I will do it,' Reuben said.

She looked at him, began just barely to smile, then understood that a smile was not called for, would cheapen the moment. 'Maybe you should think about—'

'I will do it,' he repeated.

'But Reuben, your other jobs. You should speak to Mrs Dugan.'

'I will tell Mrs Dugan.'

Nina lifted her eyebrows and looked down at her cuticles. She knew Sandra Dugan slightly – a quiet woman and nobody's pushover, a recent New York transplant who ran her business as a business: She had imported to Key West the exotic notion that a person might show up to clean two weeks in a row. 'Maybe you should *ask* Mrs Dugan.'

Reuben gave a philosophic shrug. 'It is no difference. If I ask and she says no, I quit. If I tell and she doesn't like that I tell, I am fired. It is the same.'

'But Reuben—'

'Meesus Silber, please. It is what I wish to do.'

And so it was agreed.

Reuben put his apron on and started to clean, humming Cuban songs. He dusted, he vacuumed, he cut flowers from the yard and arranged them neatly in porcelain vases. He was happy and proud. He had been singled out, called upon to serve, to care, to have the privilege of watching his friend grow stronger. He would watch him like a fisherman watches the sky, alert and knowing, the first to see a change, a danger. He would be the kind of friend he wished he had, and so perhaps become worthy of having such a friend himself.

CHAPTER EIGHTEEN

'MAYBE IT'S LIKE an Elvis sighting,' said Ray Yates. 'You know, a delusion people have to link themselves to someone famous, to feel important.'

'Our friend Augie,' said Clay Phipps, 'wasn't quite *that* much of a celebrity.'

'Local celebrity,' Yates countered, 'local delusion.'

The talk-show host had just finished work. His theme music, as usual, had made him thirsty, and now he was drinking with his buddies at Raul's. Overhead, misted stars showed here and there through the thinning bougainvillea. The relentless heat had baked most of the flowers away, they'd puckered up and fallen, fluttering to the ground like singed moths. What would survive the summer was mostly just a knuckly vine armed with thorns as sharp as fish hooks.

Robert Natchez took a pull on his rum, then clattered his glass onto the varnished table. The mention of Elvis had made him testy, as references to pop culture always did. Why did intelligent people gum up their brains with such garbage? How did such inane and trivial crap insinuate itself into the conversation of the sophisticated? 'Look,' he said, 'it's one more instance of the *Sentinel* fucking up. Why not just leave it at that?'

'You don't have to get mad,' said Clay Phipps. It was a way of egging the poet on, and it always worked.

'I do have to get mad,' he said. 'We're trying to have a civilized discussion here, and suddenly it's dragged down to the level of some Shirley Maclaine, Oprah fucking Winfrey, Nazi diet horse-shit. Tabloid television. It's cheap. It's disgusting.'

Phipps sipped his Meursault, noted how its caramel low notes came forward as the wine warmed, and tried to look contrite. 'All right, Natch,' he said, 'you pick the level of discourse.'

Natchez froze for an instant like a second-string halfback who's been clamoring all season to carry the ball and realizes suddenly he's got to run with it. 'All right,' he said, 'all right.' He cleared his throat, took a sip of rum. 'First of all, we're all agreed that Augie is dead and the newspaper is wrong. Right?'

He sought out his friends' eyes and extorted hesitant nods, though the fact was there was no more reason to doubt the published story than to believe it.

'OK,' Natchez agreed with himself. 'So how does a sick rumor like this get started? Is it just that so little happens in this town that make-believe is required to fill in the blanks? Is it some lunatic form of homage? Does it start as an innocent mistake – someone who doesn't even know them sees Nina standing for half a second next to someone who vaguely resembles Augie, and boom, right away it's the buzz of Duval Street?'

Ray Yates had been sitting with his forearms flat across the table. A thin film of sweat had glued them to the varnish, his skin made a sound like tape lifting as he shifted positions to raise a finger. 'Natch, hey,' he said, 'back up a step. What makes us so sure the rumor isn't true?'

The poet paused a beat, then visibly brightened, having thought of one of the glib but vacuous pronouncements of which he was so proud. 'Because a person gets one life and one death. And Augie's had his.'

'Very neat,' said Clay Phipps, 'but what if it just ain't so? What if he's had his one life and his one death, and it turns out he's alive again?'

There was an odd thing about Robert Natchez's bardic pronouncements: Once he'd made one he was stuck with it, he'd go to any length of logical gymnastics and verbal fireworks rather than admit that his lovely remark was finally devoid of content. 'Then, by definition,' he blithely announced, 'he's no longer a person.'

'Now you're being an asshole,' said Ray Yates.

The poet was undaunted. He was happy. He was holding center stage, and besides, ideas in which people vaguely figured held his interest a great deal more than people did. 'No,' he said. It was not exactly a denial that he was being an asshole, more a categorical disagreement with anything anyone else might say. 'Look, a person has certain prerogatives. Life, liberty, pursuit of happiness, that kind of bullshit. You think those prerogatives are boundless? No. They apply to one life, one death, one period of mourning. Once a person has used those up . . .'

Natchez fell silent and dimly realized he had no idea what he would say next. Yates and Phipps were staring at him, not drunk but not quite sober either, their eyes a little soupy with alcohol and mugginess. Beyond the knuckly bougainvillea, sodden summer clouds were massing; muted lightning bounced around inside them, indistinct and fleeting. The poet was not the type to leave a line of thought unfinished, but he understood that to go farther was reckless. It wasn't so much that he would say what he believed as that he would have no choice but to believe what he had said, since no utterances except his own could penetrate his skepticism and teach him anything. Recklessly, he continued.

'Once a person has used up his life and his death, he's got no rights left, don'tcha see? Laws don't apply or protect him, usual standards make no sense. He's an outsider more than any living person can be an outsider. An alien, a ghost.'

'How about if he's a friend of ours?' Clay Phipps asked mildly.

'Can a ghost be a friend?' Natchez shot back. 'Can a ghost be anything?'

'You're crazy,' said Ray Yates, to which Robert Natchez gave a satisfied smile.

They went back to their drinks, and the smell of the air changed. Suddenly it was carrying salt and iodine and a suggestion of dry shells. Clay Phipps poured the last of his unshared wine and turned the empty bottle upside down in the bucket of long-melted ice. 'S'gonna storm,' he said.

'S'gonna be weird,' Yates mused, 'if Augie really is alive.'

'Wouldn't be hard to find out,' Natchez said.

Phipps regarded this as a challenge aimed squarely at him, and he hid his eyes in his glass. He wanted no more

than the others to be the one to ask Nina Silver if Augie
had returned. He could think of no delicate way to
phrase the question, and he didn't want to confront her
redoubled grief if the rumor turned out to be false. But
Phipps had once upon a time been Augie Silver's best
friend. He'd been his eulogist; he'd tried, albeit feebly,
to seduce his presumptive widow. 'All right,' he said, in
the tone of a guilty man taking on a debt of penance. 'I'll
find out. I'll stop by. Tomorrow.'

The rain came just as the three friends were parting on
the sidewalk. It came down heavy but slow, in fat warm
creamy drops driven now and then by soft gusts that
blew sheets of it sideways past the streetlights while
other parts rained down straight as tap water. Ray Yates
was soaked before he'd even reached his scooter; his pink
and lime-green shirt wrapped him like a tattooed second
skin. He kick-started the little bike; the gears clattered
unpromisingly, then a spark survived the deluge and the
motor whined, making a sound like a mosquito in your
ear while you're asleep.

Key West is very flat and almost all of it is paved; the
place drains about as well as a concrete basement without
a sump, and a heavy downpour turns it almost instantly
into a paddylike landscape of uprooted garbage cans and
fallen palm fronds scudding by like rafts. Yates drove
slowly. Water came halfway up the scooter's spoked
wheels; water streamed down his legs and between his
toes, over the oozing leather of his open sandals. He
wound his way through the narrow streets of Old Town,

then was able to go just a little faster on the stretch of A1A along Smathers Beach. Dollops of rain pelted his forehead. A pickup truck went by too fast and threw an arcing wave that broke at shoulder height. By the time he'd reached his home on Houseboat Row and locked the scooter to a No Parking sign, his hands and cheeks had been slapped pink by shards of water and three postage stamps buried deep in his wallet had glued themselves to the back of his library card.

His head was down against the rain as he bounded soggily along his gangplank. He didn't see the large dark figure waiting for him there. "Lo, Ray,' it said.

Yates recognized the voice and instantly felt his bowels go soft, a jolting knife-edged heat suffused his cool soaked khaki shorts. He stopped walking and stood there breathless in the rain.

'You're late onna payment again, Ray,' the figure said. 'Tha' shit gets old.'

There are moments in life when anything you do or say is wrong, and if you do and say nothing, that's wrong too. Yates wrestled with the question of meeting his accuser's eyes, though he knew that nothing better or worse would come of it. There were no excuses to be made and no sympathy to be found: This was Bruno. Bruno was a bagman and enforcer for a Miami-based loan shark, bookmaker, and drug pusher named Charlie Ponte, and he was very good at his job. He was loyal as a Doberman and neutral as a snake, unburdened by intelligence and built like a pizza oven. 'Twice I let ya go already,' Bruno said. 'It don't look right, like I'm fucking off. Ya got twelve hunnerd bucks for me?'

The two of them stood there in the pouring rain and neither seemed to notice it was raining. The ocean was pocked, curtains of wet swirled in front of the headlights of the occasional passing car. Ray Yates was into Charlie Ponte for forty thousand dollars. The interest rate was 1.5 percent a week, and Yates had punted on two payments. The gambler had had losing streaks before, but never like this. This was the kind of losing streak from which people sometimes did not recover. 'Bruno,' he said, 'I got like forty dollars in my pocket. Friday I get four hundred something. You can have it all, every penny.'

'Ya don't take me serious,' Bruno said.

'I do. I do,' said Yates.

'Nah,' said Bruno. He sounded sad and neutral. 'On'y way you're gonna take me serious is if I hurt ya.'

Without hurry, he moved through the rain toward Ray Yates, and Ray Yates didn't budge. There is a pathetic inevitability in a confrontation between someone who is tough and someone who is not. It is not a struggle but a ritual, the weak one keeps his anguish to himself and goes down with the humble and defeated silence of some toothless creature being gutted alive by a lion. Yates blinked water off his lashes and peed in his pants. Then Bruno smashed him between his left cheekbone and the socket of his eye. The blow came so quick that the debtor didn't know if he'd been hit with a fist, a forearm, or an elbow. His head snapped back and he turned half sideways, and Bruno pummeled the exposed flank with a punch that shook blood out of Yates's lung. He went down on one bare knee and covered up as best he could. Rain and snot poured down his throat as he labored to get back his wind.

Bruno stood over him, patient as death. He reached into a pocket for his cigarettes, then seemed to notice for the first time that he was soaking wet. He threw the ruined smokes into the water and found a stick of gum instead. He unwrapped it, folded it into his mouth, then gave his quarry a casual kick in the ass. 'More?' he asked. He asked as casually as if he were offering a second helping of potatoes.

'No, Bruno,' Ray Yates whispered. 'No more.'

'"Stan" up like a man then. Ya look ridiculous.'

Yates got to his feet. The left side of his face was already beginning to swell, the eye squeezing shut at the outside corner. His knees were jelly and he leaned against the frail wooden railing of his walkway.

'Sataday it goes ta eighteen hunnerd,' Bruno said. His face was close to Yates's now, and the gambler smelled spearmint gum and garlic through the salty rain. 'Fuck we gonna do about that, Ray?'

Yates's throat clamped shut, and for a while he couldn't speak. 'Bruno,' he rasped at last, 'I don't know. The truth, Bruno? Short of a miracle, I'm not gonna have the money for another three, four weeks.'

The enforcer spit his gum. It hit Yates in the forehead then bounced into the ocean. 'That stinks. My business, that's a long time in my business.'

'Look, tack on a penalty, double the interest, anything you want. Like I told you, Bruno, it's about those paintings. Once they're auctioned there'll be plenty of cash, I'll pay off in full, I swear.'

Bruno put his hands on Yates's shoulders. The gesture was almost friendly, until he started pushing with his ramrod thumbs into the soft places behind the other man's collarbones. 'How long's it been since you won a fucking bet, Ray?'

It was a gauche question and Yates didn't answer.

'What if you lose this next one too? What then?'

'Those pictures aren't a bet, Bruno. They're money in the bank.'

The tough guy dropped his hands, moved his tongue around inside his cheek, and seemed to be considering. Then he looked up at the sky. Rain was still pouring down in big frothy drops, it ran in rivulets between his oily bundles of slick black hair. 'Gonna catch cold on accounta you,' he said, suddenly taking things personally. 'I hate that, a summer cold.'

He grabbed the front of Yates's tropical shirt, pulled forward, then thrust him backward against the wooden rail. The rail was nothing more than a two-by-four nailed onto posts, and the beefy Yates crashed through it like a bowling ball through pins. The water next to the seawall was too shallow to break his fall; knobs of coral racked his legs and slammed against his back and he lay there stunned amid the beer cans and the condoms, the turds and tampons shot out the bottoms of people's boats.

Bruno looked enormous standing on the gangplank. 'I'll see what Mr Ponte wants to do with you,' he said.

He walked off slowly through the rain, and Ray Yates lay dead still in the slimy water until he was very sure the big man wasn't coming back.

CHAPTER NINETEEN

JIMMY GIBBS TOOK UP his position on the port side of the *Fin Finder* near the stern and got ready to loop his heavy line around the bollard. It was June 1. Supposedly the season was over, yet these goddamn know-nothing idiot tourists kept showing up at the charter-boat docks and saying they wanted to go out fishing. Bargain hunters, cheapskates – that's what you got this time of year. Fat guys who drove straight through from Georgia with miniature beer cans in their hatbands; guys whose shirttails wouldn't stay tucked in and whose fumbling fingers would screw things up if they so much as tried to put a shrimp on a hook. They said they liked the heat, these out-of-season visitors, but that was so much bullshit – nobody liked it ninety-two and hazy, with last night's puddles turning to steam that made your legs sweat like hot breath on your crotch. What they liked was the cheap motel rooms, the greasy free tidbits at happy hour, the twofers in the restaurants.

It was funny, Jimmy Gibbs hazily reflected as he tightened down his line with his scored and grizzled hands: You might have thought these people, being less unlike himself, would be nicer to him, less demanding; you might have thought too that Gibbs would feel less touchy taking care of them. But somehow it didn't quite work out that way. There was no bigger pain in the ass on earth than a workingman on vacation. Worried about every dollar; his whole year spoiled if the sun didn't shine or if, God forbid, the fat fuck didn't catch a fish; always suspicious that he wasn't being treated royally enough, that the next guy up the ladder was getting treated better. Rich northerners were wimpy bastards, but Gibbs somehow found them less galling to work for. Maybe it was just that it was less hot when they were here, he didn't end the day quite so wrung out, sweat-soaked, thirsty not in his throat but in some unreachable place halfway down his gullet.

Matty Barnett, looking fine and dignified at the wheel of his boat, cut the engines. In the sudden silence you could hear the whoosh of the pelicans' wings as they gathered to beg for their loops of gut, their fish stomachs full of littler fish.

There were four clients, burned red and swollen with beer, milling around the cockpit, antsy to get off. They filed past Gibbs like he was one more piece of docking hardware, then lolled on the pier, their caps pushed back on their shiny heads. The mate cleated off his dock line and regarded them from under his damp eyebrows: four fat cheapskates waiting to be served.

The skipper stepped down from the steering station. 'Give 'em a beer,' he told Gibbs mildly.

So easygoing, Matty was. So calm, so diplomatic. It's a hot day and they're waiting for their fish; give 'em a beer and keep 'em happy.

It was just the kind of chore, having nothing to do

with fishing or the business of running the ship, that Jimmy Gibbs most hated. He delivered the beers and kept his mouth shut. Then he lifted the ice chest, jackassed it over the gunwale and onto the dock, and got ready to clean the fish.

He hosed down the cleaning board so that the splintered wood gleamed darkly in the sun, then reached into the cooler and grabbed a hogfish. Its tail was curling upward and its eye had the surprised look dead fish often have, a look of disappointment, of having been betrayed.

'Whole or fillet?' asked Jimmy Gibbs.

The four fat fishermen looked over at him and sucked their beers. Then one of them said, 'Hey, that's mine. That sumbitch had some fight in 'im, wuddn't it? Took line, lotta line. That drag screamin', oh shit.'

Gibbs stood there in the sun. His short gray ponytail lay like a rotting log against the back of his neck and dammed up the sweat coming down from his head.

'Fillet, I guess,' the fisherman finally said.

Gibbs shoved his knife in and tried to think of other things. Like money. Soon he was going to have some. The painting Augie Silver had given him was on its way to New York, and it was going to fetch a bundle. The Sotheby's people had no doubt of it. They even arranged the crating, shipping, insurance, said they'd take the cost out later. Pretty decent of them, Gibbs thought. He reached into the hogfish and disassembled it. The guts were cold from the ice and felt almost good squishing through his fingers. He spread the creature like an open book and cut the flesh away from the backbone and the skin.

Then he pulled a small yellowtail, barely legal, out of the cooler. Its stripes were still bright, its brick-red gills fanned out in search of something they could breathe.

'Whole or fillet?' asked Jimmy Gibbs.

Three of the four fat fishermen laughed. The fish guts dried on Gibbs's hands. They itched. Flies came to the dead fish and landed on the first mate's wrists.

'Ain't nothin' t'fillet on that baby,' said one of the laughing clients.

'Leave 'im whole, I guess,' said the one who wasn't laughing.

Gibbs worked. His blue shirt was soaked under the arms and along the spine. A drop of sweat fell into his eye and he had no way to rub it.

When he was halfway through the chestful of fish, one of the clients said to him, 'Yo, friend, grab us another beer.'

Gibbs just stared at him, then went back to his gutting.

Now the clients were offended, they weren't being treated well enough. You could see all four of them turn sulky, just like that. Let 'em, thought Gibbs. The trip was over, and if at the end the four fat fucks got pissy and didn't tip him, who the hell cared? He'd be well off soon, he'd be a captain, and when he was, he'd dock his boat and go sit in the shade, like Matty Barnett was doing now. No more gutting, no more scaling, no more playing barmaid.

He reached into the fish cooler again and told himself to think about the future and be happy. But he wasn't happy. There are two things that drive a poor man crazy.

One is feeling that there's no way out and the other is feeling that there is. What used to be just miserable suddenly becomes unbearable. The last grains of patience slip through the glass the fastest.

'Whole or fillet?' asked Jimmy Gibbs.

The fish on the board was the biggest of the day, a grouper maybe thirty-three, thirty-four inches, ten, eleven pounds. It was a nice fish, but the fishermen were grumpy now, they didn't whoop about it or slap each other on the back. For a few seconds no one spoke, then a loud old car went past in the parking lot and over the noise of it Jimmy Gibbs heard someone say fillet.

He put down his knife, picked up the cleaver and the mallet, and with a single blow that sent loose scales jumping he chopped the head off the fish. Grouper have massive heads, heads like bison, and once this one was severed past the hump, it no longer looked big.

'Fuck you doin'?' one of the four fat fishermen said. He said it loud enough so heads turned three, four slips away, and a lot of people Jimmy Gibbs knew were curious to see what happened. 'I said whole, goddamnit. That one was to show the wife.'

Gibbs looked down at the decapitated fish. The face was at a funny angle, there was an inch or two of blood-smeared plywood between it and the body. The cleaver blow had made the jaws spring open and the tongue was sticking out. Gibbs felt bad. He'd heard wrong, OK, it was his fault. He was choking down some evil-tasting stuff and working up the breath to say that he was sorry.

But the fat fisherman wouldn't leave it alone. He

threw his beer can down and stomped it. It wasn't quite empty and some foam shot out. 'Goddamn fuckin' people roun' here,' he said. He said it loud. 'Fuckin' locals can't do nothin' right.'

A trickle of sweat loosed itself down Jimmy Gibbs's back. Late afternoon sun glared orange on the water, a half-circle of crews and tourists seemed to be drawing closer. Gibbs itched everywhere, his hands balled up and he felt his fingernails clawing at his palms. His knife was on the cutting board in front of him, flecked with gore and sharp as a razor. He'd used a knife once on a man, many years ago. He remembered the weird red pleasure of it, the sucking resistance of flesh to the blade, the fish-eyed surprise on the face of the one stabbed. To kill someone, Gibbs had learned, was less difficult than people thought. All it took was singlemindedness and a burst of raging purity.

Sun glinted off his knife, but when Gibbs made his lunge at the fat fisherman it was the oozing fish head he picked up.

He came quickly around the table, threw himself chest-to-chest against the man who had insulted him, and thrust the amputated grouper head against his cheek. The fisherman stepped clumsily back, warding off the slime with his sunburned elbows. The head slipped out of Jimmy Gibb's hand and skipped along the pavement; gulls swooped down on it instantly and pecked away its eyes. People sprang toward Jimmy Gibbs to fend him off, but before they grabbed him the fisherman fell backward over the curb and Gibbs pancaked down on top of him like a lineman. He managed one weak punch against the ear, one backhand slap across the jaw, and was working his slime-covered hands toward the other man's throat when two guys grabbed him by the armpits and pulled him off. Gibbs jerked his shoulders and kicked the air. The fat fisherman got up spluttering. His three buddies made a token gesture to hold him back, one of them handed him his cap.

A gull tried to fly away with the grouper head, but it was too much weight, the big bird couldn't get it off the ground.

The first thing Gibbs saw as the blind white rage began to dim was the pink and mild face of Matty Barnett. He was speaking calmly to the four fat fishermen, trying to persuade them not to call the cops. 'It's the heat,' he said. 'Guys get a little crazy. Listen, trip's on me, how's that? Someone else'll finish your fish, you'll take the resta the beer . . .'

Gibbs pawed the ground. Cheapskate fat-fuck white-trash tourists: They even found a way not to pay to go out fishing.

Barnett walked slowly to where Gibbs was being held. His crinkly Santa Claus eyes were looking down, his posture was weary. He spoke very softly because there were a lot of people standing by. 'Jimmy,' he said, 'I can't have this. You're fired.'

An unfinished fight leaves a man like Jimmy Gibbs as jumpy as unfinished sex. His muscles were twitching, his insides knotted up for battle, and there was no one left to battle but himself. 'I'm not fired,' he said. 'I quit. Fuck this.' He was not in control of his voice and it got louder and rougher as he thrust his chin toward the *Fin Finder*.

'Next month I'm buyin' the fuckin' boat and you can all kiss my hairy ass.'

Barnett blinked. This was the first time he'd heard about Jimmy Gibbs buying the boat and he set it down to his former first mate's desperate swagger. 'We'll talk about that some other time,' he said, as softly as before. 'For right now you better hit the road.'

The skipper nodded and the two guys holding Jimmy Gibbs moved him out, squeezing tight against his sides like prison guards as they walked him to his rusty truck.

CHAPTER TWENTY

'YOU KNOW WHAT they're starting to say,' said Peter Brandenburg, the art critic for *Manhattan* magazine. 'They're starting to say the whole thing – his disappearance, the retrospective, this supposed miracle return – was one big cheap publicity stunt.'

'That's ridiculous,' said Claire Steiger.

'Absurd,' put in Kip Cunningham.

'Is it?' Brandenburg prodded, and he lifted his martini. For his money, which it rarely was, Coco's Bar at the Hotel France still made the best cocktail in town. The classic glass alone made it worth the seven dollars. And there were no peanuts in the mix served up in heaping cut-glass bowls. Only the more aristocratic nuts: pecans with perfect cleavage, brazils like small canoes, cashews curled like salted shrimp.

'Think about it,' the critic resumed. He wiped his fingers on a napkin, then plucked at the neckline of his woven silk vest. 'You've got a painter who hasn't painted in three years. Who knows if he can paint anymore? He dies and he's suddenly a star. A speculative frenzy kicks in. Then, just when the momentum is perhaps beginning to slow, there's a dramatic new twist: a rumor that he's back! Really, doesn't it seem—'

'Seem what?' Claire Steiger cut him off. Her fingers reached toward the nut bowl and grabbed a couple of depth charges of sodium and fat. She chomped a walnut, then seemed to realize what she was doing and dropped a filbert onto her coaster.

'Convenient,' said Brandenburg, and he managed to make the word sound dirty.

'It's hardly convenient,' said Augie Silver's agent. 'Peter, you remember what happened to prices when Warhol died, when Rothko killed himself. They take a huge leap, we all know that. If it turns out he's alive—'

'Alive, not alive,' said Brandenburg impatiently. 'I'm telling you that people are suspicious, confused, and ready to be very pissed off. It's the kind of thing that ruins people.'

'Ruins who?' asked Kip Cunningham.

Peter Brandenburg flashed him a quick glance from underneath his eyebrows and pretended not to understand the question. He was known at Coco's and it did not do for a critic to look upset, to appear to be taking things personally. But Brandenburg did look upset, if only for an instant, and only to someone who knew him fairly well. Claire Steiger saw the twitch at the corner of his eye and went at it the way a boxer attacks a cut.

'Yes, Peter,' she said. 'Who would it ruin?' She caught her husband's eye and for a second, only a second, they were allies, almost lovers, again.

Brandenburg sipped his martini. He was forty-four years old and had all the advantages that youngish/oldish age could offer. People who didn't know him assumed he must be sixty because he had that kind of power and had been in print forever. Yet there were boyish things about his looks that allowed him still to pass, in any but the harshest light, for not much more than thirty. His reddish hair had neither thinned nor faded. He was lean as he'd been in prep school, his astute hazel eyes were every bit as clear. His posture was firm and rather stiff, inviolate; he was as self-contained as something kept in Tupperware. He didn't answer the question.

'Of course,' Claire Steiger goaded, 'it was really your review that got the whole thing rolling. Is that what's bothering you, Peter?'

'I stand by my review,' the critic said.

'Well, then,' said Kip Cunningham.

Brandenburg turned petulant. 'I just don't want to feel that I've been duped. And I don't want to feel that I've been party to a hoax.'

Augie's agent ate the filbert on her coaster. 'Peter, Peter, I swear to you I've tried to get to the bottom of this. I called the house. The houseboy answers, acts like he doesn't speak English. I tried Nina at the gallery. She's got the answering machine on, she's screening calls, she hasn't called me back. She's still angry about the retrospective. I doubt she even knows about the auction—'

'Sotheby's has a certain aversion to scandal,' said Brandenburg. 'I can see reputations destroyed. I can see the whole thing blowing up.'

Claire reached out and took the critic's hand. It was not a gesture of kindness: She'd noticed many times that Peter Brandenburg did not like to be touched, it only made him jumpier. 'Peter, I assure you this is not a hoax. The tone set by your review—'

Kip Cunningham waited a beat, then reached out and patted Brandenburg's wrist. 'We've got to wind you down, old boy. A squash game and a good long steam. Whaddya say? Tomorrow, four o'clock?'

Augie Silver was feeling slightly stronger, his progress measured in the small, sweet, private victories of the convalescent.

He discovered that if he rested his eyes, just closed them for a few deep breaths now and then, it was much easier to stay awake for more than several hours at a time. He could read, could hold a book and sometimes concentrate. He found that if he stood up slowly, very slowly, he could keep enough blood in his brain so that his vision didn't go blank around the edges, so that he hardly felt the ocean dizziness anymore.

He began to wean himself off broth and return to solid food – soft food, like the peeled, sliced mangoes Reuben the Cuban was bringing to him on a tray.

'Meester Silber?' he said quietly, having softly knocked on the frame of the open bedroom door.

'Come in, Reuben,' said the painter. 'And Reuben, would you stop it already with the Meester Silber bullshit?'

The young man did not answer until he'd smoothed the convalescent's sheets so that the tray fit neatly over them and didn't pull. 'Please, Meester Silber, it is a respect.'

'I know it is, but that kind of respect I don't need. I want you to call me Augie.'

Reuben folded his hands in front of him and looked down at the floor. Then his eye was caught by the vase of flowers at Augie Silver's bedside. The morning's hibiscus blooms were starting to curl; he'd replace them with sprigs of jasmine before he left.

'Awk,' said Fred the parrot. 'J&B. Where's Augie?'

'Ya see, Reuben, even the goddamn bird calls me Augie.'

At this the young man could not help smiling shyly. The parrot was a crazy bird. And Reuben liked it when Mister Silver cursed, he wasn't sure why. Maybe because when other men cursed, cursed in English or in Spanish, there was anger in it, and mockery, and violence. But Mister Silver cursed like telling a joke, like whistling a song, it was not about anger, but freedom.

'So come on, say it: Augie.'

Reuben hesitated. To say a name was no small thing. It carried a weight, an honor. It was a kind of touch. He took a breath, then looked the painter in the eye. It was a bolder look than he had ever cast at Mister Silver and he found it not much less difficult than looking at the sun, but he knew in his heart that the saying of a name should go together with a look like that, a look with nothing hidden. 'Augie,' he softly said.

'Bravo,' the painter answered, dimly aware that this leap into informality, into the first chamber of intimacy, was as much a victory for Reuben as was conquering solid food for him. 'Now siddown.'

He nodded toward the bedside chair, and Reuben the

Cuban didn't budge. A breeze rustled the palm fronds, they scratched at the tin roofs of Olivia Street. The wet smell of mango wafted up from the tray and mingled with the baked aromas of cracked sidewalks and softening streets after a day of blistering heat.

'Reuben, you're here to keep me company. So keep me company, goddamnit. You need a written invitation?'

Again the painter gestured toward the chair, and Reuben glanced at it as though he were standing on a high-dive platform looking down at a bucket of water.

'What the hell is this about?' Augie asked. 'Is it just because you work for us? Because I'm an old fart with white hair? You think we're fancy people? What?'

Reuben shuffled his feet. He glanced at Fred the parrot. For reasons known only to itself, the bird had ruffled its feathers and the lifted edges cast purple shadows against the green. Instead of answering the question, Reuben softly said, 'You really want me to sit with you, Augie?'

'Christ, Reuben. Yes.'

Lightly, gracefully, the willowy young man settled on the edge of the chair. He didn't sit, he perched, an apron across his thighs, most of his weight still carried on the balls of his feet. 'Augie,' he said, 'the reason it is hard for me to sit with you, it is none of the things you say. It is because I think you are a great man.'

Either Augie Silver put down a sliver of mango or the wet fruit slithered through his fingers. 'Ah, bullshit,' he said, and Reuben the Cuban could not help smiling shyly.

CHAPTER TWENTY-ONE

ON THE STROLL up Olivia Street, Clay Phipps counted seventeen cats and eleven dogs. The cats were nearly all in motion – skulking over hot curbstones and slinking through the latticework under porches, stalking palmetto bugs or just being sneaky for the hell of it. The dogs tended to be princely still – laid out on the pavement with their chins on their crossed paws, panting softly, contentedly drooling, fixing passersby with the flatteringly interested glances that canines turn on humans. The day had been cloudless, with an odd desiccating wind from the east. The cactuses were gloating, they seemed to stand up straighter and taller as the palms drooped and the poincianas let their feathery leaves hang down lank as Asian hair. Finger-sized lizards clung to tree trunks and climbed the pocked sides of coral rocks; they were brown, gray, invisible until sex or vanity got the best of them and they puffed up their scarlet throat sacs, making themselves impressive and absurd.

Clay Phipps was not ordinarily a rapt observer of dogs and cats, plants and lizards. But this evening he was trying, with mixed success, to distract himself from the errand he was on. It was, on the face of it, a simple mission, potentially a joyous one, yet Phipps could bring himself to feel no joy. Everything had gotten too screwed up in his feelings toward Augie Silver, his feelings toward himself. Everything made him feel ashamed. He had tried to seduce the woman he took for Augie's widow but who may have been his wife. He was selling, at the first opportunity and with hardly a moment's hesitation, the paintings Augie had given him as tokens of their friendship.

Why was he so willing, secretly eager even, to part with those canvases? There was, of course, the nasty vulgar business of the money. It was fatiguing, a high-wire strain to live wealthily year after year while having, in fact, so little cash, so little real security. His newsletter could go out of fashion, the perks and freebies could dry up, and that would be the end of the amber-edged Bordeaux, the turreted hotel rooms. What would he do with himself? Minus the trappings, Clay Phipps would look to all the world like the small-timer, the perennial freeloader, the facile lightweight he suspected himself to be.

That was why he was secretly relieved to have Augie Silver's paintings off his walls: The pictures, like almost everything else to do with Augie, had come to seem a reproach to him, a reminder of how he'd gypped himself for want of nerve, shortchanged his life in the name of doing what was easy. They'd been earnest young artists together, Clay and Augie had. Augie had stuck to his work and eventually won through to mastery, while Clay had given up on the slow salvation of writing plays and used his skill to carve himself a blithe and cushy niche. They'd been bachelors together back when being a bachelor was rambunctious, ribald fun. Augie had emerged from the debauch with the mysterious readiness for love, for marriage; Clay had not emerged at all, just grown stale within the ever staler game. He had been left behind; no, he had left himself behind, and that was worse.

He walked up Olivia Street and was assaulted by an ugly thought: Certain things would be easier if Augie Silver stayed dead and gone. There'd be a great deal less explaining to do. There'd be no more mute reproaches. Phipps's life had in some sense shriveled to accommodate the fact of his friend's death; he was, if not happy, at ease now in the smaller space, the tighter orbit. Maybe Robert Natchez in some crazy way was right: The world closed up around a dead person, there was no room for his return.

Clay Phipps climbed the three porch steps, paused a moment to smooth his linen shirt, and rang the bell.

After a moment Nina Silver opened the door, not very wide. She was backlit by the yellowish glow of the living room, her jet-black hair was square across the bottom and perfectly framed her oval face. She smiled at Clay Phipps, but her posture was the posture of a sentry.

'Clay,' she said. It was neither unfriendly nor welcoming.

'Nina,' he said. He waited a polite interval to be invited in and was only slightly surprised when the invitation didn't come. 'I was wondering how you are. These rumors . . . It must be very trying.'

'I'm all right, Clay,' the former widow said. 'Thank you for your concern.'

There was a silence, and Clay Phipps's falseness filled it up the way a bad smell fills an elevator. Then the evening's first locusts began to rattle. Blocks away, some idiot revved a motorcycle. The family friend cleared his throat. 'Nina,' he fumbled, 'the rumors, the newspaper . . . Is it true? Is he back?'

There is a horror of lying about important things that is more ancient than morality, a kind of religious terror of tempting fate, offending the universe by denying some crucial facet of it. Nina Silver wanted nothing more than to be left alone, and there was no way she could lie about her husband being alive. 'He's back.'

'My God.'

'He's been through hell, Clay. He's very ill, he's very weak. He's not ready to see people.'

'I understand,' Phipps mumbled, feeling that he understood nothing, neither life nor death, friendship nor love, loyalty nor envy.

'Please keep this quiet, Clay. Please? We'll call you when he's a little stronger. I promise.'

'All right,' said Phipps, 'all right.'

He backed down the porch steps, he didn't know how his feet found the stairs, the sidewalk. On the way home he didn't notice dogs or cats, trees or lizards. He didn't see the misted moon or the swarms of moths around the streetlights. He was looking for something else, scanning his heart for some bright patch of gladness at learning Augie Silver was alive. The gladness should gleam, he thought, the way a pool of cool water gleams in the desert; he could steer his steps to it and be refreshed, be saved. But first he had to find it, and though he looked at nothing else as he strolled down Olivia Street, he couldn't find the glad gleam either.

When he got home he was rattled and thirsty. He grabbed an extravagant Pauillac, an '82 Duhart-Milon, and noticed that his fingers were unsteady as he sliced the lead foil. The wine poured purple and thick, it glubbed as it squeezed through the neck of the bottle. No light came through the bowl of the glass, and the first smells were black smells, licorice and tar.

Phipps took the wine to the living room and sat down on the sofa. The pale, denuded rectangles where Augie's paintings had hung put a crazy pattern on the wall. Phipps told himself he'd have the place painted soon.

Augie Silver was alive.

Phipps drank. The wine was closed up still, it tasted less than it smelled and had a steely edge. He sucked air through it. Some of the alcohol was siphoned off and different flavors seemed to move like different-colored pebbles to different places in his mouth. Amazing stuff, Pauillac.

Augie Silver was back, and Clay Phipps was one of the very few people who knew it for sure.

He poured more wine. The wall of tannins opened just a bit, glints of fruit came through like sun through the chinks of a blind. Dusty currant with an undertaste of plum, held together by a teasing astringency that did rude things to the tongue.

Augie was alive, a lot of things were changed, a lot of plans suddenly in chaos, and as Clay Phipps drank he saw less and less the wisdom or necessity of keeping it to himself.

Claire Steiger, at least, should have the information.

He lumbered to his desk, looked up the phone number of the Ars Longa Gallery in New York, and left a message with the answering service. Then he refilled his glass. The wine was getting soft and comfy as a well-used baseball mitt.

Why shouldn't Robert Natchez be told? Why not Ray Yates? They were friends, after all, they had a right to know.

Phipps made two more calls. But Natchez was at a reading and Yates was hiding from his loan shark, and he just talked to their machines. He poured out the last of the wine. He didn't think he'd broken his word to Nina Silver. Had he even given his word? He couldn't quite remember. That part of the evening seemed a different day. His conscience was not clear exactly, but shut down, benumbed. If he'd failed to find the cool, clear water of loyalty, he'd at least availed himself of a damn nice puddle of wine. His balance just a little tentative, he slipped out of his linen clothes and went to bed alone.

CHAPTER TWENTY-TWO

'DID YOU EVER SEE that experiment they do with the Ping-Pong balls and mousetraps?' Arty Magnus asked his eager but ungifted protégé, Freddy McClintock. 'They set about a zillion traps, load 'em with Ping-Pong balls instead of cheese. Then they drop in one tiny, almost weightless Ping-Pong ball. It lands on a trap and sets it off. Now you've got two balls clattering around. Then four, eight, sixteen, thirty-two, infinity. It takes about one deep breath to happen, and with all the snapping springs and flying balls and mayhem it very soon becomes impossible to figure out how the whole goddamn thing got started.'

The young reporter used the eraser end of his pencil to coax his red hair back from his sweaty forehead. 'And you're saying that's how news spreads?'

'Very good, Freddy,' said Arty Magnus. He swiveled in his editor's chair, put his feet on the air conditioner that dribbled water more than it pushed air, and wished that he was somewhere else. 'You're catching on.'

McClintock beamed. He was proud of himself for finding confirmation of the Augie Silver story, though all he'd done was put himself, quite by chance, on a collision course with the bouncing bit of news.

Ray Yates and Robert Natchez, having heard last night's messages from Clay Phipps, had convened for breakfast at Raul's. Their waitress was a lush who finished her workday at 3 P.M. and promptly repaired to the Clove Hitch bar. Making chitchat with Hogfish Mike, she told him of the miracle return she'd heard the two discussing. Curran, amazed that anyone could survive being sucked into a waterspout, told the tale to several customers, Jimmy Gibbs among them. McClintock, nosing around the charter-boat docks somewhat aimlessly, picked up the yarn from a group of skippers who had no customers that day.

'So I'll do a follow-up?' McClintock asked.

'What do you have to add?' said Arty Magnus.

'That the rumor was true,' said the young reporter. 'That I was right.'

'You think anyone gives a flying crap you were right?'

McClintock's lips moved but he found he had no answer. There were in fact some new parts to the story, but the local newshound, moving in his small domain, hadn't collided with them. He didn't know who Claire Steiger was, or that she had spent that morning strategizing with the small group of allies she despised and badly needed. He didn't know that Jimmy Gibbs, now jobless and having torched his bridges, had, in his provincial purity, called Sotheby's to ask if the auction could still be held if the painter was alive.

'Let it rest a day or two,' said Arty Magnus. He looked up and saw how crestfallen young McClintock was. That was the bitch of playing mentor: seeing people become disillusioned without getting any smarter. 'Look,' he said more gently, 'if you're right, you'll still be right in forty-eight hours. If he's alive, he'll be alive. What's the hurry?'

During those forty-eight hours, Augie Silver seemed quietly to break through some mysterious barrier that had been retarding his recovery. His ravaged body grew cleverer at relearning things, battered organs remembered their functions, and he felt a mute animal joy at the wonder of recuperation. That a broken thing could fix itself – this was as marvelous a fact as anything under heaven.

He began to sit outside in the mornings, before the days had grown too beastly hot. Reuben brought him coffee and fruit in the shade of the poinciana tree. Augie watched the shadows move across the yard, looked at cloud reflections in the swimming pool when the wind was very still. Sometimes he sketched – pencil drawings of flowers and shrubs, quick life studies of Reuben which he would sign with a flourish then give the young man to take home. When the sun got high, Augie would go inside to nap, and the naps now seemed like earned rest from some activity rather than a mere slipping backward into helpless exhaustion.

On the fourth of June, the convalescent had his best day yet. He ate. He drew. He strolled around his yard on legs that did not tremble. Midday, he took siesta and was ecstatically awakened by the tropical music of a fierce brief downpour clattering on the roof.

That evening, when Nina came home, there were

high spirits in the house. Augie's health was a shared crusade, a common mission; everyone partook of his invigoration, as though he were a racehorse. Reuben allowed himself a flush of knightly pride in his care and vigilance. Nina's face softened, the tension in her jaw diminished as she stroked her husband's forehead and found it neither cold nor feverish.

For a little while they sat out by the pool, the three of them. Nina had a glass of wine. Reuben accepted a bit of rum. Augie asked for Scotch and was allowed a few drops in a lot of water. 'Cutty Sark,' said Fred the parrot as he perched on the back of a lawn chair.

'Bullshit,' said Augie. 'H-two-O.'

The sky dimmed and deepened to a jewel-box blue, and Reuben the Cuban got up to leave.

Augie Silver, the green parrot perched upon his shoulder, began the long slow stroll to bed.

Outside the front door, just on his right as he exited, Reuben found a small bakery box with a card taped on top. He picked it up and brought it in to Nina. 'Look what someone left,' he said.

Nina opened the card. Small neat handwriting she didn't recognize said, 'A Speedy Recovery.' Inside the little box was a single Key lime tart, the authentic kind that's yellow, not the tourist kind that's green.

'How nice,' said Nina. 'I wonder who brought it.'

Reuben shrugged and smiled. He didn't know, but it made him happy that there were others who agreed that Augie Silver was a great man and who wished him well. He said good night again and slipped away.

Nina took the tart out of the box and put it on a plate.

Augie loved Key lime, anything Key lime. She was happy
to get more food into him, coax another few ounces back
onto his frame. She carried the treat toward the bedroom, and before she'd even reached the doorway, she
sang out, 'Dessert, Augie. Someone brought dessert.'

Augie was already in bed, he had the sheet pulled
halfway up his sunken white-haired chest. He'd lit the
hurricane lamp on the bedside table; it cast a weird light
on the parrot's belly as the bird side-stepped on its perch.

'I want to make love with you, Nina,' the painter said.
'I want to try.'

His wife swallowed, couldn't breathe, couldn't move.
The last light made soft blue boxes of the windows. A
barely visible wisp of smoke came through the chimney
of the lamp. Nina tried to say something but Augie put a
finger across his own lips and she didn't get as far as
making words. They held each other's eyes a long
moment, then Nina absently put the plate down on the
bedside table and began to undress. She'd almost forgotten this part of nakedness: being seen, becoming ready.
Lamplight played on her flanks, gleamed on her breasts
and cast shadows in her hollows, and for the first time in
a long time she felt beautiful.

She got into bed next to her husband. His skin was
hot and taut, as if pinched and tucked against his bones,
but it was still his skin, she recognized it, she nestled
close against his chest. They kissed, and through his lean
lips, parched and cracked, she remembered the way of
his kissing, the taste of his mouth was as it had always
been. He touched her and their bodies remembered
things together, struggled back from loss, pain, grief,

disease, redeemed each other from deadness and laughed at incapacity from the high vantage of long love.

Afterwards they cried a little in each other's arms, and after that they slept, slept so soundly that they didn't hear a scuffling as Fred the parrot came down off his perch and ate the Key lime tart, and didn't hear the feathered thump as the bird dropped stone dead on the floor.

PART THREE

CHAPTER TWENTY-THREE

FRED THE DEAD PARROT lay on Augie's side of the bed, but it was Nina who saw him first.

As she sidled sleepily to the bathroom in the half-light of 6 A.M. she glimpsed but did not recognize the stiffening bundle on the floor. It was not till the return trip back to bed that she understood what she was looking at. She squatted over the expired pet and examined it. Fred's eye was open, staring at the ceiling, the lens glassy and thick. The green feathers had pulled in neat as fish scales, and the claws were rounded down as though grasping desperately for some perch in eternity. Nina lifted the bird before figuring out exactly what she would do with it. She held it a moment, noting its fluffy, hollow-boned lightness, then put it softly on her dresser.

For herself she felt no great grief. The bird was noisy, as devoid of tact as a Parisian; the occasionally funny things it said were witless accidents and did not amuse her. But she felt a pang for Augie. She was afraid the bird's demise would depress him, would slow his recovery. As though to fortify him against the loss, she climbed back into bed and softly pressed herself against his taut dry skin.

In the dim light she had not noticed the pecked-at

161

Key lime tart; in fact the arrival of the Get Well offering in its string-tied bakery box had been greatly over-shadowed by the momentous event of making love, and she had nearly forgotten about it. She saw no great mystery in the bird's having died. Parrots were long-lived creatures, but mortal, after all. Things went wrong with them, they caught viruses, succumbed to cancers, just like people. The bird had died and that was that.

Augie woke up shortly after seven. He blinked in the direction of the vacant perch but did not immediately realize anything was wrong. Nina brought him juice and coffee. To make room on his bedside table, she carried away the mutilated pastry and last night's glass of water; she was thinking about how best to break the sad news to her husband and didn't pay particular attention to the mundane chores her hands were doing.

'Coffee in bed,' Augie was saying. He was smiling, he woke up cheerful. He sipped the hot brew a little awkwardly, brown drops clung to his unruly white mustache. 'Makes it all worthwhile just to get coffee in bed.'

Nina sat softly next to him and stroked his hair. 'Darling,' she said, 'something happened to Fred last night. I found him dead this morning.'

Augie frowned and sighed. He sipped coffee and looked out the bedroom window. It was a flat still morning, the breeze had yet to rouse itself, and neither plants, people, nor even lizards seemed quite awake yet either. 'Smart bird,' he said at last.

'He's here,' Nina resumed. 'Do you want to see him?'

Augie nodded, and Nina brought him the dead bird

the way a mother brings a sick child a favorite doll. The painter took the rigid parrot and laid it against his shoulder. He stroked the sleek green feathers, kissed the top of the beak where the flat hard nostrils were, then stoically handed the stiff bundle back to his wife.

'Should we bury him?' Nina asked.

Augie pressed his lips together and shook his head. 'That wouldn't be doing him a favor.' In Key West, not even people got buried; their caskets were stacked three-high in concrete hurricane-resistant mausoleums. The ground was so rocky and the water table so near the surface that even shallow holes filled almost instantly with a gray seepage that oozed through the limestone like milk through a sponge. 'Just wrap 'im up and toss 'im.'

Nina took the corpse to the kitchen, swaddled it in newspaper, and dropped it in the trash, where it lay oblivious among the mango peels, the coffee grounds, the squashed tart in its foil shell.

It was not until hours later, when she was at her gallery and losing herself in the savingly precise task of cutting a mat, that the truth of what had happened flooded in on her with the sudden slow momentum of a car crash. Her breath caught, her stomach knotted. Her hand slipped, the knife zigged crazily across the drafting table and clattered to the floor. Nina didn't pick it up. Paralyzed by an awful certainty, she stood there pale and rigid; and the sunlight coming through the gallery window held no cheer but only a viscous gluey weight.

*

'Lemme make sure I have this straight,' said Detective Sergeant Joe Mulvane. He sat on a corner of his desk and let the thick part of one beefy thigh hang over the edge. His knee almost touched a file cabinet. The tiny office had no window, and a greasy oscillating fan was pushing the stale air around. 'Your bird died and you think someone is trying to murder your husband.'

Nina Silver squirmed in her aluminum chair. OK, it sounded ridiculous. Probably she hadn't done the best job of explaining. But how could she be expected to be cool, organized, thorough? She was panicked. She'd dropped everything, locked the gallery, and ridden her old fat-tire bike as fast as she could to the undistinguished building that served as city hall, police headquarters, and Key West's central firehouse. She'd dashed up the handicapped ramp, sprinted a flight of anciently linoleumed stairs, followed the faded arrows to the police part of the premises. She'd arrived sweating and winded. Instant airtight logic was a little too much to ask on top of that.

'Sergeant,' she said, 'I'm telling you – that tart was poisoned.'

'If we had it we could test it,' said Mulvane. 'Or if we had the bird.'

'I know, I know,' said Nina. 'But I told you. I didn't think. I threw it away. The housekeeper took the trash out – I checked with him. The garbagemen came. The tart. The bird. They're gone.'

Mulvane drummed lightly on his desk with the fingers of one hand. Of all the kinds of people who settle in Key West, not the least numerous are those for whom Key

West would seem the most unlikely place on earth, a purgatory almost, and Joe Mulvane was one of these. He had a pale freckled complexion that could not stand the sun. He was thickly built with larded muscle; you could picture him shoveling snow in a T-shirt, and the heat was for him as much a torment as it is to a long-haired dog. He was not a bigot, but nor did he exactly revel in human diversity. He belonged, it seemed, in a blue-collar suburb south of Boston, a place where people had basement workshops and basketball hoops in the drive-way; yet he was restless, perverse, and spirited enough to flee where he belonged.

'Look, Mrs Silver,' he said, 'I understand you've been under a lot of strain—'

'Don't condescend to me, Sergeant,' the former widow cut him off. 'I'm not a child. I'm not a hysteric. The fact is there are a lot of people who would profit from my husband's death.'

Mulvane pursed his lips and lifted his red eyebrows. When paranoiacs started ascribing motives, it could sometimes get interesting. 'Like who?'

'Like anyone who owns one of his paintings. Anyone who wants to see the price go up.'

'Ah,' said Mulvane. 'Someone who's selling.'

Nina nodded.

'OK,' said the cop. 'So who's selling?'

'I don't know,' said Nina. 'I don't know if anybody is.'

The detective frowned. For a moment it had almost seemed he had a thread. 'Let's back up a step. How many people have pictures?'

Nina shrugged and could not quite rein in a quick sigh of frustration. She admired her husband's profligate generosity – and it had often driven her batty. Forget the money; money, they'd always had enough. But here he had a significant body of work, maybe a great body of work, and he was so casual about it, so careless. Almost as if it didn't matter. And that of course was the crux of it. To Augie, it *didn't* matter. Life mattered. The work was incidental, a by-product, a residue.

'In Key West?' she answered at last. 'Maybe a dozen. Maybe twenty. Altogether, probably a hundred. Maybe more.'

'That's a lot of killers,' said Mulvane. 'Your husband suspect anyone in particular?'

'He doesn't know,' said Nina.

'Doesn't know what?'

'That someone tried to kill him. Look, he's very weak, he's had a heart attack. He can't find out.'

Mulvane scratched an ear, let out a bigger breath than it seemed the tiny office could hold. 'All right,' he said, 'all right. Let's start at the beginning. This tart. You don't know who brought it.'

Nina said, 'That's right.'

'You just found it by the door.'

'No. I didn't find it. It was brought in to me.'

'Ah. Who brought it in?'

'The housekeeper. Reuben. But Sergeant, really—'

'Reuben,' said Mulvane. 'Cuban?'

There was something a little rancid in the way he said it. 'You don't like Cubans?' Nina asked.

'Mrs Silver, I'm a homicide cop. I don't like anybody.'

'All right, then. He's a spick. He's a queer. What else would you like to know, Sergeant?'

Mulvane looked at her. She was artsy but she was prim. The short neat hair. The quiet classy jewelry. She was no longer short of breath and now that she had settled down she was precise and logical as a watch. He leaned forward over her, and in the tiny office the effect was of a mountainous cresting wave about to break. 'What else I'd like to know,' he said, 'is if there is even one small possibly relevant fact besides the fact that it was this queer Cuban who handed you the supposedly poisoned goody.'

Nina bit her lip, then shook her head in a defeated no.

Mulvane shrugged, then reached into a damp shirt pocket and produced a slightly soggy business card. 'Call me when there is.'

'But Sergeant—'

'Mrs Silver, listen. I'm not unsympathetic, I'm really not. But we don't do preventive medicine here. Real murders, people murders, we take care of those first. Dead parrots – call the ASPCA.'

Nina's hands were crossed in her lap. She took a deep breath, then pressed her palms down on her knees and got up from the chair. Grudgingly she took the business card. It was a paltry thing but it was all she had. She said, 'Thank you, Sergeant,' and she turned to go.

When she was halfway through the open doorway Mulvane spoke again. 'That houseboy, Mrs Silver. He have any paintings?'

CHAPTER TWENTY-FOUR

THE RAZOR GLINTED in the dappled shade beneath the poinciana tree.

Reuben the Cuban held it by the yellowed bone handle and for a moment kept the blade poised a couple inches above Augie Silver's upturned throat. Through the thin skin of the painter's neck, the blue and lightly coursing jugular could be quite clearly seen. The funnel of the windpipe stood out fibrous as the gizzard of a chicken. Augie's breathing was shallow but even, his eyes were trustingly closed. Here and there doves were cooing, a hummingbird blurred against the hibiscus. Reuben held his breath and brought the cool and well-stropped blade a centimeter closer. The artist seemed oblivious to the approaching steel, he gave a slight twitch as though in sleep and a sinew fluttered beneath his ear.

'You sure you want to do this, Augie?'

'Go ahead,' the painter said without opening his eyes. 'Get it over with.'

'But the beard looks good. Makes you look like Papa Hemingway.'

'I used to be plenty macho, Reuben. I've caught enough fish and drunk enough alcohol. I don't need to look like Papa Hemingway.'

The younger man shrugged and bent over Augie. With his free hand he pulled the skin along the jawbone, and he began to shave his neck. The dry white hair was light as cornsilk, it drifted onto the old sheet in which Augie was shrouded, and some of it continued falling to the ground. Now and then Reuben rinsed the razor in a basin of hot soapy water. He worked in silence for a minute or two, but there seemed to be something on his mind. 'Is this what macho is, Augie?' he asked at last. 'To catch fish and drink a lot of alcohol?'

Augie smiled and Reuben felt the skin move. 'Part of it,' the painter said. 'Also you have to know how to fix things, cars and such. And you have to fuck a lot of women till it hurts and now and then punch someone in the nose.'

Reuben stood poised with the razor and considered. 'I am not macho,' he confessed.

'Me neither anymore,' said Augie. 'It's a phase.'

The young Cuban went back to his barbering. 'You used to punch people in the nose?' he asked.

'No,' said Augie. 'But not because I didn't want to. Only because I was afraid they'd hit me back.'

'To be afraid,' said Reuben. 'This is not macho.'

'No,' said Augie. 'But everybody is.'

Reuben rinsed the razor. The sun was near its zenith, it made a steely mirror of the swimming pool. The tree the Cubans call Mother-in-law made a rattling complaining noise although there did not seem to be a breeze. Reuben looked at Augie's chin. It was odd to be shaving someone else, to be paying such unflinching pore-by-pore attention to another's face, and there was something deeply naked about Augie's skin, pale under the beard, splotched pink from the tug of the blade as the hair was scraped away.

'You have fear?' Reuben didn't exactly mean to ask the question, he just heard himself asking it.

'Damn straight,' Augie said. He was going to leave it at that, but there are certain questions that are like siphons, they suction off truth and once the flow starts it continues of itself. After a moment Augie went on. 'I used to have a terrible fear of falling short somehow, disappointing myself in some final way, some way that could never be fixed. I'm not afraid of that anymore. No, that's a lie. I still am. But much less. What the hell. But I was terrified of dying down in Cuba, I'll tell you that. Among strangers. Without even saying goodbye to anyone . . . And you?'

Reuben hesitated. It was his own fears that had led him to ask about Augie's, yet he was unprepared to have the question turned around. He rinsed the razor, looked away a moment. His eyes burned. 'I fear to be alone,' he said.

English words, Spanish syntax. Augie didn't quite know how to take it. Feared to be alone in a room? Or feared to live his life alone? Augie decided to address the longer-lasting terror.

'You'll find someone,' he softly said. 'You're a caring, loving man, Reuben. You'll find somebody worthy of you.'

Reuben didn't answer. For himself he didn't mind crying, but he was there to help, not to ask for help, and he didn't want to impose his crying on Augie. He pressed his jaws together, then tried to smile. Gently, he pulled the skin along Augie's jaw and went back to shaving him.

But his hand was trembling just a little, the razor veered from its proper angle and sliced through the skin of the painter's chin. With a nauseating vividness Reuben felt the blade pop through the flesh. For a second the cut place was paler than the skin around it, then it filled with a line of blood that formed a fat red drop at its lower verge. Reuben pulled the razor back and looked with shame and horror at what he had done. He had let his own pain conquer him so that he had hurt his friend. Frantically he began apologizing while his free hand reached for a cloth to dab the wound.

Augie turned his head away. 'It's only a nick,' he said. 'I used to cut myself all the time.'

But Reuben was not to be comforted. He was sorry in English, he was sorry in Spanish. The tears that he'd choked back now broke loose, the drops were thick as Augie's blood. He fretted with the cloth over the painter's cut chin, got it splotched with blood in half a dozen places. The red blots made him feel queasy, and without a word he dashed into the house to fetch a fresh clean towel.

He had just passed through the open French doors when Nina entered from the front. She saw him with the ferocious midday light glaring at his back. She saw that his face was tormented with some terrible guilt. She saw the razor in his hand, the bloodstained cloth. She lurched forward as though she might perhaps attack him, and she screamed. Or thought she screamed. But before the sound had left her throat she had passed out cold and crumpled to the cool bare wooden floor.

Reuben stood there, tears drying on his cheeks, the razor dangling from his fingers.

The sight of Nina fainting had baffled him but also brought back his composure the way a dreadful piece of news can make a drunk man sober. Suddenly it seemed he had a lot to do, and he wasn't sure of the order he should do it in. He had Augie outside, half shaved and bleeding. He had Nina here, blanched, unconscious, her legs folded under her in a way it seemed they should not go. He put the razor and the bloody cloth on the kitchen counter. He approached Nina and tried to lift her to the sofa. She was limp and unhelpful as a sack of rice, and he dragged her more than carried her. He slipped her shoes off, then grabbed the razor and a new towel and went back out to Augie.

Augie didn't seem to have missed him. He was relaxing under his sheet, contentedly baking in the stressless all-over warmth of hot shade. The blood on his chin had thickened to the consistency of jam, solid enough to stem the tide of further bleeding. Reuben resumed his apologizing and Augie told him gently but firmly to shut up.

'For Christ's sake, Reuben, you make it sound as if you'd slit my throat.'

After that the young man worked in silence. Water glinted in the swimming pool, lizards did push-ups on the pitted coral rocks. Dry white hairs fluttered down from Augie's face, they were almost light enough to float away like motes of dust.

Inside, Nina was coming back from the small death of a fainting spell.

Her brain turned on like an old television, the kind that started with a single point of quivering light then popped into a grainy gray in which void images moved like ghosts. One fact filled the screen: Reuben, this peculiar young man she'd trusted and even loved, had killed her husband and it was her fault absolutely for throwing them together. Her own life was finished, that much was clear. She'd forfeited it by this amazing blunder, this astonishing misjudgment. Her eyes opened of themselves, she looked out at the world she'd disowned. She saw the French doors, the flat indifferent light above the pool. The cloth with Augie's blood on it still lay crumpled on the counter. There was nothing left to do but go outside and find the body.

She sat up. Her veins had lost their will and the blood emptied down through them as if through rain spouts; she again grew light-headed. After a moment she stood on legs that no longer seemed her own and moved slowly toward the open doors. She did not allow herself an imagined vision of Augie dead, yet she was assaulted by a lunatic memory of drawing class: a tilted oval standing for a human face, balanced on a stem of neck at an angle that could only be true in death.

She stood in the open doorway now and saw Augie, clean-shaven, shrouded in a sheet but very much alive.

Reuben had his back to her as he finished Augie's sideburns, and it was her husband who saw her first.

'Darling,' he said. He reached up and rubbed his own smooth cheeks. 'I wanted to surprise you.'

'You did,' she said. She struggled to smile and struggled to move forward without letting Augie see that anything was wrong.

'You're very pale,' he said to her. 'Do you feel all right?'

'Hm?' she said. She glanced quickly at Reuben and he understood he should not speak. 'Just feeling a little peaked.'

Augie took her hand. 'Upset about Fred.'

It was not a question and Nina didn't have to answer. Instead, she took Reuben's hand with her free one. She felt she owed him that, and more, for the secret and grotesque insult of suspecting him.

The young man put the razor down and solemnly beamed at Nina's touch. Augie smiled softly. It seemed to him that the three of them were sharing a moment of mourning for the fallen parrot, and to complete the circle he took Reuben's other hand. They were silent for a while as the sun beat down. Doves cooed and blue butterflies flew past, and by the linking of their fingers a pact was formed that was no less sacred for the fact that each of them had a different notion of what the moment was about.

CHAPTER TWENTY-FIVE

IN THE CONFERENCE ROOM at Sotheby's, everything had a name.

The chairs were not just chairs, they were Barcelona chairs. The lamps were Corbusier, the long blond tapered table was Eero Saarinen. The overhead lights were the same that Mies designed for the Seagram Building, and coffee was poured from a Bauhaus pot represented in the permanent collection of the Museum of Modern Art.

None of this was affectation. It was business. In the world of antiques and collectibles, provenance was all. Who designed it? What was the vintage? Had the creator had the grace and the savvy to die and thereby join the Pantheon of bankable reputations? The auction houses had a clear mission to enhance the wealthy public's concern, not to say obsession, with questions such as these. It was all done to enlarge appreciation of the finer things.

Funny thing about the finer things, though: Their value could change dramatically while they themselves became neither finer nor less fine. And this was precisely the phenomenon being discussed in the Sotheby's conference room on the morning of the sixth of June.

Campbell Epstein, head of the Painting Department, flicked the white cuffs of his blue-striped shirt. 'We're thrilled, of course, that the artist is alive,' he said. 'Delighted.' He said this in the direction of Claire Steiger, as if he was paying her a personal compliment. But Epstein didn't look delighted. Nerves had put a yellowish tinge in his slightly hollow cheeks, crinkles gathered between his eyes from the tension that fanned in a scallop pattern across his forehead. 'But it does put a radically different complexion on the auction.'

'I should think,' muttered Charles Effingham, the chairman of the board. Effingham hated meetings. He hated coming into the office at all. He was sixty-four years old, unabashedly a figurehead, and absolutely perfect in that role. Upper-crust British, with a shock of white hair generally described as leonine and an American wife typically characterized as incredibly rich, he served his shareholders best at charity balls, golf tournaments, regattas. Absently, he now riffled through the glossy four-color catalogue that had already been printed at vast expense for the Solstice Show. He found the pages devoted to the works of Augie Silver. Next to each illustration was listed the painting's size, approximate date of execution, medium, and Sotheby's most expert guess as to the value. He read the numbers, then stared at Campbell Epstein over the tops of his elegant half-glasses. 'Rather utopian, these estimates,' he said.

The head of Paintings swallowed so that the knot of his yellow tie bobbed upward above the gold collar pin then quickly subsided like a dying erection. 'Sir, may I be candid?'

Effingham gave forth a soft harrumph. Among his favorite peeves were these spasms of veracity that sometimes overwhelmed executives at meetings. What did they accomplish except to clinch the case that they were talking hogwash the rest of the time?

'The painting market is in a doldrum,' Epstein went on. 'That's common knowledge. The Silver estimates are optimistic, yes. But our hope was that record-breaking prices for this one artist would buoy the entire show, would spawn a sort of chain reaction—'

The chairman cut him off. 'There'll be a chain reaction, all right. When the actual bids fall egregiously short on the Silvers, a chain-reactive pall will descend. There'll be the sad sound of closing wallets. Paddles will come to rest on well-upholstered laps. The bottom feeders will be most grateful.'

The conference room fell silent save for the subtly maddening hum of the overhead fluorescents. Shoes slid softly over the Bokhara rug, someone rattled a Rosenthal cup back into its saucer. Claire Steiger felt that the moment had come to go on the offensive. 'Am I the only one here,' she said, 'who believes the Augie Silver canvases will hold their value?'

She panned her soft brown eyes around the table, and for a moment none of the half-dozen men seated there took up the challenge. Finally, Campbell Epstein said, 'Claire, your faith in your client is touching. But the estimates were based on the assumption—'

'That you had a hot dead painter on your hands,' Claire Steiger said.

Epstein's tie did its little dance, he glanced nervously

at his boss. Effingham looked interested for the first time all morning.

'Well,' the dealer resumed, 'I'm arguing that you now have something better. A miracle man. The publicity will be incredible. And on top of the reviews we already have? The Brandenburg alone—'

'Rather embarrassing for Peter,' came a nasal voice from the far end of the table. It belonged to Theo Stanakos, the director of public relations. Where other people had a brain, Stanakos had a switchboard, a tracking station for gossip in and gossip out, a radar screen on which were etched the trajectories of news, opinions, careers as they took flight, arced, and fizzled.

'I don't think I follow you,' Claire Steiger said. 'Are you suggesting his review was not sincere?'

'I'm saying it was too sincere,' Stanakos said. 'A great deal too sincere. So unlike Peter to get swept up in the emotion of the moment. Or any emotion. He got choked up at the thought of writing a eulogy, I suppose. But now – it seems so excessive. Gushy. Smarmy. Don't you agree?'

'No, I don't agree. I think Peter Brandenburg got it right, and it makes no difference whatsoever if it was a eulogy or a midlife appraisal. What he said would have been said ten years ago if Augie Silver was more ambitious, if he pushed—'

'Claire, Theo,' Campbell Epstein interrupted, 'I think we're getting off the point.'

'We are *not* getting off the point,' Claire Steiger shot right back. 'The point is that Augie's price will hold because his reputation is made, it's assured. The momentum—'

'A living artist can always muck it up,' Charles Effingham put in. He spoke softly but there was something incisive about the Oxford accent, it cut right through the flabbier consonants of the other speakers. 'Every collector is aware of that. This year's genius is next year's buffoon. Look at Schnabel. You can't sell him and you can't even have him on your wall without looking like an idiot. It's a nuisance.'

'But an artist only mucks it up by continuing to paint,' Claire Steiger argued. 'Augie Silver hasn't worked in years—'

'He could always start again,' said Effingham.

'He won't,' said the agent, with greater certainty than in fact she felt. 'I know him. He's—'

'What does *he* think about the prices?' put in Theo Stanakos.

Damn him, Claire thought. Damn his bitchily sharp way of cutting through to what someone doesn't want to talk about. 'I don't know,' she admitted. 'I haven't spoken to him.'

'Odd,' said the chairman.

'He's ill. He's weak. His wife is hiding him—'

'Then presumably,' Effingham went on, 'he doesn't even know his works are being offered.'

Claire Steiger struggled to control her voice. 'If he knows, he doesn't know, what's the difference? The point is that in terms of reputation, in terms of output, he's . . . he's—'

'As good as dead?' suggested Theo Stanakos.

Charles Effingham shook his noble head. 'In this business nothing is as good as dead.'

179

There was a pause. Someone's stomach gurgled, the sound was like the last swirl of water going down a half-clogged bathtub drain.

Campbell Epstein cleared his throat. 'Right. But we still have the question of whether we revise the estimates downward, and if so, how to do it most discreetly and with least damage.'

The chairman of the board looked quickly at his Cartier watch. 'I have a luncheon to get to,' he announced, and the spry old fellow was on his feet before the short statement was completed.

Epstein rose with him and tried to smile. The attempt was accompanied by a sharp convulsive pain in the gut. The head of Paintings understood corporate shorthand. He knew the chairman had just washed his hands of the Solstice Show, the event whose success or failure defined Campbell Epstein's performance for the year. His job, which he hated far too much to be able to imagine losing, seemed now to hinge on whether Augie Silver living was worth anywhere near as much as Augie Silver dead.

CHAPTER TWENTY-SIX

ROBERT NATCHEZ, dressed all in black, sat alone in his tropical garret. From the jungly lot next door came the musky smell of decomposing leaves, the utterly baffled clucks and screams of citified chickens that had blundered into this patch of wild and were unable or unwilling to escape.

An old lamp threw stale yellow light across the poet's desk, put a brown glow in his glass of rum. At his elbow lay a grant application that had grown limp in the steamy air. The South Florida Rehabilitation League was offering two thousand dollars for a poet to teach haiku to crack addicts in halfway houses. Natchez didn't like haiku, found its modesty fake, and he wasn't crazy about crack addicts either. Their eyes were a spooky red and they had a lot of tics. Their shoulders twitched and their noses ran. They tended to like crack more than life, and Robert Natchez, given his own passionate morbidity, would have had a tough time mustering the conviction to talk them out of that preference. But he needed the money.

He needed the money, yet his one Augie Silver canvas still hung on the wall above his desk.

This was because there were other things that Robert

Natchez needed more. He needed to feel exceptional. He needed to maintain the rigid priestly purity that justified him as the final arbiter of right and wrong. He needed to feel superior to Phipps, to Yates, to everyone who had run out to hock his Augie Silver paintings, and as he had lately realized, he needed maybe most of all to triumph in some final way over Augie Silver himself. Augie the sudden darling of the marketplace. Augie the lightweight who had somehow bamboozled the critics with the illusion of substance. Augie whose lucky and so far inconclusive dance with death had cast a falsely dramatic light on what was in the end a small, conventional, bourgeois talent.

Natchez sipped his rum, breathed deeply of the molasses fumes that blended with the lewd and fetid smells of the rotting flowers from the lot beyond the alley. Fine, he thought, as he glanced once more at the application angled on the blotter: Let Augie be the sweetheart of the trendoids from New York, the moneyed philistines with their vapid pictures in their vapid houses filled with vapid conversation. He, Natchez, would fill a nobler, more heroic role: Poet Laureate to the addicted and the retarded, troubadour to the incontinent and the insane. Now here was a mission: bringing haiku to the doomed, sonnets to the senile, nonsense verses to those pure and damaged souls beyond the iron grip of sense. This would be no mere dabbling, no whore's diddling in the gross lap of commerce. It would be a liberation.

Yes. And he, Robert Natchez, would be a Liberator.

The word excited him, warmed his chest like a sudden

image of remembered sex. Poet and Liberator. He swigged rum, pushed his chair back on its hind legs, narrowed his eyes as if contemplating some grand vista, as if orating to a rapt multitude. Liberator. Freeing men from their slavery to a wan and mediocre falseness. Pointing the way to a new order where reigned a more muscular and savage truth, where the authority of the artist was untrammeled and supreme.

Liberator. Isn't that what the greatest of his forebears had always been? Bolívar. San Martín. Even Fidel. Robert Natchez felt a sudden brotherhood with these men who had bloodied themselves in glorious victory over the smugness of wealth and choked tradition. It was exalting, this sudden sense of kinship, and it was odd: Natchez's family had been American for five generations, Hispanic pride had been for him the merest remnant of an echo. Now suddenly that echo was resonating, swelling, doubling back on itself as though whispered in an oval room. He was Robert Natchez, of hot and ancient Iberian blood.

Natchez. It was a strong name and a proud one. But Robert? This gave the Liberator pause. What kind of name was Robert? It was bland, white, uncompelling, neutered. Then there was Bob, a name he'd always loathed, a name for a bait-shop assistant or someone's idea of a funny thing to call a dog. No, these names were unworthy of his newfound vocation, they were names he'd let himself be saddled with too long, but they had never been his true name. His true name was Roberto. In an instant this was clear to him, the realization was as bracing as a north breeze that put to flight the drooping and complacent clouds.

'Roberto.' He said it aloud, rolling the R's, imparting a sensual and manly fullness to the O's. The sound reflected off his pitted walls and delighted him. He said his name again, closing down his throat to create a certain raspiness, a hint of threat and implacable will.

He swigged rum. His skin itched with excitement, with a wet sticky sense of having just been born. He skidded his chair close in to his desk, picked up his pen, and held it so hard it chafed against the small bones of his fingers. Grandly he pushed aside the application form. This was no time for trivialities, it was a time for poetry, for manifestos. With trembling fingers he grabbed a fresh sheet of paper and began to scribble down the creed and testament of this new man, this Liberator, Roberto Natchez.

Jimmy Gibbs opened the rust-pocked door of his bachelor-size refrigerator and looked inside with no great appetite. The dim bulb revealed four cans of beer, one sad misshapen stick of butter with toast crumbs on it, some shriveled carrots, a leprous mango, and one-quarter of a slightly sunken Key lime pie, not the tourist kind that's green but the local kind that's yellow.

He grabbed a beer and the pie and sat down at the nicked Formica table. Outside, tree toads were buzzing in the thick air, the sound mixed unpleasantly with the ugly hum of the ugly orange crime-deterrent streetlights. Not far away tires were crunching over the white gravel byways of the trailer park. The trailer park was on Stock Island, the wrong side of the tracks if there had been any tracks. It was where the help lived, and Jimmy Gibbs never forgot that for a moment. The black women who made the beds and swabbed the toilets in the hotels downtown. The new Cubans who were busboys. The eighth-grade dropouts with their green teeth and goofy smiles who did lawns sometimes, other times tree work, deliveries till they crashed the truck, pools till they fucked up the chemicals and someone got a rash, at which point they got fired, stayed drunk two, three days, then started asking around again.

Then there were the boat guys, the fishermen and the mates. Jimmy Gibbs was one of those until a week or so ago, and from day to day, as his torn hands healed and his aching back unknotted, he remembered it as being a much better job than he'd thought it was when he'd had it. It was healthy outdoor work, had a lot of independence to it. Got him out on the water, paid him a decent if not a handsome wage, let him do what he was good at. That was the main thing, he realized now, as he used some beer to unstick pie crust from his gums. He knew what he was about out there. From icing the bait to battening down at the end of the day, he knew what he was doing.

Well, that was history. He couldn't go back to those docks. He wouldn't. Not after his big blowup and the quiet kiss-off from Matty Barnett. Not after his confident brag that he was coming back to buy the boat. He'd settled things with that one, no denying it. Not that he hadn't spouted off plenty of times before, made a lifelong hobby out of fucking up. But a person's life, he thought, was a lot like fishing line, it had a lot of give, a lot of stretch, but there came a time when the stretch was all played out, the suppleness was gone, you gave one small tug too many and the whole thing snapped, went dead and weightless in your hand. That's how his life felt now, dead and weightless like a snapped line, the fish gone, the battle over way too soon and without even the satisfaction of having been fairly beaten.

And why had it happened? Why? Jimmy Gibbs stared out the little picture window of his trailer, out at the miniature front yard made of gravel and the maze of circuit boxes and crisscrossed wires beyond, and it seemed ever clearer that it happened because he'd been given false hope by a Yankee, an outsider. That goddamn painting, the promised windfall that now fell short. All bets were off – that's what Sotheby's had told him, although they said it prettier than that. And meanwhile he'd gone over the edge. Bitterly, Jimmy Gibbs remembered Hogfish Mike's whispered counsel on the eve of Augie Silver's memorial: *He's not your bubba*. Well, Hogfish had been right, and he, Jimmy Gibbs, had been stupid to imagine that something good might come from a few friendly moments between a Yankee and a Conch. He'd made a basic and humiliating error – he'd believed the outside world might help him out. And now Augie Silver had cost him his job and his final chance at amounting to something. Maybe he hadn't meant to mess him up, but screw it, intentions didn't matter, results did. And the result was that, as usual, the rich outsider came up roses and the local guy got fucked.

It wasn't fair, it stank. Augie Silver somehow buys himself a second life, and Jimmy Gibbs loses his last best shot at the only life he's got. Two lives to none: The accounts didn't balance, that was pretty goddamn clear. Augie owed him. He ate pie and drank beer, and his tightly pulled-back graying hair crawled in outrage. The way things stood, it wasn't right. It wasn't right at all.

CHAPTER TWENTY-SEVEN

THE DEATH OF FRED the parrot changed the cadences of conversation in the Silver house. It used to be that silent beats were rare; the bird would fill them with imbecile pronouncements that added nothing but, like trills in music, eased the way from one line to the next. Now there were empty moments, it was as if Augie and Nina and Reuben were still holding a place for the departed pet, though from day to day the pauses grew briefer, time was squeezing shut around the lost one, as time does.

But if Nina was worried about the bird's demise impeding her husband's recovery, she needn't have been. Augie was getting better every day, his vigor leapfrogged over itself, and the pace of his recuperation was accelerating. His appetite was coming back and had far outstripped the wimpy tastes of convalescence: Now he wanted oysters, strong cheese, steak. He drank Guinness like an Irish baby, and a hint of something almost like roundness began returning to his clean-shaven cheeks. Reuben had cut his hair, and, shorter, it had recaptured some of its waviness and spring, the tinsel dryness that had made him look like Father Time was gone. On the ninth of June, the two-week anniversary of his return, he asked Reuben to set up an easel, and he stood at it to draw. Beneath his baggy khaki shorts, the sinews in his scrawny legs flexed with a remembered strength.

With vitality comes restlessness, however, and on that evening, blissfully unaware that someone had perhaps tried to poison him, Augie told Nina he was tired of being quarantined, he was ready to get out on the street, to resume his life, to see some friends.

They were sitting on the love seat near the pool. Nina looked away on the pretext of following the flight of a dragonfly as it skimmed across the water. But the dragonfly vanished and her dilemma did not. She had vowed to shield her husband from all worries; this was the way to save his life. But serene ignorance could be very dangerous now that Augie, sociable Augie, was antsy to reclaim his place at the hub of his circle.

'You don't think it would be too—'

Augie stroked her short neat hair and interrupted. 'Really, darling, you don't have to coddle me quite this much.' There was a pause, and when the painter spoke again it was in a playful tone his wife had not heard for many months. 'Here's what I'm gonna do,' he said. 'Tomorrow, seven-thirty, I'm just gonna pop in at Raul's. Perfectly casual. *Hi guys, what's new?* Won't that be a pisser?'

That night the oblivious painter slept profoundly. His wife stared at the ceiling, at the slowly turning fan whose soft blur riveted her gaze but failed to quell her racing mind. The thin white curtains billowed softly in the moonlight and passed along the damp cardboard smell of closed and shriveling flowers.

In the morning her eyes itched, her skin felt slack, and she had a headache that throbbed with every heartbeat. She got up alone and made coffee. She sat alone at the counter and drank a cup. Her husband was back but now this new aloneness was upon her, aloneness with her suspicions, with what to her was certainty and to others might seem madness. She looked for a bright spot and found none: Either someone had tried to kill her husband and might try again, or she was losing her mind.

Promptly at eight, Reuben knocked at the door. She let him in. He took one look at her and asked if she was ill. By way of answer, she fixed him with a stare that frightened him. There was pleading in it, and also desperation, but more than that, the young man felt, there was a fierce and merciless probing of his worthiness. He struggled to survive that gaze, to muster a limitless and joyful yes to whatever it was that was being asked of him. He held his dark eyes open, tried to put his heart in their black centers. He must have passed the awful test, because after a long moment Nina said, 'Reuben, I have to talk to you. There's no one else I can talk to, Reuben.'

She led him through the house and out the back. Her steps were measured and oddly cautious, as if she was trying to assure herself she was still in contact with the ground. She skirted the pool, had made it almost to the pillow of shade cast by the poinciana tree when she stopped abruptly, like a person with a heavy suitcase who can't go one more step. Reuben was taken by surprise when she wheeled around, he walked into her words as into a hailstorm. 'Someone's trying to murder Augie.'

Reuben said nothing. He put the amazing statement into Spanish but it remained incomprehensible. His mouth opened just slightly and stayed that way.

'I know it sounds crazy,' Nina said, and Reuben allowed himself silently to agree. Her voice was a throaty whisper, her gray eyes, usually placid, were red-rimmed and wild. Reuben at that moment was more afraid for her than for her husband.

She grabbed the young man's wrist and pulled him toward a chair. She sat leaning close to him, her hands on her knees and her head pitched conspiratorially forward like an asylum patient hissing paranoid lies about the staff. She told Reuben about the pecked-at tart, the connections not seen until later. She told him about going to the police, about Joe Mulvane's refusal of involvement; she explained as best she could about the logic of the art world and why the value of Augie's work was set to plummet. She realized in some bone-deep way that if she was enlisting Reuben's help she could hold back nothing and spare him nothing: She told him that she had suspected him.

'Yes, Reuben. When I saw you with the razor, when I fainted . . . I thought you'd slit his throat.'

Reuben took this in. It hurt badly, the pain of it scoured his insides like a rough cloth full of salt. What had he done to deserve his friend's mistrust? Had his own friendship been imperfect? Or perhaps it was necessary to be mistrusted, to feel the shame and the burn of it, as a passage to a deeper trust.

'I did you a terrible injustice,' Nina went on. 'For this you have to forgive me.'

191

'There is nothing to forgive,' the young man said. 'There is nothing to be sorry when you are protecting your mate.'

Nina seemed to take comfort from this, and Reuben was happy. 'No,' she said, 'there isn't. But Reuben, I can't protect him all by myself. I can't. I need other eyes, other ears. I need someone to talk to. Will you help me, Reuben, will you help me protect him?'

Reuben leaned so far forward, it almost seemed that, knightlike, he might go down onto one slim knee. He made bold to take Nina's hand. He didn't know if she was any longer sane. He didn't know if Augie was in true danger. But none of that mattered to his pledge. His pledge was between himself and his yearning, a contract with the ideal, untouchable by circumstance. 'With my life,' he said.

CHAPTER TWENTY-EIGHT

'I REALLY DON'T NEED a baby-sitter,' said Augie.

It was just after seven that evening. The artist was wearing baggy shorts and an ancient denim shirt with fraying buttonholes and paint dabs on the sleeves. His white hair rose and fell in random waves, his deep blue eyes were bright with the prospect of some good talk with his friends; he seemed almost his old self, minus forty pounds and most of his robustness.

'I only drive you there,' said Reuben. 'I wait outside.'

'You're not a coachman,' said Augie. 'I don't want you to wait outside.'

There was a pause, a stalemate in the living room. Nina had asked Reuben to accompany Augie to Raul's, and, by God, Reuben wasn't letting his friend go out alone.

Augie sighed, defeated. 'All right,' he said, 'you'll drive me. But none of this waiting outside bullshit. You'll come in, you'll have a drink.'

'No,' said Reuben, 'I be in the way.'

This time it was the younger man who lost the stare-down.

'OK,' he said, 'I have a drink. But at the bar. I leave you with your friends.'

They got into the old Saab and drove the ten blocks to Raul's. Reuben, a fretful and unpracticed driver, never got past second gear and was hunkered over the steering wheel all the way.

The cafe was crowded, noisy, roiled with the converging currents of people eating on the early side and people extending cocktail hour to the late side. Waitresses slid by with big trays of iced oysters, loud drunks clamored for more beers. Augie, unaccustomed to the clatter of dishes and the press of bodies, felt both invigorated and drained as he picked his way among the tables. Reuben peeled off at the bar, laid claim to a corner stool while waving away the cigarette smoke, and the painter continued toward the alcove under the knuckly bougainvillea, where he knew his friends would be.

He saw them before they saw him, and he was comforted, reassured somehow, that his companions had stayed within the small snug orbit afforded by island life, that certain things about the universe had stayed in place, were still familiar. Clay Phipps still wore long linen trousers that crinkled up behind his knees. Robert Natchez still dressed all in black, in token of some showy grief or theoretical outlawhood. Ray Yates, more local than the locals, still wore faded palm tree shirts and drank tequila.

Augie, unseen, crept up to their table and said, 'Hi guys, what's new?'

Conversation stopped, faces froze, there was a slow distended moment of some nameless guilt, as though the three seated men were kids caught doing something dirty. The awkwardness went on just long enough for Augie Silver to have the first faint inkling that something had gone wrong among his friends. Like rusty musicians, they were off the beat somehow; gestures were stiff, smiles tentative, nothing flowed.

But then Clay Phipps, gracious if not tranquil, was on his feet. For a moment the two old friends stood back and appraised each other in the brave and galling way that old friends do, each seeing in the other the deflating but tenderness-inspiring evidence of his own aging, his own mortality. To Augie, Phipps looked paunchy and somewhat dissolute: a bald, distracted man whose earlobes were stretching and whose shoulders were folding inward. To Phipps, Augie looked decrepit, dried up, stringy as a sparerib; there was something wrenching and undignified about the empty skin around his knees.

They were a couple of fellows on the cusp of being old; they moved together and embraced.

Reuben discreetly but unflinchingly watched them from the bar. He saw, as Augie could not see, the uneasy, ashen look on Phipps's face, a look not of joy but shame.

Yates and Natchez had stood up as well, they reached handshakes across the table that was bejeweled with rings of condensation from their glasses.

'Ray,' said Augie warmly. 'Bob.'

The poet could not help wincing at the bland and Anglo syllable. He looked at Augie hard and said, 'Roberto.'

Augie thought he was kidding, though he didn't see

the joke. 'I go away a few months, and you have an ethnic reawakening?'

Natchez didn't laugh, didn't answer. He just resumed his seat, and Augie was more baffled than before. He decided to try his luck with Yates. 'And Ray,' he said. 'Or Raymond. How're things with you?'

The fact was, things were worse than they had ever been, but the talk-show host didn't feel like going into it. He gave a beefy shrug accompanied by a head tilt that brought into the light the lingering remains of the black eye Bruno had given him the week before. A greenish bruise was ringed by purple clotting; it was hard to overlook.

'Walk into a door?' Augie asked him.

By way of answer, Ray Yates said, 'Siddown, have a drink.'

The painter was settling into a chair when the waitress bustled over. Her name was Suzy, she knew Augie only as a customer, a friendly face, yet she put a hand on his shoulder and smiled broadly when she saw him, and he could not help thinking that this stranger seemed more unambiguously glad to see him than did his closest friends. He ordered a Scotch and water, weak.

'Weak!' exclaimed Clay Phipps as Suzy walked away. 'My God, man, you must really have been through something. Tell us.'

So Augie nursed his watery cocktail and told the story. He knew he'd be asked to tell it many times, it was already taking on a life of its own. It was a story with three characters, even though they were all called Augie. The burly, vigorous Augie who had gone off sailing on that unmenacing day in January was not the same as the mindless half-dead Augie floating away from Scavenger Reef, nor was he the same as the chastened re-emerging Augie who was spinning out the yarn. The name was like a briefcase, monogrammed but hollow, the only thing that stayed the same as the contents were shuffled in and shuffled out. 'So here I am,' the latest Augie concluded, 'back where I started, beat to hell, and in some weird way happier than I've ever been.'

He broke off. Bar noise flooded the silence, the sun-seared bougainvillea rustled with a papery sound. Then Roberto Natchez said, 'A charmed life.'

The comment was not generous. It was sour, grouchy, warped by the annoyance people tend to feel at the excessive good fortune of another. Augie looked at the poet not in accusation but with mute inquiry: Was he jealous even of another man's near death? Natchez's face told him nothing; he glanced at Yates and Phipps and came away with the unsettling feeling that the poet had somehow spoken for all of them, that all were envious of his adventure, his resilience, that his return in some dim way affronted them. Suddenly Augie was depressed, confused. He wanted to believe that he was only tired, maybe the noise and the smoke and the unaccustomed sociability were draining him too much, overloading him and skewing his perceptions. But sitting there among his buddies he felt more exiled, more cast adrift, than when he had been lost at sea.

'I think I'd better go,' he said, and no one tried to talk him out of it. 'Doesn't take much to exhaust me.'

He rose amid uneasy smiles, paused for handshakes

that fell short of being hearty, and slipped out past the bar. Reuben the Cuban, vigilant and silent, slid gracefully off his barstool and was ready to take him home.

The next day, in answer to a call from Augie, Clay Phipps came to visit.

He arrived at the door with beads of sweat strung along his bald pink head and a bakery box neatly tied with string in his hands. Reuben took the box and held it like it might contain a bomb. He remembered the Key lime tart; he remembered the guilty look, the Judas look, on the heavy man's face when he and Augie had embraced.

Augie, fresh out of the shower, came into the living room and said hello.

'I brought some cake,' the visitor said. 'Want some cake?'

'Later,' said Augie, 'later. I want to talk.'

He led the way through the painting-strewn house, out toward the backyard. Reuben wondered why a fleeting look of disappointment had crossed Clay Phipps's face when Augie declined the pastry. Maybe it was just that the husky man wanted a slice himself. Or maybe there was some other reason.

Augie motioned Clay Phipps toward the love seat where the family friend had felt up Nina, but he slid away from the illicit spot and took a single chair instead. He settled in, then nodded toward the west end of the pool. 'That's where I delivered your eulogy. Set up a lectern so I wouldn't fall in if I swooned.'

'Nina tells me you praised me out of all proportion.'

'It's easy to be generous to the dead.'

'And extremely difficult to be fair to the living.'

This was a throwaway, a random bit of repartee, but Phipps felt sure it was somehow aimed at him. How much did Augie really know?

'Clay,' his host went on, 'about last night . . .'

'What about it?'

Augie pushed some breath through his teeth, it made a hissing sound. 'Is it just me, or was there some unease, some tension . . .'

Phipps frowned. He didn't especially want to answer, nor was he content to let Augie go on probing. 'Well, you know, the shock, the suddenness . . .'

Augie stroked his chin. 'I'd like to think it was only that. But I felt . . . I felt . . . unwelcome.'

It hurt to say the word, and Augie looked down when he said it. His looking down made it easier for Phipps to tell a lie.

'Nonsense,' he said. 'Ray and Natch, they seem to have a lot on their minds these days, they've been distant with me too.'

The painter considered, decided not without conflict to be satisfied. 'OK,' he said, 'OK. Death, you know, I guess it's made me touchy.'

Phipps saw an opportunity to change the subject. 'Touchy but happy. Last night you said you were happier than ever. How come?'

Augie looked around his yard, smiled at the oleanders and the pendant bundles of poinciana flowers. 'I used to take myself too seriously,' he said. 'I didn't think I did,

199

but I did. This whole thing about not painting. Maybe it could pass for modesty, but it was arrogance, pretension. I mean, what gave me the chutzpah to think I *had* to be that good? So I'm not Vermeer – who cares? The paintings you have, Clay – am I wrong to think they give a certain pleasure?'

Phipps squirmed, gestured vaguely, made a soft harrumphing sound. Augie went right on.

'So I'll paint as well as I can paint, and the hell with it. The people who are happy are the people who get up in the morning and do their best, don'tcha think?'

The question hung a moment in the hot thick air. It was precisely what Clay Phipps thought; and precisely what Clay Phipps had never done. Augie knew that. Was he goading him? Was he mocking him now not only by example but by precept? Or was Phipps, in his guilt and his festering disappointment, simply that determined to take offense, to find or imagine scraps of justification for turning against his friend?

Reuben, moving soundlessly and with his low-slung self-effacing geisha's grace, appeared near the two men and offered them something cold to drink. 'A beer?' he said. 'A glass of wine?'

'And there's the cake,' said Clayton Phipps. 'It's apricot.'

'Ah,' said Augie. He seemed to be considering. 'Will you have some?'

'Me?' said Phipps, as if he was being singled out in a crowded room. 'No, I've just had lunch. I brought it for you.'

Augie pursed his lips, pulled his eyebrows together. A

lot went into a man's decision about whether to have a piece of cake. Was he hungry? Would the sweetness be too cloying in the heat? Did he want the coffee the cake cried out for? Reuben leaned far forward on the balls of his feet, so far forward that he had to flex his toes as hard as he could to keep from falling over. For one mad instant it seemed to him that he should throw himself on Clayton Phipps's neck, wrestle him to the ground, and unmask him at once as the would-be killer. But he waited. He didn't want to make a scene in front of Augie; besides, if Augie said no to cake there would be no emergency.

The painter frowned through to the end of his deliberations. Then he said, 'Yes, I think I'll have a piece. A small one.' He paused a half-beat, then added, 'Sure you won't join me, Clay?'

Phipps shook his head and Reuben didn't like the shadowy smile that slithered quickly across his face.

The young man glided back to the house and paced around the kitchen. He took a knife and cut through the string around the bakery box. He opened the package and looked inside. He saw a neat arrangement of apricot halves, round and orange as just-risen moons, overlaid with a glaze like tinted glass and bordered with a butter-rich marzipan crust. Reuben liked sweets. His mouth, one of the body parts that didn't know what was good for it, watered perversely even as his mind recoiled. He shook his head and swallowed, then brought down the top of the box like the lid of a coffin. He got the stepstool and put the cake on the highest shelf of the least-used cabinet, hid it like a gun from a curious child. He put a bottle of mineral water and two glasses on a tray and went outside again.

'The cake,' he announced, 'I'm sorry, you can't have any.' He poured water for Augie and Phipps, handed them their glasses.

'Whaddya mean, I can't have any?' Augie asked. His body had readied itself for cake, the taste buds were prepared, the passageways open, and now, goddamn it, he wanted something sweet.

'The cake, it will make you sick,' said Reuben. He spoke to Augie but looked at Phipps, and Phipps seemed unable to stay still in his chair.

'Reuben,' Augie said, 'I'd like a piece of cake.'

The young man balanced his tray, bit his lower lip. 'The cake, I didn't want to say this, is full of bugs.'

'That's impossible,' blurted Clay Phipps, who suddenly seemed far more exasperated than was called for by a spoiled cake. 'I just bought it. It's from Jean-Claude's. It's—'

'It's the tropics,' Augie interrupted with a shrug. OK, he'd live without the cake. 'There are bugs here.'

'Well, damnit,' said Clay Phipps, 'there shouldn't be! Not in a fancy cake from a fancy baker. I'll bring it back.'

This, Reuben had not counted on. But for Phipps to take the cake away was out of the question. The cake was very important. The cake was evidence. It would end the danger to Augie and would prove that Nina was not crazy.

'I'm sorry,' Reuben said. 'The cake, I put it in the garbage. The compactor. The cake it is squished.'

Phipps tisked, threw a damp leg over the opposite

knee. Reuben turned back toward the kitchen, wondering if he had seen, along with Phipps's exasperation, a hint of something like relief that the cake had been destroyed. But Augie saw only his visitor's annoyance. He watched him writhe and sweat, and gently mused on how easily rattled people were before they got on terms with death.

'It's nothing, Clay,' he softly said, and he put a hand across the other man's forearm.

'But it was a gift,' the visitor said miserably, and immediately wished he hadn't used the word. It was a gift like Augie's paintings had been gifts, and he, Clay Phipps, was always doing just the wrong thing where gifts were concerned, gifts always seemed to be the litmus test that pointed up his smallness, the unintentional and unchangeable lack of generosity that was poisoning his life. Gift. The word and Augie's all-forgiving touch made him feel as loathsome as a serpent, and as spiteful. He sipped his mineral water, mopped his forehead, and wished that he was home, alone.

CHAPTER TWENTY-NINE

JUNE WAS A SLOW TIME in Key West, slow for culture as for everything else, and from week to week Ray Yates had a tougher job finding guests and events to fill up time on Culture Cocktail. The seasonal people had gone north, taking with them to the Vineyard or to Province-town their harpsichords, their loose-leaf binders of les-bian love poems. Road shows didn't come south in June, and no booking agent who wanted to keep a has-been pop act would send them to this off-season purgatory of heat, humidity, and empty seats. So Yates muddled through with the occasional self-published author, a psychic or two, and the local impresarios who spoke with relentless enthusiasm about the upcoming winter season, a million years away.

Still, the talk-show host loved going to the studio, loved it even more of late. It was a haven, a cloister, a funkily pristine cell sealed off from the world of loan sharks and mildew, losing bets and sudden hammering downpours. The studio walls were soundproofed, heavily padded in vinyl like a Barcalounger all around. The lights were recessed and soft as stars. Wires were taped down, chair casters always oiled; nothing rattled, nothing squeaked. Intercourse with the universe beyond was blessedly one-way: Yates's voice went fluently forth and nothing came back in. It was safe, it was controlled, and the host had come to crave his time in the studio like a therapy junkie craves his time on the couch, as the only respite from the mayhem and disquiet of his other waking hours.

And now Yates was just finishing the show. The guests had left; he was wrapping up with an improvised and not terribly persuasive ramble on the pleasures of the rainy season. He glanced up at the clock above the engineer's window, and in one crammed and befuddling instant he saw two things: He saw that it was twenty seconds before seven, and he saw that Bruno had invaded the production booth.

The huge thug stood there behind the triple-thick glass, his massive arms crossed over his breakfront of a chest. He had commandeered the engineer's headset, the earpieces drew attention to the way his neck tapered to his head. The quailing engineer, a trouper, managed to hit the switch that started Yates's theme music, and Bruno's face took on an expression that was uncomprehending yet transfixed, it bore the small-brained ecstasy of an ape at the opera.

The ecstasy didn't last long.

'Yo, crumbfuck.' Bruno said it through the intercom, and at the moment the barking voice bounced off the soft walls Ray Yates's cloister was desecrated, his safe haven was spoiled forever.

The violation made Yates mad; he mustered a flash of feistiness that felt heroic but vanished as quickly as a hot pee in a cold ocean, chilled to nothing by his fear.

'We got a meeting tuh go tuh,' Bruno barked. 'Ya ready?'

It was buggy in the vacant lot at dusk, but Roberto Natchez, dressed in black, didn't seem to notice. Mosquitoes buzzed unharassed around his hair, landed on his neck and bit; tropical roaches the size of mice slithered among ground-hugging vines and over red-veined roots the thickness and consistency of garden hoses. Fetid puddles between jagged chunks of ancient coral sent forth a nasty smell of sulfur. Undaunted, the poet continued on his mission. In one hand he held a wire cage, in the other a bag of popcorn.

He found a small clearing, knelt, and set his trap.

He sprinkled some kernels to draw his prey to the first chamber of the cage. A more generous helping lured the quarry to the second, narrower compartment. The mother lode of popcorn was piled temptingly on the far side of a small spring-loaded platform attached to the trip wire that would slam the door.

Content with his snare, Natchez retreated to the shadow of his building and waited. It was time, he had decided, to put theory into practice. Credos, manifestos were necessary, of course; they provided the rigorous logic without which human activity was just so much pathetic silliness, so much blundering around. Still, at some point there was no substitute for action; action alone could prove the rightness and integrity of intellect.

It was perhaps three minutes before the chicken appeared from underneath a canopy of weeds and started walking jerkily, obliquely, toward the popcorn. In the dim mix of fading dusk and distant streetlight, the bird looked dull brown and unkempt; its leg feathers were ragged and there was something unseemly, slatternly, about the drunken way it waddled. Roberto Natchez felt exhilarated: He watched the chicken and realized he would have no trouble killing it.

No trouble at all, and that was fitting. He was a true artist, and the true artist shrank from nothing. The true artist protected the pure from the impure, the worthy from the fake. There was between those things a gulf as broad and absolute as the gulf between life and death, and to perform his sacred duty the artist had to know both sides of that dread chasm. He had to be willing to hold death in his hands. Only then could he consign the true and the false to their proper places.

He watched the chicken. It had reached the far end of the ribbon of bait and cautiously, deliberately at first, was beginning to eat. It dropped its head, grabbed a kernel with its beak, then vigilantly stood erect again and looked around before it began the strenuous and unattractive job of chewing. Its horny jaw labored up and down and sideways, shreds of popcorn fell out the edges of its mouth.

The feeding gained momentum, the bird's vigilance soon gave way to gluttony. Now the chicken ate like a famished child, never lifting its eyes from the food; on its yellow feet it followed the zigs and zags of the popcorn trail and soon had entered the outer chamber of the trap.

Here it paused, and Roberto Natchez held his breath.

For what seemed a long time, the bird just stood there. Could it be that it was sated? Was it bothered, perhaps, by some change in the light as it filtered through the slender wire bars? Caught up in the clenched and sanguinous excitement of the hunt, Natchez narrowed his black eyes and willed the chicken onward.

The chicken obeyed. It dropped its head and pecked at the little pile of popcorn at its feet, then, before it was halfway finished, seemed to be distracted by the bigger pile on the far side of the metal platform. It edged forward, placed a single three-clawed foot on the trigger, then leaned over daintily and not without a certain grace, rather like a dancer bowing low across one leg. Natchez watched and felt his bitten neck grow hot with anxiety as kernel after kernel disappeared and still the trap did not clatter shut. Then, finally, inevitably, the chicken over-reached itself. Straining to seize the last few morsels, it brought its other foot onto the steel plate; the trip wire let go with a muffled twang and the door fell closed with tinny finality.

Roberto Natchez exhaled like a dragon. He was just slightly dizzy and he saw gold-green streamers behind his eyes. He did not feel the ground as he strode forward to claim his prize.

The chicken was still eating, did not seem to know that it was doomed. Not until its captor bent low and cast his giant shadow did the bird realize anything was wrong. Then it wheeled in its small space and saw that its escape was blocked. It retreated, squawked, flapped its futile wings so that its feather tips raked unmusically against the bars. It leaped in an aborted takeoff and banged its narrow head against the top of the trap. The poet considered the moment, examined his emotions. So this was how it felt to be in charge, to be enforcer, judge, and executioner. He liked it.

Squatting down, he opened the cage and gingerly reached inside. The bird shrieked and pecked at his fingers. The beak was half sharp, like the tines of a fork; the feel of it was less painful than bracing. He thrust his hand in more decisively and grabbed the chicken by the neck. He felt vertebrae beneath the scraggly feathers as he pulled his victim through the wire door.

It had been Roberto Natchez's intention to make the killing ceremonial, to invest it with the dignity and slowness of a rite. He realized now with a certain self-embarrassment that that would be impossible. The chicken, its red eye fiery with terror, squirmed and swelled, and Natchez was amazed at the quantity of senseless stubborn life that pulsed within it. Its wings pressed against his grip in bony supplication, its absurd pebbled legs still tried to run. To hold the creature was appalling; its relentless squawking was a mayhem that made a travesty of any sort of pomp, and Natchez admitted that the bird and not himself was dictating the pace of its decease. Less like a priest than a butcher, the poet pushed the chicken flat against the ground and with his other hand he made a motion like opening a jar of jam and wrung its neck.

The bird shat a yellowish paste between Natchez's black sneakers. It went rigid for a moment, a final rippling wave ran through its frenzied muscles. Then, belatedly, it seemed to realize it was dead. The tension left the carcass, Natchez felt the bones shift against the will-less meat.

He stood up, the slaughtered chicken dangling from his hand. His shirt was soaked with sweat, he felt a violent exultation mixed with fleeting nausea. He lifted the corpse to the level of his eyes, peered at it, and was gratified to discover that he felt not a whisper of remorse. He flung the bird a few feet into the tangled weeds, retrieved his wire cage, and went home to his garret to drink and write.

CHAPTER THIRTY

AT THE ECLIPSE BAR, Detective Sergeant Joe Mulvane sipped ale from a frosted mug and with his free hand pulled his damp blue collar away from his moist pink neck, the better to expose the mottled skin to the chill breath of the air conditioner. He swallowed, let forth an exaggerated *ahh* of satisfaction, then went on with his story.

'So this pretty little Cuban boy comes in,' he said. 'A strange bird, lemme tell ya. Walks like Daryl Hannah, talks like José Jimenez with some night school and a lisp. He's all excited, he's twitching. He's got this cake, apricot, he's holding it like a fucking hand grenade. It's poisoned, he's sure of it. This on top of the paranoid broad who comes in the other day. I mean Arty, you been here longer than I have. Who *are* these people?'

Arty Magnus sipped his wine, then dug his elbows deeper into the thickly upholstered bar rail, an armrest that conduced to drinking and reflection, mostly drinking. One of the very few things he liked about being a newspaperman was the chance it gave him to shoot the shit with cops. Information. Everybody needed it, and in more discreet places there was never enough to go around; in Key West, which was about as discreet as a public bathhouse, there was generally too much. Information was cheap as local mangoes and about as firm.

'The Silvers?' said the editor. 'Some of our leading citizens. He's one of the very few people down here who isn't jerking off when he calls himself an artist. She's one of the very few people still trying to run a quality business on Duval Street instead of doing T-shirts and schlock. Maybe they're strange like artsy-strange. But lunatics? No. The Cuban kid, him I don't know.'

'I do,' said the fellow who'd come in with Arty Magnus and was sitting on the other side of him. His name was Joey Goldman, he was slightly built with dark blue eyes and wavy black hair, and he had the earpiece of his sunglasses hanging over the pocket of his shirt. The other two men looked at him like they hadn't expected him to contribute, hadn't expected him to know much.

'Yeah,' Joey went on. 'He used to work for us. Before he went full-time for the Silvers. Worked in our Cleaning Division.'

He said this rather grandly, in the manner of the newly successful. Joey Goldman was an oddity in Key West, a place where many people of more privileged background came to fail, to give up, to go pleasantly down the tubes. He'd come from dubious roots, some thought criminal roots, and with a little luck and more savvy than anyone thought he had, he'd become a businessman of substance, a wheeler-dealer in real estate. In this his questionable past had served him well: It was axiomatic that it was easier to rob a place if you had a guy inside. Why shouldn't this logic extend to legitimate business? Who knew before the housekeeper when an owner was thinking of making a move, selling out or trading up? Thus the Cleaning Division was what might be thought of as the clandestine intelligence arm of Paradise Properties, Joey Delgatto Goldman, boss.

'So what's his story?' asked Joe Mulvane. 'The Cuban kid.'

Joey sipped his Campari, dabbed his lips. 'We got like sixteen, eighteen people cleaning for us,' he said. 'Most of 'em I couldn't tell ya nothin'. But Reuben I can, I'll tell ya why I remember: The first day he came to us he was black and blue. Beat up. Big bruise on his neck, one eye not open all the way. So shy he could hardly talk. Leanin' away like a terrorized cat. Sandra's askin' 'im the usual questions. *Where d 'ya live?* He lives with his parents. *How old are ya?* He's twenty-three, twenty-four, somethin' like that.

'Then I cut in, I couldn't help it. "Hey Reuben," I say, "who beatcha up?" With this, he shoots me a look that really gets my attention, a look I recognize. It's a look – how can I describe it? – it's not hostile, it's not even strong, but it's defiant, it tells you he doesn't care who you are, what he needs from you, you're out of bounds. And right away I know that whoever beat him up is in his family. I just know it. Look, he's obviously gay. Lotta old-style Cubans, a *maricón*, they get ugly, it's like a blot onna family honor. I understand something about families, trust me on that. The closer they are, the harder it is to be different. So I feel for the kid. I look at Sandra. Sandra looks at me. The kid is hired and he works out great. Reliable. Honest. Loyal.'

'Loyal till he quits,' put in Mulvane.

'I got no problem with that,' said Joey. 'I mean, all we did, we gave 'im a job. The Silvers, they practically became his family, ya know, took over from the asshole family and became the good family. We all know how that works. He did the right thing.'

There was a pause for drinking and reflecting, mostly drinking. The sounds of shaken ice and barroom blather came forward as the old industrial air conditioner shuddered, coughed, then shut down for a rest. Mulvane finished his ale with an appreciation that bordered on reverence and pushed his mug forward for another.

'But wait a second,' Arty Magnus said. 'Can we cut to the chase scene here? The cake – you said the Cuban kid was all excited about a cake. Was it poisoned?'

'Sent a slice down to the lab,' the detective said, but his eyes were searching for the bartender and he wasn't going any farther till his warm and empty glass was replaced with an iced and filled one.

When it was, he licked the foam then casually announced, 'Yeah, it was fulla poison. Nasty shit too. Sugar. Butter. Cholesterol, enough to make your heart slam shut. A regular time bomb. I took it home, ate it with the wife and kids.'

'Painting again?' said Claire Steiger. 'Augie, I think that's terrific. Only—'

'Only what, Claire?' Augie said.

She shifted in her poolside chair. It was early evening. She and Kip had arrived in Key West barely an hour before. They'd checked into the Flagler House, showered and changed, and now were straining the muscles of their faces to look congenial, to make it seem like this ferocious guarding of their interests was a social call, almost a pilgrimage. A fading light shimmered in the gummy air above the pool. Overhead, the palm fronds hung dark and limp, they sifted the wan gleam of a hazy dusk.

'Only maybe it would be better,' the agent said, 'if people didn't find that out just yet.'

Nina, sitting on the love seat with her husband, pursed her lips. She was over feeling qualms about her gut mistrust of almost anything her former mentor said. 'Why, Claire?' she asked. 'Why does it matter?'

The dealer's brown eyes were soft, her full lips managed a smile, but she could not quite hold back her hand from reaching for another bit of Brie, of which she'd told herself she'd have no more. She slipped the fat cheese into her mouth and shot a quick glance at her husband. He'd arched an eyebrow perhaps a quarter-inch then dived into his gin. Certain things you could count on in life: Round Jewish women reached for food at moments of exasperation, angular WASP men grabbed at cocktails. The couple swallowed their respective medicines and then the wife went on. 'Augie, Nina – there's a big auction at Sotheby's ten days from now.'

'The Solstice Show,' said Nina.

'Yes. And a lot of Augie's works are being offered.'

Augie said nothing. He'd had paintings auctioned before, and he didn't see that it had much to do with him. What did it matter if old forgotten canvases from

215

the gallery's holdings and from collections in New York were shuffled around in exchange for cash? He was on to other things, it was the new work that he cared about.

Nina was not quite so placid. 'The auction's in ten days, Claire, and we only find out now?'

The agent groped for some high ground. 'I tried calling weeks ago,' she said. 'You never got back.'

Augie didn't have the stomach for a squabble. 'Really,' he said, 'what's the difference?'

Kip Cunningham, who would not accept the notion that mere bankruptcy cast the slightest doubt on his expertise in business, could not help chiming in. 'It's just, you know, better not to advertise a fresh supply—'

Augie shushed him with a small wave of his hand. 'I totally understand,' he said. 'And frankly, it's all the same to me if people find out today or next month or never. I'm painting to paint, not to get talked about.'

'But what if people ask?' Kip blurted.

Augie sipped his Guinness, let a bit slide frothily past his gullet. His body was working again, his pipes were flowing, his mouth was tasting, and there was a sacred delight in this that overwhelmed all petty and non-visceral concerns. 'If they ask,' he blithely said, 'I'll tell them.'

Kip and Claire, still allies in debt, if little else, zoomed in quickly on each other's eyes.

'It might be better—' the agent began.

Nina cut her off. It is a weighty thing to know another person's moves so well that a single phrase can bring on rage, can create the bitter certainty that one is being manipulated, bullied, used. For Nina the awareness was especially galling because she could still remember, though the recollection baffled her, when she had wanted to be Claire Steiger: tough, assured, no one's fool, a creature of the city. Amazing, Nina thought, the number of false starts and wrong desires that could be crammed into something as short as a lifetime. 'Surely you're not going to suggest he lie?' she said.

'No, of course not,' the agent waffled. 'But for example—'

'Claire,' said Augie Silver, 'I'm much too superstitious not to tell the truth. The little talent I have, I'm not going to jinx it by denying it. Look, you don't want people to know I'm working, just keep people away from me. You can do that, can't you?'

'The press? Nobody can do that, Augie,' said Claire Steiger. 'You know that.'

The painter shrugged and sipped his stout. He looked up at the sky, pulled in a chestful of jasmine-scented air, felt his body in the love seat, and savored the nearness of his wife's hip next to his. Claire Steiger, whose skill it was to make people want things, understood that Augie no longer wanted anything she could do for him or sell him, and this was very frustrating. You could not manipulate someone who truly didn't care. You could only go around him, or over him, or find some way to remove him from the loop. The agent stole a quick glance at her husband and saw a flat dead desperation in his eyes that she prayed to God was not reflected in her own.

CHAPTER THIRTY-ONE

THERE IS SOMETHING about being ushered into a dark Lincoln full of mafiosi that makes a person feel sick to his stomach.

There are a lot of ways they can kill you right there in the car, and none of them are pretty. Piano wire around the neck. Ice pick through the base of the skull. A point-blank shot that singes skin in the instant before it stops the heart. Ray Yates tasted bile. He was no dummy, he knew what the shrinks said about compulsive gambling and the death wish. They were wrong. He gambled for excitement. OK, maybe humiliation had something to do with it. Maybe he got off on the pang of losing, that confirming disappointment that was bracing as a pinch on the scrotum. But you had to be alive to feel that. This was something the shrinks seem to have overlooked.

'Take 'im tuh duh gahbidge?' Bruno asked.

The man in the front passenger seat considered. He was a small neat man, with short gray hair that was too perfect and crescent sacs the color of liver beneath his eyes. 'Nah, take 'im tuh duh shahk.'

There was another goon in the back seat with Ray Yates. At this he smiled and sucked wet air between his teeth and gums. 'Yeah, Mr Ponte, great. Been a while since we fed the shahk.'

The Lincoln lumbered slowly out of the alley, wound its way through the narrow cobbled downtown streets. Barefoot dirtbags in droopy-ass jeans wandered here and there among tourists wearing short shorts the colors of lemons and limes. A guy went by on a unicycle with flashing lights among the spokes. This, Yates thought, was the town he'd wanted to fit in with. A town of easy eccentricity, funk without violence, harmless farting around. How had he managed to turn it sinister for himself?

The big car passed a Do Not Enter sign, then turned down a passageway barely wider than itself, and Yates, who'd thought he knew every byway in Key West, lost track of where he was. The car stopped. He was ordered out, there was barely room to squeeze. Bruno turned the lock on a green-painted metal door that was the only break in a wall of crumbly brick.

'We got keys,' the other thug explained. He smiled, sucked his teeth. 'We got keys for everywhere. Get the fuck inside.'

He gave Yates a push into the dark building, and the first thing the debtor noticed was the smell of fish. Not dead fish; live fish, the slime and seaweed smell of live fish swimming in aerated saltwater. Someone hit a light switch. Revealed was a room of buckets and mops, ladders and freezers. At the far end was a metal staircase, the top of which could not be seen.

'Sal,' said Charlie Ponte to the thug who sucked his teeth, 'grab some fucking fish.'

Sal went to a freezer. Bruno pushed Ray Yates toward the stairs. Heavy feet made a dismal ringing sound on the steel steps, a clamor that bounced off the walls of the closed aquarium and came back sounding drowned.

The stairs went up two stories and ended at another door. Bruno opened it and grinned. Then he shoved Yates through. The talk-show host found himself standing on a metal grid, maybe six feet square. Around the platform, waist high, was a railing, and beyond the railing, two feet away and one foot down, was the lip of the vast tank that held the aquarium's prize attraction, an eleven-foot hammerhead called Ripper. The tank was dark. A murderous silence hovered over it. It smelled like blood and clams. The others piled in behind Ray Yates. The thug called Sal was carrying two frozen bonito, maybe ten pounds each. There was a small spotlight on the feeding platform; Charlie Ponte turned it on.

'Sal,' he said, 'trow our friend a fish.'

Sal tossed one of the bonito, and before it hit the water, the shark exploded through the surface, its monstrous sideways dildo of a head thrashing, its unspeakable mouth wide open to reveal its double rows of razor teeth. Sharks are not neat eaters. They don't bite cleanly, they tear, they shred, the sharp chaotic hell of their mouths reduces food to strings and tatters. Ray Yates watched the frozen fish disintegrate. The shark thumped the water for more. Salt spray flew above the tank, roiled water viscously lapped.

'Get up onna fucking railing, Ray,' Charlie Ponte said.

Yates didn't move. Ponte walked slowly up to him

and back-handed him hard across the cheek. Then he nodded to his boys. They lifted the debtor by the armpits and sat him on the rail. He held it, white-knuckled, fighting vertigo. The shark was circling at his back. The rough texture of its silver skin glinted in the light, the obscene gashes of its gill slits sucked and spilled out water.

'Ray,' said Ponte, 'you're like very close to being dead. You know that, right?'

Yates swallowed, nodded. The railing was cool, it chilled his bowels.

'And why?' Ponte continued. His voice was just slightly louder now, it came through the splashing and sliced roughly through the dark building with its secret nighttime life of fish. 'Because you're a weak piece a shit. No control. A fucking bed wetter.'

'It's never been like this before,' Yates whimpered. 'I've always paid. Bruno knows that.'

Ponte looked at his goons. 'And what's Bruno, the fucking credit bureau? Ray, you're poison. You bet on a horse, the horse falls down. You bet on a fighter, he pisses blood. Now you're inta me for forty-somethin' and I hear you're betting on a fucking painter. This is a new one on me. How the fuck you bet on a painter?'

Bruno and Sal obediently chuckled. Sal held the other bonito by its tail and tried not to let it drip on his shoe as it defrosted.

Yates sat. Drops of spray were wetting his back, and he could not shake the image of the shark rising up on its tail and biting his ass off. 'It's not a bet. I own these paintings.'

'Yeah. So?'

'Week and a half from now, they'll be sold. Sotheby's. New York. They're worth a lot of money. Hundreds of thousands.'

Charlie Ponte looked down through the open grid beneath his feet and sadly shook his head. When he spoke again, it was to Sal and Bruno. 'He's holdin' out on me. I hate that. Turn 'im upside down.'

Sal put aside the thawing fish and the two goons grabbed Ray Yates. The debtor wriggled but not much: There was nowhere to go but two stories down to a stone floor or into the fishbowl with the shark. They hoisted him then turned him like a roast, laid him out so that his upper thighs were across the rail and his torso was hovering in space. His hands gripped the top of the shark tank, he wondered if the ragged teeth would flash and hack his fingers off. He pulled his face back as far as he could from the roiling water, but still he smelled fish blood and an awful musk. Ponte moved alongside and spoke to him calmly.

'Ray, I hate a guy that sells me short. You think I'm stupid? You think I don't read the paper? Those paintings ain't worth what you say. Who knows if they're gonna sell at all? You lost again, Ray. You're fucked.'

Yates's back was cramping, his eyes were starting to tear. 'I'll get the money,' he rasped. It was all he could think of to say.

'Yeah? How?'

If people were punished for thoughts, the world would be a jail. Yates held himself above the shark tank and looked down at the water. The silhouette of the grotesque and hungry hammerhead snaked through it like the shadow of death. There seemed one way and one way only for Yates to get the money, and in that moment of infinite fear and infinite selfishness there was no doubt that he would cash in Augie Silver's life to save his own, the only question was the nerve and tact it took to do the deal.

'I thought ... I thought he was dead,' the gambler stammered.

'Yeah,' said Ponte. 'I know that's what you thought.' He leaned back against the railing, calmly lit a cigarette. 'Like usual you were wrong.'

'I could end up being right.'

'Fuck's that supposed to mean?'

Yates's voice was soft. 'Mr Ponte, you take the money. From the paintings. Keep all of it.'

For a moment Ponte said nothing. His expression was midway between offended and amused. He took a puff of his cigarette then threw it into the shark tank. Then his upper lip abruptly pulled back and he pummeled Ray Yates in the kidney. The blow sent a searing pain up his back and a hot surge through his tubing.

'You mizzable fuck,' the mobster said. He pointed at Yates as at a species of lizard and spoke to his boys. 'The legitimate world. There it is. No self-control. No balls. Won't even clean up its own messes.' He turned his attention back to the writhing debtor. 'Scumbag, you think you can hire me, just like that, to kill for you?'

Ray Yates tried to breathe. The air smelled like the inside of a fish and there seemed to be big splinters underneath his ribs. But he had somehow moved past fear, fallen through the bottom of it into some horrid but clear place that was like already being dead. 'You're gonna kill, Mr Ponte,' he said, in a voice grown weirdly even, weirdly certain. 'You kill me, you get nothing. You kill him—'

The debtor's words were swallowed up in a watery mayhem. At a nod from Charlie Ponte, Sal had thrown the second fish into the tank. The hammerhead rocketed up to meet it, its appalling face came so close to Ray Yates's that he could see the bilious color of its yellow eye, the bent, in-sloping arrowheads of its vile teeth, could hear the sickening crush and grinding of its jaws. A wave flew up around the thrusting shark, it arced and billowed like a wake thrown off a boat. It drenched Ray Yates as the shark plunged downward, and by the time the gambler could see and hear again, his tormentors were gone and he was left to scramble down from his precarious perch alone.

CHAPTER THIRTY-TWO

KEY WEST IS JUSTLY FAMOUS for its sunsets, but most people do not realize that its moonrises are at certain seasons equally sublime. In summer, the waxing moon migrates toward the southern sky. When full, it emerges powdery salmon from the flat and open waters of the Florida Straits. Those waters, in the humid, windless dusks of June, take on an unearthly texture, part mirror, part soup, and dully gleam like brushed aluminum. If one is very lucky, one can sometimes see the very first lash of light as it peeks above the tabletop horizon. The mottled moon takes a long time to climb out of the ocean, and once it has, its color changes, lightens every moment, like a big wet yellow dog as it shakes itself and dries.

Saturday the twelfth was the full-moon evening, and Augie Silver, feeling spry and restless, took it in his head that he wanted to go to see it. 'Come on,' he said to Reuben an hour or so before the great event. 'We'll throw an easel in the car. I'll sketch awhile, and who knows – it might be one of life's great moonrises.'

They were in the backyard. Augie had been reading and Reuben was picking up the sticky brown pods that fell from the poinciana tree. 'I think maybe it is cloudy,' the housekeeper said. But it wasn't cloudy. It was perfectly clear, albeit with the electric shimmer of a summer haze.

Augie looked at him. 'You don't want to go?'

This was difficult for Reuben to answer. He wanted to do whatever Augie liked. But his mission was to keep the painter safe. Then again it was hard to protect someone if he could not know he needed to be protected. Nervously, the young man wiped his hands on his apron. 'We can go. Only—'

'Only what?'

'Only, Nina—'

'It's late night at the gallery. We'll be back way before her. Maybe we'll bring home stone crab for dinner.'

So Reuben loaded the old Saab. He laid Augie's easel and pad across the back seat. He put in a cooler of mineral water in case Augie got thirsty, some fruit in case he got hungry. He put in a jacket, though a jacket was unthinkable in the unyielding mugginess. He noticed nothing unusual on Olivia Street. Dogs lolled next to car tires. Bicycles went past. Here and there clean undented convertibles were parked, their frivolous colors, tinted glass, and lack of rust marking them as rentals. The palms were still and limp, even the Mother-in-law tree was silent.

It was seven-thirty when they set out, Reuben driving, slowly. The light was soft, the roads were quiet. What traffic there was, was mainly heading the other way – downtown, west, toward the gaudier, commoner spectacle of sunset. On White Street, old Cubans sat on mesh chairs in front of empty stores and slid dominoes across the cardboard boxes that served as makeshift tables. On Atlantic Boulevard the pink and aqua condos stood like blocks of giant candy. Australian pines lined the wetlands, looking dejected and enduring, like people who are always moaning and complaining yet will outlive all their friends. The air smelled of frangipani.

'You know,' said Augie, 'sometimes I forget how much I love this town.'

'Is a nice town,' Reuben said, without taking his eyes from the road. He leaned slightly forward over the steering wheel. He regarded driving as a grave adventure that required all his concentration. He took no notice of the turquoise convertible with tinted glass that stayed a steady hundred yards behind him, moving at a sightseer's pace with its top up.

'It's very ... specialized,' Augie said. He considered this as they turned onto A1A. The road was twenty feet from the Atlantic Ocean and maybe eighteen inches above it. 'There are towns, you know, for making money. Towns to start a career. Towns to go to college. Towns to raise a family. Key West is no damn good for any of that. Key West is to feel good and be happy. That's all. Don'tcha think?'

'*Si*, yes,' said Reuben absently, his attention riveted to the pavement. 'Augie, where you like me to stop?'

'Over past the airport,' Augie said. 'Where the island curves around. You get the biggest sweep of water there.'

Reuben put his blinker on a long time in advance and started driving even slower. Alongside A1A – a continuation of it, really – there is a broad concrete promenade that in certain places fronts the beach and in others ends directly at the seawall. This promenade is used by bicyclists and joggers, prostitutes both male and female. Windsurfers sometimes park their vans there, fishermen sometimes leave their pickup trucks along it and launch their dinghies over the rampart. At the spot Reuben finally edged off the road, there was no sand, the green water came right up to the barricaded island. Beyond the thigh-high wall, scattered mangroves perched atop their tangled cones of roots, stilts and egrets gawked around for food.

'Good,' said Augie as Reuben turned off the Saab's ignition and the turquoise car slid slowly, silently past them and continued north. 'This is good.'

Reuben sighed with relief that the drive was over. Then he clambered out and reached into the back for Augie's easel. The painter, still brittle and unaccustomed to sudden movements, took a moment to unfold himself from the car. His knees were stiff beneath the ever-present khaki shorts, his shoulders felt tight inside the faded purple shirt. He stood with one hand on the Saab's warm roof and looked around. In the west, the sun was an orange ball that had lost its fire and dangled just above the low shrubs of the salt marsh; the sky above it was streaky green. In the east it was a different sky, satiny, already dim and sweetly modest, as if a shy bride was turning off the lights before she would receive the moon.

Augie meandered. That's what he always did, it was some fundamental part of his looking at the world, some basic ritual of settling in. He wandered to the seawall, he wandered to the edge of the road. He wandered past the car, backtracked, then did a lazy pirouette and sauntered off again. Reuben zigged and zagged behind him, the easel on his shoulder. Finally the painter found the place that felt right to his feet and looked right to his eyes. He put his hands in his pockets and sniffed the air; it had the good mud smell of limestone and the tang of sun-baked shells.

The pad and easel appeared in front of him and the artist started to draw. He sketched a feeding egret, captured the unlikely splayed angle of its stick-figure legs and the lightness of the feathered crest raked back from its head. He caught the shrewdness of the lidless eye and the strength in the darting neck that could unravel and strike as fast as any snake.

Reuben moved a respectful twenty feet away and watched. He was in awe of Augie working, not just the skill but the mysterious boldness it took to draw a line, the confidence and the belief that were needed to leave a mark. Reuben knew that he himself would never have such boldness. He liked to make small changes in things that already existed: arranging flowers, plumping pillows, setting dishes perfectly on a table; he made things more beautiful and it pleased him. But to start from nothing . . .

'Reuben, look,' said Augie, pulling the young man out of his thoughts. He gestured quickly toward the west, abandoned by the sun, then made a sweep across the flatly glowing water to the east. 'Should be any minute now.'

The painter smiled, excited, and Reuben was happy for him and happy for himself, happy to have a friend who, even though his hair was white, even though he was not young, was excited at the thought of seeing moonrise.

They watched, scanning the horizon for a telltale gleam. On the seafront promenade, life streamed by around them. A jogger pushing a stroller ran past Augie's easel. A knot of screaming mopeds zipped by on the curbless shoulder of A1A.

Then Reuben noticed a turquoise car driving slowly toward them on the broad walkway. In Key West, a town of hazy boundaries, where storms confused the ocean with the land, where friendships sometimes crossed over into hatreds, where sidewalks slipped without a curbstone into roadways, it was not unusual to see a car among the joggers. Everyone wanted front row on the sea, and Reuben's only fear was that the vehicle, now perhaps a hundred yards away, would intrude on Augie's moonrise.

Reuben didn't want to let that happen, and imagined that by vigilance he could prevent it. He watched the car and left the blank and promising horizon to his friend. The painter, rapt, gazed toward the east. The air was dead still and the temperature of skin; a pair of ibis flew down and landed with a skipping splash. The tires of the turquoise car made a sudden squeal just at the instant that a blood-red cuticle of moon poked through its dark envelope of ocean. Augie turned and pointed, his face ecstatic, as the murderous vehicle hurtled toward him. Reuben, low, lithe, afraid of nothing, threw himself across the car's trajectory. His shoulder caught Augie in the solar plexus and the two men flew over the seawall and into the mangroves as the easel was reduced to matchsticks and the indifferent moon threw red beams that skipped across the water and tracked the turquoise convertible in its escape.

PART FOUR

CHAPTER THIRTY-THREE

'HE SAVED MY LIFE,' Augie Silver softly said to Nina.

It was around 10 P.M. Reuben, bruised and soaking wet, had gone home. The painter was propped on pillows in his bed. It had taken him a long time to get his breath back as he lay stunned among the mangroves and the fleeing birds, and now he was unpleasantly aware of the weight of his lungs; they heaved in his chest like sacs of lukewarm gelatin. His arms ached, his leg muscles twitched in their loose wrappers of empty skin. His wife sat next to him and stroked his dry and feverish forehead.

'Damn drunk drivers,' she muttered.

Augie briefly closed his eyes, swallowed, opened them again. 'Nina,' he said. She waited for him to continue, and as she waited she glanced toward the window. As on the evening Augie had come back to her, the thin curtain was blanched by moonlight and billowed softly on an unfelt breeze. He took her hand. 'Nina, listen. I don't think it was a drunk. And I don't think it was an accident.'

The former widow pushed out breath as though to speak but found she had no words. Augie paused, then with great effort lifted himself onto his elbows.

'I didn't want to say anything,' he went on. 'I wasn't sure. I didn't want to scare you. But ever since Fred, that tart, now this business with the auction . . .' He looked at Nina's face, her wideset slate-gray eyes, and understood that no more needed saying. 'You knew?'

'I suspected. I didn't want *you* to worry. Manny Rucker said—'

'Aren't doctors fabulous?' Augie interrupted. 'They prescribe no stress and think life is gonna obey their orders.'

He managed a parched smile that his wife could not return.

'I went to the police the day Fred died,' she said. The words, long overdue, spilled out now. 'They thought I was crazy. They told me to call the ASPCA. Maybe now they'll believe—'

'Believe what? That someone tried to run me over with a turquoise convertible? Half the cars in town are turquoise convertibles. Rented and identical.'

'At least they'll know you're in danger.'

Augie tossed his head on the pillow. 'So what will they do? Put a patrolman at the door? Keep me under house arrest for my own protection? For how long? There's only so much—'

'Augie,' said Nina, and there was a letting-go in her voice, a half-groan like muted thunder very far away. 'I've been so afraid. I've been so afraid for so long now.'

She leaned against him and he held her. The only comfort he could offer was the attempt at comfort, and in giving it he could almost forget that he was terrified as well. But then another thought occurred to him. He pictured Reuben, odd, shy, swishy Reuben, streaking across the path of the speeding car, his own young body perhaps three feet from its fender as it throttled toward them. 'And Reuben? Reuben knew?'

'He knows,' said Nina. 'I had to tell him.'

Augie slowly shook his heavy head. 'Reuben is amazing.'

Joe Mulvane was a man who knew how to fill a doorway. His broad shoulders in their out-of-place suit jacket nearly brushed against both sides of the frame, his thick thighs prevented any light from slicing in between his legs, and his mordant posture made it clear that he did not appreciate being called with a paranoid tale at 8 A.M. on a Sunday morning and asked to pay a mercy visit.

Nina Silver greeted him, looking prim, composed, not obviously hysterical. She led him in and offered him coffee, which mollified him somewhat. He leaned against the kitchen counter as she poured him a mug. He jerked a thumb toward the living-room walls. 'These your husband's paintings?'

Nina nodded, then braced herself. People always felt obliged to make some comment. It was a nuisance.

'They're big,' said Mulvane.

'Yes,' said Nina Silver. She handed him his coffee, led him through the living room and out the French doors to the pool.

Augie was sitting there, an untouched slice of melon and a plate of mango muffins set in front of him. His color was bad, a yellowish gray, and his skin hurt, his body throbbed like a headache all over. 'Darling,' said his wife, 'this is Sergeant Joe Mulvane.'

The painter didn't rise, just held out a hand. 'Hi, Joe,' he said. 'Augie.' He said it with the same sort of utterly disarming informality that had allowed him to sit on Nina Alonzo's office desk the first time they had met. People should rest when their feet were tired. They should call each other by easy names. Why not? Mulvane seemed to understand. He slipped off his jacket and took a chair without waiting to be offered one. He drank his coffee.

'Have a muffin, Joe,' said Augie, offering the plate. 'I'm not hungry.'

Mulvane, a Bostonian, knew from muffins, although they didn't have mango way up there. He broke off a piece and appraised its texture.

'Joe, listen,' Augie went on. 'I'm sure my wife was right to call you, but I can't help feeling we're wasting your time. There's so little to go on. I didn't see the driver or if he was alone. I didn't see a license plate. Neither did Reuben.'

Mulvane swallowed a piece of muffin, looked quickly for a napkin, then discreetly licked his fingers. 'But both of you – you and Reuben, I mean – are sure it was intentional?'

'The guy sneaked within thirty yards of me and floored it.'

'And it was one of those turquoise ragtops?' the detective asked.

'Spanking clean,' said Augie.

'That's a renter,' said Mulvane. He blinked his sandy eyelashes, looked around the Silvers' yard. The swimming pool and plantings reminded him how perilously enviable the well-to-do Key West life could be. 'And you're not aware of any enemies?'

Augie shook his head.

The detective thought back to his first conversation with Nina. 'But you have a lotta friends,' he said.

Augie looked down, his color went a shade more sallow, his deep blue lighthouse eyes went dim. 'Yes,' he said, 'I do. And in some crazy way, that's what bothers me more than anything. That it could be a friend.'

Mulvane dove into his coffee. He was a homicide cop; hurt feelings did not come very near the top of his list of human tragedies. Yet there was something in Augie's pain that got to him. An intimate betrayal was itself a kind of murder. 'Well, let's not assume—'

Nina cut him off, following her own insistent train of thought. 'What else could it be? The paintings. The prices.'

The artist recoiled at the words but could not deny them. Murder, after all, generally came with a motive.

The cop had a piece of muffin in his hand and realized suddenly that he had lost his appetite. He put it back on the plate. 'Maybe you should call the auction off,' he suggested.

'Impossible,' Augie said. He wore a look Nina was not sure she had ever seen in him before, a look not exactly of helplessness but of sour despairing. 'There's this huge machinery already cranked up. Sotheby's. Advertising. Sellers. Buyers. My agent.'

'Agent?' said Mulvane. 'What's he do?'

'She,' said Augie. 'Shows the work. Publicizes. Coordinates.'

'Takes a cut?'

'Of course.'

'She's in New York, this agent?'

'Based there,' Augie said. 'She was here a couple of days ago.'

Seemingly from nowhere Mulvane produced a small and crumpled notebook and a cheap and capless pen. 'What's her name?'

Augie squirmed in the heightening sun as though he himself had suddenly come under suspicion. 'Joe, really—'

'Claire Steiger,' Nina said. 'S-t-e-i-g-e-r. She was here with her husband, Christopher Cunningham. Goes by Kip. They were staying at the Flagler House.'

'Did they rent a car?' the detective asked, the butt of his pen against his freckled lower lip.

Nina looked at Augie. Augie shrugged. Neither had noticed how their visitors arrived.

'When did they leave town?'

Augie shrugged again. 'They might still be here, for all I know.'

Mulvane took a last pull of his lukewarm coffee, held the ear of the mug with the pen and pad still twined between his fingers. Then he slid his chair back and got up.

'Sergeant,' said Nina, rising with him and trying to keep her tone free of panic, 'are you going to help us?'

Mulvane made an involuntary sound that was halfway between a sigh and a growl, the gruff and weary complaint of one who always seemed to end up caring more than he wanted to and doing more than he told himself was worth it. 'Officially, no,' he said. 'We have two open murders and a suspicious suicide on the books. I go to the chief, he's gonna tell me no crime has been committed, leave it alone. I'll do what I can. But quietly.'

'Thank you,' Nina said.

The beefy detective waved the gratitude away like a fly. 'First thing,' he said, reaching for his jacket, 'make a list. Anybody here in town who has paintings—'

'They're friends,' said Augie. 'The pictures were gifts. They wouldn't be selling . . .'

Mulvane didn't want to be around while Augie dragged himself to the bitter end of that line of reasoning. He kept on talking to Nina. 'I don't care how much you think you trust them – I want the names. Call me later. We'll check car rentals. After that . . .'

He hunched his shoulders, and the movement made him realize that his cop-blue shirt was already damp, another sweaty day in Key West had begun. He squinted toward the sun, it rudely pawed its way like hot hands between palm fronds and through the gaps in branches. He glanced at Augie and Augie met his eyes but didn't say a word. A lousy thing, thought Joe Mulvane, to be bumped off by a friend; and since he didn't have anything to say to make it seem less lousy, he walked unescorted through the Silver house and back into the relentless sunshine on the other side.

CHAPTER THIRTY-FOUR

THE WAY IT WORKED, the cars were put in neutral and then hooked one by one to a conveyor chain. The chain ran under a metal groove that was like a knife gash in the earth. There was an electric eye that started the water when the cars pulled even with the washing frame. Then the jets hissed all around, above the cars and on both sides. The water came out hot but went lukewarm almost instantly as it vaporized. It vaporized into little fuzzy globes like dandelions, and sometimes rainbows cropped up in it; the vapor moved but the rainbows hung in space where they had started. After that the brushes came down, they squeezed in softly but insistently like a fat aunt's arms and didn't let go till they had felt the car all over.

Then the water stopped and the car paused in the metal shed between the wash frame and the rinse frame. That's where Jimmy Gibbs stood, in the clanging, a steamy place between cycles. He wore green rubber boots and held a rag. He worked the vehicles' starboard side, and his job was to rub away the dirt and stains too stubborn for the brushes; the birdshit that sometimes needed scraping with a fingernail, the exploded bugs that congealed to the color and consistency of baked-on egg.

People wanted a clean car when they rented. Spotless. That fact had been drummed into him from the instant he'd applied for this idiotic job. Didn't it matter if the engine pinged, didn't matter if the body rattled. The car had to look good, festive, vacationlike for the off-season deadbeats with their cheapie vouchers and their plastic nose protectors. Was it part of what made it feel like vacation, Gibbs wondered, to look as ridiculous as possible? To wear a nose protector, a flowered shirt, and to drive around in one of these silly-looking ragtops in their frippy Florida shades of plum, persimmon, turquoise?

Wave on wave the cars came through the shed, a dreary parade of dripping doors and fenders emerging from a fog of mildew and the smarting stench of strong detergent. Gibbs's toes itched maddeningly inside his rubber boots. He'd wanted to work barefoot, give his cracked and soggy dogs some air. The boss wouldn't let him; some insurance bullshit. That was the thing about working on land – there was always some rule, some regulation, some suit making it his business how you had dealt with the fungus between your toes. They blocked you from the light, these land jobs; they stank up the air worse than fish guts ever could. In all, going from sea to land seemed a terrible descent, a punishing demotion.

Jimmy Gibbs had come down in life. He admitted it, in some crazy way he savored it, it confirmed the way he'd always figured things would turn out. Except he wasn't finished yet – that's what no one realized. He had a plan, and this jerked-off job was part of it. A big part. Gibbs had to laugh. Could anyone imagine that he was standing melting in this metal hell of steam for the four-fucking-thirty-five an hour they were paying him?

Another turquoise convertible rolled dumbly up to him and waited to be scrubbed. He clutched his fraying rag and attacked a patch of guano on its windshield. All alike, these rented cars, alike as fish in a school. That was the worst thing about them, and the best. Gibbs rubbed some limestone grit off the vehicle's sleek flank as the conveyor yanked it past him. Hell, he thought, these cars aren't even from a place; on the bottom of the license plate, where the home county was stamped, these just said Lease. Lease County, famous for its cheapskate deadbeats. Cars from nowhere, going nowhere.

Unlike himself. Jimmy Gibbs was moving up. He'd sunk low, he'd sink a little lower still, but after that he knew what he was springing to the top. This job was going to do more for him than the boss man with his dry hands and his tie clip could ever have imagined. With a wet hand Gibbs patted the yard keys in his pocket. Satisfying, the feel of those keys. He raked a forearm across his streaming hairline and turned back, just slightly refreshed, to the unending line of ridiculous convertibles.

At around four o'clock that afternoon, the telephone rang at the Silver house. It was Joe Mulvane. He'd done some checking up on the list of names that Nina had called in to him a few hours before. She switched on the speakerphone in the living room so that she and Augie could listen together, sitting on the couch. With the speaker on, Augie thought, it seemed less like talking on the phone than listening to the radio, passively taking in a news flash not on one's own life but on some stranger's.

'The agent and her husband,' Muldane said, 'they checked out of the Flagler House around two P.M. yesterday.'

'Ah,' said Nina. 'So they were gone.'

'No,' said Mulvane. 'They didn't fly out till nine-thirty. But they didn't rent a car. I checked both names.'

Augie let a long breath out.

'Of course,' the detective went on, 'there are other ways to get cars. Theft is popular. Fake IDs. But in the meantime, somebody did rent. Ray Yates. Rented a ragtop, turquoise, Friday night, and hasn't been seen or heard from since.'

'Maybe he went on vacation,' Augie said.

'His employer didn't know about it,' said Mulvane. 'I called the station. Yates phoned in yesterday morning, he didn't say from where, and told them he didn't know when he was coming back.'

'Can you find him?' Nina asked.

The answer was quick and definite. 'No. I checked his boat, I asked some neighbors. I don't have the resources to do more.'

There was a pause. Augie caught himself staring at the speaker and felt suddenly pathetic, having a conversation with a plastic box, looking to the box to solve his life for him.

'Maybe we can find him,' Nina said.

Mulvane cleared his throat. It was a skeptical sound that seemed to go with the lifting of eyebrows, the

245

rolling of eyes. 'We might be dealing with a killer here,' he said.

The words hung in the air; Augie tried to get his mind around them. Ray Yates a killer? It seemed preposterous. But then, was it any more unlikely than the notion that the would-be murderer was his agent, or Clay Phipps his oldest friend, or any of the other buddies with whom Augie had drunk and sailed and fished and eaten? No, Yates was neither more nor less fantastic as a villain than the others. As in a nightmare, everywhere was taking on a tinge not only of horror but of a dread perverted flatness; all things were equally misshapen and equally possible. The painter, suddenly dizzy, let his head swim backward onto the settee cushion.

After what seemed a long time, Mulvane continued. 'If you learn anything, through friends, whatever, call me. Don't do anything crazy.'

The plastic box seemed to be waiting for an answer, but Augie and Nina just stared at each other, and after a few seconds Joe Mulvane hung up. A moment passed, then the dial tone kicked in. It was a rude and ugly sound, urgent as a siren as it blasted through the reedy speaker. Nina got up silently to turn it off. 'What now?' she said.

Augie blinked up at the ceiling. Fear and battlement had combined in his brain to produce something verging on indifference, a numbness that allowed for certain threads of clarity running through a fabric whose larger pattern had stopped making sense. 'Let's call Natchez,' he suggested. 'He'll know where Ray is, if anybody does.'

Nina dialed. Then she switched the speaker on and nestled next to her husband. The phone rang two times, three times, and on the fourth it was picked up; there followed the telltale pause of an answering machine.

Then the poet's voice, somber and imperious, filled the Silvers' living room.

'You have reached the home and workplace of Roberto Natchez,' it said. The R's had a lot of tongue, the O's were round as sea-tossed stones. Augie and Nina stared first at each other, then at the phone.

'I do not often take calls,' the message continued. 'I make no promise to return them. I have much to do. You may leave a message if you wish.'

In the short space before the beep, Augie tried without much luck to collect his thoughts. 'Natch, it's Augie, call me' was all he could manage to say.

Nina went to the phone, pre-empted the intrusion of the dial tone. 'He sounds deranged,' she said.

Augie didn't answer. He was thinking at that moment not about Natchez's sanity but his own. Not so many months ago, he'd been walloped on the head, had a concussion and amnesia. His brain had been blood-starved, sun-baked, desiccated. How sure could he be that he'd ever quite recovered? Suddenly he was scared in a different way than he had been before. He leaned forward, put his elbows on his knees. His voice was soft and a little shaky.

'Nina,' he said, 'if something was wrong with me, with my mind I mean, you wouldn't hide it from me, would you?'

She moved to him quickly, her feet made no sound

on the floor. She squatted down in front of him and took his hands. 'I don't understand.'

'I would want to know. If I was going crazy, if I *was* crazy ... Promise me you'd tell me, you'd help me understand that much at least. Promise.'

She held his eyes. In her gaze was love and respect and no false kindness.

'Good,' said Augie. 'Good. 'Cause, Nina, all of this is seeming very strange to me.'

CHAPTER THIRTY-FIVE

IT WAS THE SAME SHY, modest Reuben who knocked first, then unlocked the front door of the Silver house at eight o'clock on Monday morning. Heroism had not changed him, because it hadn't dawned on him that he was a hero. What he'd done did not require courage, as he saw it, but only vigilance and loyalty. Those qualities the young man did credit himself with having, but he didn't regard them as anything that should be thought of as rare. They were the basic things a friend should be. If bold acts followed from them, it was only because circumstance had allowed a friend to be a friend.

He was surprised, therefore, when Augie, dressed in shaving coat and slippers, came sweeping out of the bedroom and took him in his arms. The painter pressed the housekeeper's lean chest against his own, swayed with him a moment as in a slow dance, and kissed the top of his head. 'Reuben,' he murmured. 'Reuben, what a fellow you are. *Machissimo.*'

The young man allowed his hands to rest lightly on his friend's back, his cheek to lie against the painter's shoulder. Augie smelled like soap and toothpaste, the moist warmth of a shower was still pulsing off him in waves. Reuben was happy. He felt that he was getting back more than he possibly could have given. When Augie at last withdrew from the embrace but still held on to Reuben's arms, the young man's eyes were gleaming, his heart was healed, his lips arced in a small smile that was as solemn as it was joyful.

'You are feeling all right?' he asked.

Augie did not immediately answer. Rather, he spun toward the living room, an unaccustomed manic edginess making his movements angular, abrupt. 'Today?' he said. 'Today I feel fine. Full of fight. But yesterday, Reuben, yesterday was one of the worst days of my life.' He perched briefly on the arm of the sofa, then sprang up again, weakly but not without a certain jauntiness. 'Did you ever have a day, Reuben, when it suddenly seemed that you'd been kidding yourself your whole life long, that you've been mistaken about everything and everyone, that everything you've believed in has been wrong?'

Reuben looked at him. He was sorry Augie had felt bad, glad that Augie was telling him. It did not occur to him that maybe the question was not meant to be answered.

'No,' he said.

Augie pulled up short.

'The things I believe,' Reuben went on, 'there are not many, but I never doubt them. Maybe they are not possible. But I know that they are right.'

The words soothed Augie like a rubdown; the tightness went out of his posture and he sat. 'Yes, Reuben,' he said abstractedly. 'Yes. Damnit, that's exactly as it should be.'

There was a long silence except for the dry rattle of

the palm fronds, the soft scrape of leaves against the tin roof. Then Reuben said, 'Where is Nina?'

'In bed,' said Augie. 'She had an awful night. Come here, Reuben. Sit down.'

He patted the sofa next to him, and the housekeeper very tentatively parked himself on the edge of it.

'I know what's going on, Reuben,' the painter said. 'Nina and I have spoken. We've talked to the police.'

The young man looked at the blond wood floor between his feet. 'Were we wrong—'

Augie waved the question away. 'Not at all, not at all. But Reuben, here's the thing. Yesterday I was so glum, so rattled, I almost forgot to be pissed off. Then all of a sudden I said to myself, Wait a second, someone's trying to kill you, and your reaction is to get depressed? That's too much philosophy where your balls should be. So I got mad. Very mad.

'Reuben, the auction is one week from today. Between now and then, I'm gonna find out who's after me, I'm gonna find out why, and I'm gonna put that person out of business. I don't know how, but I'm gonna do it. Nina's closing the gallery for the week. We'd like you to be here with us. Can you move in for a while?'

The young man puffed with pride and sat up very straight. 'Of course,' he said. 'Of course. Later on I'll get my things.'

Then he stood, moved lithely to the kitchen, and put his apron on. Hero or no, it was still his job to dust, to do the dishes, plump the pillows, and arrange the flowers.

*

251

Art happens when a person of talent is seized with nervous energy and discovers that he or she has nothing to do except create.

At around 9 A.M., pacing aimlessly along the blind paths of his newfound rage, Augie decided he wanted to paint. He wanted to work on something big, something bright, something that would confirm him in his resolve while at the same time providing respite from his preoccupation and his fear. He asked Reuben to scavenge through the storage room and pull out the largest easel he could find, along with a huge canvas, eight feet by five, that had been stretched and gessoed ages ago and never used.

Not till the canvas had been set up in the shade of the poinciana tree did Augie have the faintest notion of what the painting's subject would be; and then he knew at once. It would be a picture of Fred, an *hommage* to the murdered parrot who had died as a proxy for its master.

'Green,' the painter said to Reuben. 'I'll need a lot of green. And a ladder. I'm starting at the upper left. There's jungle there, can you see it, Reuben? Vines with purple flowers. And berries tempting as tits. Parrot heaven. Maybe some monkeys peeking out, very small.'

He climbed the ladder, his wizened legs twitchy in the khaki shorts, and he began to work. Extravagant leaves appeared, veined and pendant; suggestions of muted sunlight filtered through from everywhere. Augie hummed as he painted; he didn't seem to know it. He smacked his lips as here and there he plopped down dollops of bright red among the foliage: succulent fruits full of sun-warm juice. He painted, and he thought of nothing, yet in that fecund blankness certain things became clear to him. Suddenly he understood that whoever was trying to kill him was an awful coward. A poisoned tart that killed a bird, a car as murder weapon; these were craven stratagems, and in that realization was both a comfort and a warning. Augie now felt confident that no one would confront him, no one would appear before him with a loaded gun. He understood too that no ploy, no deceit would be too abject or too crass for this enemy. He painted. The gloriously tangled canopy of leaves took shape, trumpet flowers in orange and magenta were strung along the vines, and after a couple of hours Augie realized quite abruptly that he was happily exhausted. He came down from the ladder on stiff knees, handed his brush and palette to Reuben, then walked on feet that tingled to his bed.

When Augie awoke from his nap, Reuben had already set lunch on the shady table near the pool, and Nina, who had slept late but was still frazzled and unrested, was on a rave.

'I tried calling Robert again,' she was saying. 'Same crazy message. And I just think it's really shitty that he doesn't even return the call.'

Augie looked down at the plates of sliced fruits and cold seafood. Painting made him hungry. That was one of the things he loved about it. 'Maybe he's away. Maybe he didn't get the message.'

'It's not like we're wasting his precious time with chitchat,' Nina went on. 'If he knows where Ray is . . .

And come on – he's not away. He's got no money and nowhere to go. He's just being—'

'Being what?'

'Being arrogant. Being secretive. Being himself.'

They ate. Augie sucked meat from a crab claw, then, as if thinking aloud, said softly, 'I thought you liked Natch.'

'I've enjoyed him at moments,' said Nina grudgingly. She nibbled at a wedge of avocado. 'But everything seems different now. I just feel so let down, so disappointed in them all.'

Augie frowned at his food. He knew what she was saying, he'd felt it too. He passed along another of the unsought consolations that had come to him while working. 'Nina,' he said, 'someone is trying to do something terrible to us. That doesn't mean everyone is guilty.'

'No?' said his wife. She put her fork down, dabbed her mouth on a napkin, then fixed her husband with a naked stare. 'Then why do I feel that they are?'

CHAPTER THIRTY-SIX

THE STAIRWAY UP to Roberto Natchez's third-floor garret was narrow and steep and smelled like dead flowers mingled with onions simmered long ago. Heat spiraled up along the banister and collected in a shimmering mist beneath the wire-strengthened skylight cut into the sunstruck metal roof. It got hotter with each step, and even the young and slender Reuben was damp between the shoulder blades by the time he reached the poet's door. He mopped his forehead on his handkerchief, took a moment to collect himself, and knocked.

Natchez looked up from the blank sheet of paper angled exactingly in front of him. He did not get many visitors, and he hid from himself the truth that he was grateful and curious to have one now, telling himself instead that he was annoyed at this interruption of his labors. He put down his pen with a show of irritation, then stood and examined himself briefly in the full-length mirror tucked in a dim alcove near his desk. Content that his black shirt was presentable, he walked the two steps to the door.

He saw Reuben standing there and felt a flash of disappointment. He'd imagined a more important-looking caller. 'Yes?' he curtly said.

'I am sent by Mr and Mrs Silver,' Reuben said. 'They would like to speak with you.'

'I know they would,' said Natchez, as though it was obvious that everyone wanted to speak with him. He turned away and the momentum of turning carried him once again into his living room. Reuben decided to regard this as an invitation to enter, and he followed the poet in. Natchez wheeled on him. 'I got their messages,' he said.

'So why you don't call back?' pressed the messenger. 'They speak of you as a friend.'

Natchez squelched a pang of guilt before it could register as such, and went on the offensive. 'And who are you?'

'I am Reuben.'

Natchez nodded sagely and as if somehow vindicated. 'Spanish.'

'American.'

The poet nodded again, a condescending smirk spreading across his mouth the way a drop of sludge smears itself across a puddle. He was standing near his desk now, and when he spoke he did not look right at Reuben, but a little off to the side. 'American,' he scoffed. 'That's what the new ones always say. American. They say it with pride, as if it were some great accomplishment to come here and be used.'

'I am not used,' said Reuben. 'I do what I want to do.'

'Of course,' said Natchez, sneering. 'You want to run errands for the Anglos. You want to clean their toilets. You want to pick up the crumbs from their tables.'

Reuben found the lecture boring; he'd heard it before, in neighborhood bodegas, from old men playing dominoes. What did interest him, though, was the question of why Natchez didn't look at him while he lectured. He came a half-step farther into the living room and realized that the poet was watching himself in the mirror: practicing his delivery, but practicing for what?

'You want to work for bad wages,' the liberator droned on. 'You want to call your bosses Mr and Mrs Anglo while they call you—'

'I call them Augie and Nina,' Reuben said. He said it softly but with a delight that exasperated Natchez. He turned away from the shadowed mirror and looked at his visitor with quiet fury.

'Well, you tell Augie and Nina that I'm very busy just now and I'll call them when I can.'

Reuben stood his ground. He glanced around the poet's apartment. It was dusty, dim, starved for sunlight, air, and furniture polish. Termite droppings flecked the windowsills, limestone grit put a dull gray coating on the floors. 'I won't,' he said.

'You won't what?' said Natchez.

'I won't tell them that. It is too important. Do you know where Ray Yates is?'

The poet put his hands on his hips, checked his posture in the mirror, and took a tone as superior as any rich Anglo could possibly muster. 'What gives you the nerve—'

'I ask you a question,' Reuben shot right back. He wasn't trying to mimic Natchez, but he also put his hands on his hips, and the effect of the two of them standing there was faintly ludicrous. 'Where is Ray Yates?'

Like most bullies, Roberto Natchez was ready to cave in at the first sign of real resistance. He dropped his hands and shrugged. 'I don't know.'

Reuben considered. He had his answer but it was an empty answer. He looked down at the floor and wished someone would wash it.

But now suddenly Natchez seemed eager to volunteer more information. It galled him to be asked a question to which he did not know the answer; it galled him to have given in to this fey little spick who spurned his liberator's message. He was ready to take out his pique on Ray Yates, who wasn't there to defend himself. 'Ray Yates is a very weak person,' he said.

Reuben said nothing, just sucked shallowly at the fetid heavy air. Natchez glanced sideways, tugged at the placket of his shirt, and orated.

'He lacks self-discipline. And, like many people of privileged background, he imagines there will always be someone to fix things for him. Someone to step in and write a check or make a phone call to some powerful friend who owes a favor.'

Reuben stayed quiet and watched a gekko slink along a cobwebbed baseboard.

'He gambles,' Natchez went on. 'Heavily. Your kind employers – Augie and Nina – they know that? I'll bet they don't. He's a sneak about it. Even I didn't know how heavily he gambles until a couple of days ago. He's pathetic.'

'Last Friday night he rents a car,' Reuben ventured.

'Yes,' said Natchez. 'To run away. To hide. He's in trouble with his loan sharks. A mouse in trouble with the snakes. He's got to stay in a little hole somewhere until he pays them off.'

'How will he pay?' asked Reuben, but he knew the answer before he'd finished the question. Natchez, smirking, lifted a heavy eyebrow toward his single Augie Silver canvas.

'It's so perfect,' the poet said. 'The mouse will pay the snakes with the money that some vulture will waste on a picture by a—'

Reuben interrupted to spare himself the pain and rage of hearing Augie insulted. 'You hate everyone,' he said.

It was not a question. Roberto Natchez did not bother to deny it. Rather, he straightened his back and appraised himself in the mirror, took his own measure as arbiter of all things. 'I hate weakness,' he said. 'I hate fakes. I hate people who think that by fooling themselves they can fool the world. I hate—'

'You hate Augie?' Reuben asked.

Natchez paused, raised a finger in the manner of a preacher, then elected not to answer. He attempted a small ironic smile, but it stalled halfway through the muscles of his face and locked into a death's-head grimace. Reuben could not help falling back a step. The room suddenly seemed more suffocatingly close than it had been before, as if the air itself had melted away and left behind some noxious residue of stinging dust and the infernal swampy vapors of rotting vegetation. Reuben swallowed, his mouth tasted vile. With effort, he tore his eyes away from the poet's evilly contorted lips; he had to look at something else, anything else. His flitting eyes glanced at bookshelves, sooty windows, then came to rest on a wire cage standing end-up in a corner of the room.

The poet's gaze caught up with Reuben's, his grimace was transfigured to a scowl of diabolic pleasure. 'I catch chickens,' he explained. He paused, showed teeth, cinched in the corners of his eyes. 'Then I kill them. I wring their necks.'

'For food?'

'For moral exercise.'

Reuben blinked, recoiled. He felt shaky on his feet, he groped for some idea or image that would steady him and pictured the Silvers' yard, a place of sun and breeze and smells of living things. 'Why should a chicken die—' he began.

The poet cut him off, his scowl leavened but made no less horrible by the beginnings of a twisted grin. He moved toward Reuben, herded him to the door to be sure he'd get the last word in. 'The same reason a chicken should live,' he said. 'No reason. No damn reason at all.'

CHAPTER THIRTY-SEVEN

'BAD NEWS,' Claire Steiger said, her voice weary and clenched as it crackled through the speakerphone. 'Lousy news. Peter Brandenburg smells a journalistic coup. He wants to do an interview with you, peg it to the auction.'

Augie was sitting on the sofa sipping tea and contentedly perspiring. He'd done a good day's work on the picture of Fred the parrot, the effort had left him feeling blithe and light. 'Was a time,' he said, 'you would have opened champagne on news like that.'

His agent ignored him. 'He wants to fly down there in the next day or two. Get the piece done fast, to run next issue. That means it hits the newsstands Sunday night and goes to subscribers Monday morning. Which means that by the time the auction starts at ten o'clock, the whole world knows you're painting again.'

Augie said nothing; it was all the same to him. Nina paced silently near the phone, concentrating less on her former boss's words than on her tone. There was something in it that Nina didn't think she'd ever heard before: a grudging acknowledgment that maybe she could not control events. At this, Nina felt a kind of triumph; she was not proud of the feeling, nor did it surprise her.

What did surprise her was the flash of sympathy she felt as well: Take the ability to control things away from a person like Claire Steiger, and what was left of her?

'I tried to talk him out of it,' the dealer resumed. 'He went on a tear about how the critic has to stand above commerce and blah, blah, blah. It's not like Peter to get so righteous, so shrill. It's almost like he's being spiteful.'

'Why would he be?' asked Nina.

The agent paused, there was a seething helplessness in the silence. When she spoke again, something had snapped, her voice was both whiny and ruthless. It made Nina think of the terrifying girls she had sometimes seen in city playgrounds, remorseless girls who would fight harder and dirtier than any boy, biting and kicking and going after eyes with their fingernails and never saying uncle.

'He's a bitch,' Claire said of Brandenburg, 'and I have no idea what's on his mind. But Augie, I'm asking you one last time, please don't do this interview. Stall. Sandbag. Do whatever—'

Nina cut her off. 'Claire, there'll be other paintings, other auctions. Why not think about the long term—'

'For me this is the only one that matters,' Claire Steiger interrupted in turn.

'But if you're representing Augie's interests?' said his wife.

'That's just how it is,' the agent said. 'Don't ask me to explain.'

Nina paced, unappeased and unsatisfied. 'Claire,' she pressed, 'I think you should explain.'

For a moment the humid air seemed to oscillate, pulled first one way then the other by the tug of wills. But when the agent spoke again, her position had only hardened, her tone grown still more steely. 'Augie, Nina, there will be serious consequences, dire consequences, if this auction falls flat.'

'Consequences for whom?' pressed Nina.

Some static came through the speakerphone, but the agent didn't answer. Augie and Nina looked at each other, their eyes grabbed like only the eyes of longtime mates can do, affirming for the millionth time a concord much profounder than mere agreement. 'Claire,' said Augie, 'nothing personal, but your advice doesn't mean that much to me right now. We'll let you know.'

Pants are handy things but they never fit exactly right.

On thick-built men like Joe Mulvane, they tend to bind around the thighs, the back seam has an annoying tendency to crawl between the buttocks. When such men sit and lean forward, say, against a bar, the waistband of their trousers binds them in the belly, while at the base of their spines an unattractive gap appears and seems to tug their shirttails out as well as to create a natural channel for sweat to pour. A belt doesn't close the trench in back; it only presents a retaining wall that bites into the flesh below the navel.

About the only benefit a belt provided a man like Joe Mulvane was that it gave him a place to hang his beeper – and most of the time he wished the beeper had never been invented. He was sitting at the Clove Hitch bar having an end-of-workday beer with Arty Magnus when the goddamn thing went off. Conversation died in a wide swath all around them; everyone had a morbid urge to listen in on the latest carnage when a homicide cop got beeped. Hogfish Mike Curran did a quick turn with his rag and mopped up condensation in Mulvane's direction. Even the gulls and pelicans standing on the nearby pilings fell silent for the moment. But the message was nothing gruesome. It was Augie Silver saying simply that he thought the two of them should talk.

The detective went back to his beer. A week before the summer solstice, the sun was still white hot at nearly 6 P.M. and cold beer seemed God's kindest gift to sweltering humanity.

Arty Magnus, reluctant journalist, felt a fleeting impulse to attend to the business of his newspaper. 'Augie Silver,' he said. 'The slightly famous painter with the dead parrot.'

'Yup,' said Mulvane, and left it at that.

Magnus nipped at his gin. He was a stringy guy, gangly even, and he liked the heat. He liked extremes. If you lived someplace hot, let it be hot. Let the streets melt, let exhausted air conditioners explode. 'Joe,' he said, 'can I ask you a question?'

Mulvane just looked at him without pulling his lips very far from his beer.

'Augie Silver – there something going on here I should know about?'

'That's two questions,' said Mulvane. He sucked the last of his brew and stood up so that the gap closed at the back of his pants and the cloth blotted the sweat that had run down. In all, it was not a pleasant sensation. 'I'll see ya later,' said the cop.

'If Yates is in bad hock with his loan shark,' reasoned Mulvane, 'that's a big problem for him. He might rather make it a big problem for you.'

'He has paintings,' Nina said. 'And he rented a turquoise car.'

'But in the meantime,' the detective said, 'it's the agent who seems antsier than anybody else.'

'She has the most to gain,' said Nina. 'And I don't see why she's got this shoot-the-moon attitude about this one auction.'

'And then there's the crazy man,' the cop added to the tally. 'The chicken slayer. What's his angle?'

'He is evil,' Reuben said.

Mulvane nodded. He knew from evil. 'But there's no money motive?'

'His painting is still on the wall,' said Augie. 'Reuben saw it. Besides, mere greed would be too bourgeois for Robert. He'd have to find a way to make it philosophical.'

The four of them were sitting in the backyard near the pool. The sun had slipped below the level of the trees, the drooping fronds absorbed the last of the day's battering, and the dappled air that filtered through seemed no temperature at all. Fat summer clouds towered here and there. Their bottoms were lavender, they were voluptuous with swelling curves, and they roamed the sky like sniffing dogs, deliberating as to where they'd drop their rain.

Mulvane sipped his beer. He felt suddenly irritable, out of his depth. Conniving art dealers. Philosophical poets who choked chickens. Key West was a weird town, and the weirdness extended even to why and how inhabitants got murdered. Mulvane wanted to bring the discussion back to more familiar grass-roots criminality.

'The other people on your list,' he said. 'Jimmy Gibbs. You know he once killed a man?'

There was a general recoil, but less so than there would have been a week ago. People could get used to anything.

'I knew he'd been in trouble,' Augie said. 'I didn't know ...' His voice faltered, he gestured weakly, he thought about the time he'd spent on the water and at the Clove Hitch with the gruff, grumpy, always-bitching-and-moaning Jimmy Gibbs. Damnit, he enjoyed the guy.

'Was a long time ago,' Mulvane said. 'Almost thirty years. And supposedly there were some mitigating cir-cumstances, maybe he was even justified. But still, there are people who can kill and people who can't.' He raised his beer; the timing made it seem like some macabre toast to homicide. 'So who else?'

He glanced from face to face and Reuben piped up. 'Meester Pheeps. Who brought the cake.'

'Right,' said Joe Mulvane. 'That excellent poison cake.'

'Come on,' said Augie, 'he's my oldest friend. And he isn't selling his paintings.'

Mulvane put his glass down on the low iron table in front of him and glanced at the painter from under his eyebrows. 'How do you know?' he asked.

Augie was drinking white wine. It looked greenish in

the fading light. The artist gave a nervous little laugh, and squirmed. 'Look,' he said, 'I started giving him pictures – Jesus, it must be twenty, twenty-two years ago . . . And I've spoken with him, we've talked. I mean, he had a chance to tell me, he would have said something . . . And it's not like he's strapped for funds. At least I don't think he is . . . No, he would have told me, I know it.'

There was an embarrassed silence, a pained silence such as might surround a person who'd just come to suspect a spouse's infidelity that had been long before surmised by others. Nina reached out gently and put a hand on Augie's wrist. Reuben pulled a deep breath in, as though trying to take the hurt into himself and thereby cleanse the air.

Joe Mulvane softly cleared his throat. 'Try to find out for sure,' he said.

Augie nodded. He slumped down in his chair, his thin bare knees splayed out. Far away there was thunder, the sound was less heard than felt. It was dim enough now for the headlight bugs to glow, they flew by slowly, their red eyes bright before their blurring wings.

Nina steeled herself to press on. 'And we've yet to decide about this interview,' she said.

'Pros and cons?' said Joe Mulvane.

'The argument against,' said Nina, 'is: Do we really want any more attention? The argument for—'

'The argument for,' Augie roused himself, 'is that, goddamnit, I will not be cowed.' He was forcing himself upright in his chair; he pressed down on its arms so that his bony shoulders hunched up almost to his ears. 'I keep silent, I hide – whoever's after me, they've won. I won't roll over.'

'Who cares who wins?' said Nina.

But Augie went right on. 'Besides, why should we imagine that this auction passes and suddenly the threat is over? There'll be other auctions, other shows, other reasons to kill me. Something like this doesn't just go away.'

'He's right about that,' said Joe Mulvane. 'As a rule.'

'So you're saying he should do the interview?' Nina asked.

The detective fended off the suggestion with the lift of a meaty hand. 'I can't give protection, I'm not giving advice. Look, you do the interview, you're raising the stakes, putting yourself out there—'

'Setting a trap,' said Augie, 'with myself as bait.'

'Something like that,' Mulvane resumed. 'It's a risk. Keep quiet, maybe you're protecting yourself, maybe you're just prolonging things. It's a tough call.'

'I'm doing it,' said Augie.

Nina sipped her wine. Reuben checked around to see if anyone needed another drink, a fresh dry cocktail napkin. Off to the east, lightning made orange pulses inside a purple cloud.

'Well, listen,' said Mulvane, 'if your mind's made up, I'll say one thing. General rule, there's two ways to stay out of trouble. Say nothing to nobody or say everything to everybody.'

'Meaning?' Augie said.

'Meaning that if you're doing interviews, don't just talk to this one guy, talk to everyone who's interested.'

Augie could not help giving forth a little laugh. 'Joe, I think you have an exaggerated notion of how many people give a damn about me.'

'Local paper does,' said the detective. 'This I know for sure.'

Augie shrugged. 'OK, I'll talk to the local paper. World famous in his hometown. Why not?'

CHAPTER THIRTY-EIGHT

THAT NIGHT Augie Silver couldn't sleep.

He lay in bed and watched the lazy turning of the ceiling fan, listened to the fleeting showers that hammered briefly on the metal roof then stopped as abruptly as if someone had turned off a faucet. He looked at his sleeping wife, now and then brushed a stray hair from her face. At around 5 A.M. he slipped out from under the thin damp sheet.

Nina roused herself enough to ask if he was all right.

'Fine, darling, fine,' he said. He leaned over with some difficulty and stroked her shoulder. 'There's something I need to do.'

'What?' she asked fuzzily.

'Go back to sleep,' he whispered.

He pulled on his khaki shorts and a blue work shirt with paint spots on the sleeves. Then he tiptoed through the hallway, past the closed door of the guest bedroom where Reuben was now staying. From a basket on the kitchen counter he took the key to the lock on Nina's old fat-tire bicycle, and he left the house.

Key West is a very quiet place at 5 A.M. A soft electric hum spills out of the pinkish streetlights; if a cat wails, fighting or fornicating, you can hear it many blocks away. Augie's tires made a nice sound, a sticky sound, as he slowly rode and, nub by nub, the rubber treads were stretched off the damp asphalt. The high parts of the streets had steamed themselves almost dry; along the curbs were shallow puddles that would be gone by daybreak. Nothing moved. The waxy flowers of the night-blooming cirrus gave off an uncanny lacquered gleam.

Augie's legs were tired by the time he'd pedaled the eight flat blocks to Clay Phipps's house. He gave himself a moment to recover before he pushed open the wooden gate and climbed the four brick steps to his friend's front door. Then he knocked.

He waited, taking in the salad smell of moist shrubbery and the short-lived freshness of air with the coral dust washed out of it by rain. He knocked again, hard enough so that his knuckles hurt, and in another moment a light came on inside and Clay Phipps opened the door.

He looked confused, jowly, and not his best. He was wearing pajama bottoms, blue-and-white-striped silk; his pink stomach was bare and puffy, his soft chest showed the beginnings of unpretty breasts. The top of his bald head was blotchy with sleep, his side tufts were wispy, long, and tangled. 'Augie,' he muttered. 'What the hell—'

'We have to talk,' the painter said. 'I'm coming in.'

He slipped past the other man, brushed lightly against his gut while passing. He strode firmly through the entrance hall and confronted the six naked rectangles on

271

the living-room walls. They were only dimly lit by the entry light and yet they glared. Some were high, some were low, some were tall, some were wide. The centers of the rectangles were very white and seemed not meant to be exposed, they were like the parts inside the bathing suit. Along the edges were lines of soot and grime, nasty suggestions that nothing was ever quite clean. Augie gestured toward the rude blanks and looked his old friend in the eye. 'Clay,' he said. 'Why?'

Phipps was not yet totally awake, but he was awake enough to know what he was being asked. He blinked, glanced around his living room as if it were a stranger's house. He sighed, walked heavy-footed and obliquely toward a chair, and sat down on the edge of it. He said nothing.

'Why, Clay?' Augie repeated. 'Why all of them?'

Phipps stayed silent. He put his elbows on his knees and ran his hands across his head, but his sparse hair came away no less disheveled than before.

'Money?' Augie asked. He waited a beat then answered his own question. 'No, I don't think so. You've always liked to pamper yourself, but I've never known you to be greedy. If you needed money, you'd sell one, two – you wouldn't sell all six.'

Phipps kept quiet. Augie locked his hands behind his back and looked up at the ceiling as if puzzling out a problem in the higher math.

'Were you just showing off, Clay? Is it as simple as that? Were you hoping to get kissed up to as a big collector, invited to some fancy East Side parties?'

Clay Phipps tried to speak, but all that came out was

a low rasp, a sound like someone stirring gravel with a spoon. He tried again. 'Augie, we all thought you were dead.'

The painter moved away from the guilty wall and stood above his friend. 'I don't want to sound like a sentimental fool,' he said, 'but it seems to me that that might be a reason to keep the fucking paintings. A little something to remember me by.'

'I don't need pictures to remember you,' Phipps said weakly, but it sounded smarmy even in his own ears and it evoked nothing but an icy stare from Augie. A moment passed and then Phipps spoke again. He spoke so softly that Augie had to lean down low, straining in the pre-dawn quiet to catch the words. 'Or maybe it's that I didn't want to remember you.'

Augie straightened up. He felt a pain that was also a relief; the decay of a lie had been scraped away, a nerve was open to the air. 'Ah,' he said, 'a bit of naked honesty creeps in. How bracing. How rare.'

'I need a drink of water,' Clay Phipps said. Abstract-edly, almost as if sleepwalking, he got up and padded barefoot toward the kitchen. Augie dogged his steps.

'You thought I was dead,' he said to Phipps's back. 'Well, I had some things wrong too. I thought I had friends to come home to.'

Phipps switched on the kitchen light. He was a fastidious bachelor and the place was neat. A single place setting had dried in the drainboard. Wineglasses gleamed on a shelf. There was a handsome wooden knife block on the counter with every knife in place. 'You do,' he said as he drew a glass of water from the cooler.

'Bullshit,' Augie answered. He watched his old friend gulp down his drink, watched his throat pulse with swallowing and his belly stretch a little farther, and he was suddenly seized by a physical revulsion mingled with an aching and useless compassion not just for Clay Phipps but for all things human. Drinking water and pissing urine; getting old and getting fat; disappointing friends and being disappointed; all of it a noisy and befuddled prologue to the lonely act of dying. 'Clay, what did I do to you? What did I do that you need to forget about?'

Phipps leaned back against his kitchen counter. He blinked down at the floor, he scratched his scalp. The sleepiness seemed finally to fall away from him and was replaced by a whining defiance, a complaining that had gone unspoken for far too long and turned rancid. 'You want to know, Augie? You really want to know? You shamed me. You shamed all of us. Me. Yates. Natchez. You made us feel like shit.'

They locked eyes. The kitchen was narrow and they were standing very close. The knife block bristled near Phipps's right elbow. Augie said nothing.

'I don't think any of us realized it until you disappeared,' the heavy man went on. 'Until we thought you died. It's like ... how can I explain it? When you were around, we figured we were your friends, we must be like you. Then you were gone, and it was very clear we weren't like you at all. You had your work. You had your marriage. You had your way of getting on with people, different kinds of people, making everybody feel good. We had none of that. Not really. And the worst thing, the humiliating part? We didn't even know we didn't have it – you had it for us.

'You feel betrayed, Augie? *I* feel betrayed. When you hit the reef, we *all* hit the reef. Don't you see that? This pleasant little life we had down here, we thought there was some heart to it, some depth. But no, it only seemed that way because you buoyed it up. You had an obligation . . .'

Almost casually, almost as if the gesture were an accidental fidget, Augie reached for a knife. His left hand moved forward abruptly but with no special quickness. It went past Clay Phipps's flank and seized the biggest handle. The blade was long and thin, the flexing metal rang softly as it was whisked out of the block. Phipps fell silent, his breath caught with a strangled gurgling sound. He tucked his chin and the loose flesh underneath it began instantly to tremble.

'Someone's trying to kill me, Clay,' said Augie. 'Is it you?'

Phipps didn't answer. He stared at the knife, his eyes throbbed in and out of focus. Augie held it loosely, carelessly; it glinted in the electric light, and the point was a few inches from Phipps's bare pink stomach. He arched his back and tried to shrink, he leaned back hard against the counter and squeezed the edges of it with white fingers.

'You think I'm going to stab you, Clay? Terrible thing, a guilty conscience. Hold out your hand.'

Slowly, warily, Phipps lifted his eyes. He let go of the counter edge; his palm made a moist sound as it came away. He presented his soft plump hand and Augie gently placed the knife in it. 'Feel better now?' he asked.

Phipps just stared at him.

'I asked you a question,' Augie went on. 'Answer it.'

Phipps blinked. He remembered to breathe, but he seemed as baffled and as terrified to find the knife in his own hand as he had been to see it in his friend's. 'Augie, Jesus Christ—'

'All right, let's try a different question. You want me dead, Clay?'

The refrigerator switched on; the sudden noise was shocking. Somewhere far away a dog yelped. Outside the small kitchen window the darkness was changing from pure black to a veiled and grainy purple. All at once the knife felt not just brutal but unutterably obscene, disgusting, in Phipps's hand. He turned and put it on the counter, and when he faced Augie again he was crying. The tears didn't fall, they just made his irises look melted, smeared; the rims of his eyelids were bright red and the corners of his mouth began to quiver.

'I've wished you were dead,' he said softly. 'Once you'd gone, once the secret was out about how small my life is, how alone I am, how ridiculous . . .' He shook his bald head, lightly slapped his belly with a mix of self-mockery and affection without respect. 'Yeah. I've felt maybe there'd be less to be embarrassed about, less to feel like a failure about, if you didn't exist.'

He paused, dragged the back of his hand across his eyes. He sniffled, and then, through the wet and childlike noise, he gave a little laugh. The laugh carried a bleak but genuine amusement. He pinched the bridge of the nose, then made a dismissive gesture that seemed to take in his striped pajamas, his tender pink feet, his neat kitchen with his cookbooks and his saucepans and his wooden spoons. 'But Augie, for God's sake, I'm not a killer.'

Augie stood back and appraised him. Phipps's face would not stay still. His mouth held the bleak smile for just a moment, then collapsed, folded down as if he would begin to sob. The eyes crinkled with the last pinch of a laugh, then clouded over in shame, and finally opened wide and liquid with a naked hope: the hope that he would be forgiven.

Augie didn't know if he could come across with that forgiveness. If it happened, it wouldn't happen by decision but by feeling, and the feeling needed time to ripen or to shrivel.

He turned without another word and walked quickly through the denuded living room and out into the humid purple dawn.

CHAPTER THIRTY-NINE

WHEN HE GOT HOME it was almost seven.

Rays like a crown were spiking up the eastern sky, and the curbside puddles had dried. He locked the blue fat-tire bicycle in front of his house. He opened the door and saw Nina pacing in the living room and drinking coffee. Her eyes were flat and tired.

'Augie,' she said, 'you shouldn't have gone out alone.'

'I know,' he said. 'I had to. I'm sorry.'

'You went to Clay's.' It was not a question.

'He's selling his paintings. All of them. He's ashamed of himself and he wants to be friends again.'

Nina held her coffee mug in both hands. Her head was tilted at an inquiring angle.

'It isn't him,' said Augie.

'You're absolutely sure?' said Nina.

'No. Not absolutely. But he had his chance. I'm exhausted.' He went to her. She didn't budge. 'Mad?'

'Yes.'

He rubbed a hand over his face, the skin felt rubbery. 'I don't blame you,' he said.

He went to the bedroom. Reuben was there. His hair was wet from the shower, and he was plumping Augie's pillows. How did he know just what Augie wanted and how did he do it so fast? Reuben was amazing.

Augie didn't bother to undress. He slipped under the sheet, pulled a pillow over his eyes and ears, and when he woke up it was noon.

Nina was mostly over being angry, though she exacted a promise that Augie would run off on no more reckless errands. They had lunch, and then the painter asked Reuben to set up the big easel in the backyard and to carry out his partly painted canvas from the storage room. He was ready to return to work on the *hommage* to Fred, a heroic portrait of a noble bird against the backdrop of a mythic forest.

He took his brush and palette and climbed the ladder under the shelter of the strangely dainty poinciana leaves. He began to paint and he began to hum. The jungle canopy took on texture and humidity. Weird rootless flowers sprang to crimson life in the damp and crumbly crevasses between branches. Unknown huge-eyed creatures – antic crosses between cats and bats and squirrels – flitted half-hidden in the camouflage of light and shade. Here and there a flash of searing sun shot through; bulbous fruits and pregnant pods swelled with excess of vitality. The foliage shaped itself around a monumental absence, held itself open, breathless and fluttering in expectation of the something that was missing, till the picture seemed to cry out for the colossal presence of an outsize parrot, a prodigious parrot in splendid and extravagant plumage.

Augie was mixing colors, humming, chuckling to himself, when the phone rang. He didn't hear it, nor did he see Nina walking toward him until she was standing almost directly underneath the ladder.

'Peter Brandenburg's on the line,' she said. 'He wants to fly down tomorrow morning and do the interview in the afternoon.'

'Fine,' said Augie, 'fine.' He was thinking about birds and vines and jungle, he didn't want to distract himself with journalists and interviews. But then he remembered the suggestion Joe Mulvane had made. 'Tell him there'll probably be someone from the *Sentinel* along.'

Nina shielded her eyes from the sun and frowned up at him. 'He won't like that,' she said. 'Big New York critic sharing time with some reporter from the local rag.'

Augie shrugged. 'I hate giving the same answers twice. If he wants the interview, that's the ground rules.'

Nina was momentarily exasperated, then a small and enigmatic smile crossed her lips. When she'd thought her husband was dead, she'd made of him, if not a saint, then someone milder, less rambunctious and unmanageable than in fact he sometimes was. She'd almost forgotten what a stubborn bullheaded pain in the neck he could be when he was working, when he was strong. She shook her head and went back to the phone.

Augie mixed pigments, concocted an unabashedly ferocious shade of acidy lime green, and began the arduous and endlessly amusing job of trying to give the flightless paint the fluff and lift and airiness of feathers.

*

'Matty been around?' asked Jimmy Gibbs.

'More'n you have,' said Hogfish Mike Curran. Losing Gibbs as a regular was no great financial loss to the Clove Hitch, but still Hogfish spoke in the slightly wounded tone of the barkeep who has been abandoned.

'Been busy,' said Jimmy Gibbs.

Curran doubted it but kept that opinion to himself. A few seconds went by, then Gibbs blindsided him by saying the real reason he'd been away. 'Besides, that little scene the other week . . . I just ain't felt like bein' at the docks.'

A sudden wave of fellow feeling swept over Hogfish Mike. 'I gotcha, bubba. Have one on me?'

In the instant after the words had left his mouth Curran understood two things: He understood that he'd been ambushed, worked around to the offer of a freebie, and he understood that Gibbs, being Gibbs, would try to stretch the offer.

'Jeez, Hogfish, thanks. A shot and a beer, if you don't mind.'

The bartender wheeled around, grabbed a longneck and poured a slightly grudging shot of no-name bourbon. When he spun back toward Gibbs, the former mate was watching a fishing boat come into the Bight, watching the way it chiseled out a wake and the way the green water went foamy but flat behind it, and there was a no-bullshit sadness in his face that made Curran feel a little mean for not giving him more alcohol.

But then Gibbs brightened – brightened even before he'd put the cold beer to his lips. His eyes flashed, and in the first instant Hogfish Mike thought it was a twinkle of innocent mischief. In the second instant he decided he'd been half right. It was mischief, but the sadness was still there, mixed in with it, giving it a snarl and a weight and an angry drive that meant trouble.

Gibbs sipped his beer. 'Ain'tcha curious why I'm lookin' for Matty?'

Hogfish looked away, watched a cormorant baking its wet wings on a piling. 'My business,' he said, 'it don't do to be too curious.'

'Yeah, yeah,' said Gibbs. 'Well, I need to make sure the *Fin Finder* is still for sale.'

'Far as I know it is,' said Curran. He paused, then crossed his ropy forearms and leaned in a little closer. 'But Jimmy, what good's it do ya? That auction thing, the painting – you told me it was all screwed up.'

Now Gibbs was having fun. He'd managed to pull Hogfish in. He sipped beer, watched a cloud of gulls trail out behind a returning boat. A mate with a rubber apron and no shirt was cleaning the catch. 'Is screwed up,' he said at last. He swigged again, then gestured toward the swarm of flying scavengers plucking entrails from midair. 'But there's more'n one way to gut a fish.'

The twinkle in Gibbs's eye had become a glower, he was clutching his beer bottle like it was a bludgeon, and Curran didn't like the look of things at all. He put his hands flat on the bar and leaned in even closer. 'Jimmy, you ain't gonna go and do somethin' stupid, are ya?'

Gibbs let go of his beer, grabbed his shot glass, and tossed the bourbon down. Then he grimaced. His gums had seen enough alcohol over the years so that a shot of booze no longer made them burn; still, the grimace was part of the ritual of drinking, a visible reminder that the shot had registered. He waited for his face to settle back down before he spoke. 'Nah, Hogfish, nothin' stupid. For a change, in fact, I'm doin' somethin' smart.'

CHAPTER FORTY

Arty Magnus did not often pull rank on his subordi-
nates. It made for bad morale around the newsroom,
and besides it was extremely rare for there to be a story
that the editor had the faintest interest in personally
covering.

But when Joe Mulvane called late on Tuesday to say
that Nina Silver had asked his advice about who her
husband should speak to at the paper, Magnus decided
to assign the interview to himself. *Famous painter returns
from dead to real or imagined attempts on his life.* This was
a cut above the promotional pap and small-town politics
usually covered by the *Sentinel*; this might be of interest
more than a few mile markers up the road. Freddy
McClintock, the eager and deficient young reporter,
would briefly sulk at his boss's usurpation, but he'd get
over it; young reporters always did.

The interview was scheduled for three on Wednesday
afternoon.

In preparation, Reuben had taken down most of the
paintings that had hung in the Silvers' living room since
the eve of Augie's memorial. The painter no longer
wanted them there. If he was bothering to give interviews, he didn't want to talk about the past but the future

– the new phase of his work that was being exuberantly launched with the huge odd portrait of Fred.

Not quite finished, the flamboyant canvas had been moved near the sofa, it leaned back on its spattered easel and dominated the house. There was a lot of birdness in it, Augie thought, but he allowed himself to feel there was more in it as well. God knows how, he had managed to put some disturbing knowledge into the parrot's red eyes, some wisdom about the lush and sensual death grip that was the dark side of the seduction of the tropics. Then again, it was hardly a tragic painting. In fact, minus the solemnity that seized people when they thought they were beholding Art, it was more or less hilarious: a giant bird the color of some sickening candy, out of all proportion to a berserk forest full of fake fruits and sham creatures . . .

'Nina, what the hell am I supposed to say about this thing?'

She patted his arm as he leaned back on the couch. 'You'll think of something clever, something quotable,' she said. It was a quarter till three. Ceiling fans were giving an illusion of freshness to the stultifying air. Reuben was putting up coffee. Nina looked with pleasure at the oleanders in their vases. She was glad people were coming to the house. It was nice to have some distraction, to be doing something, anything, besides worrying about her husband dying.

Punctually at three, a pink taxi pulled up in front of the Silvers' home and Peter Brandenburg got out. Fussily handsome and almost as tan as a local, he was wearing an off-white linen suit over a shirt of cotton oxford; he carried a notebook bound in cordovan leather, along with a German tape recorder of space-age design. He paid the driver, straightened the collar of his jacket, and was approaching the porch steps just as Arty Magnus pulled up on his bicycle. It was brutally hot and Magnus was wearing shorts and sandals. In his bike basket was a cardboard-covered spiral notebook, the kind with the wire that always catches things. 'Hi,' he said. He held out a hand as he deployed his kickstand.

Nina had apparently been right: Brandenburg seemed miffed at having to share his interview time and appeared to loathe his small-town colleague on sight. He shook hands briefly and limply. 'Peter Brandenburg,' he said. '*Manhattan* magazine.'

This last was without doubt an act of aggression, meant to establish his dominion over the other man. Magnus, a graduate of Columbia Journalism, did not roll over.

'Arty Magnus. Key West *Sentinel*.'

They went together to the front door. Reuben ushered them through to the living room, where they stood awkwardly for a moment, dwarfed by the painted parrot and uncertain who should speak. Magnus introduced himself, shook hands with Augie and with Nina, and Brandenburg, in another gambit to assert his preeminence, made it clear that they had met before. 'You've lost weight,' the critic said to the painter.

Augie ran a hand over his sunken chest and wizened tummy. 'I've put a fair bit back on,' he said. 'But sit down, sit down. Coffee? Wine? What would you like?'

'Nothing for me,' said Brandenburg. He picked a solo

chair, took a gold pen from an inside jacket pocket, and started setting up his tape recorder.

'Coffee'd be great,' said Magnus. He plopped down on the edge of a love seat and shook a stub of pencil out of the spiral binding of his notebook; the metal flange that held the eraser had been bitten flat.

There was a moment's small talk, then Peter Brandenburg crossed his legs, straightened his linen trousers, cleared his throat, and gestured noncommittally toward the looming canvas. 'Why don't we begin,' he said, 'with your decision to start painting again. How did that come about?'

Augie ran a hand over the crests and troughs of his wavy white hair. 'Well, it happened when I was stranded down in Cuba—'

'You were shipwrecked, weren't you?' put in Arty Magnus. 'Marooned?'

'Yes,' said Augie. 'Right. I guess I really should begin with that. Back in January . . .'

The New York critic briefly shut his eyes, shifted impatiently in his chair. He was there to talk about art, not shipwrecks. He knew as much of the shipwreck tale as he needed and he had a tight deadline to meet. Besides, he'd already decided what the gist of his story would be; all he needed was some quotes to flesh it out.

'. . . so by the time I came around,' Augie was concluding, 'I'd decided I'd been a perverse and arrogant ass to give up painting. I felt that I was shirking in some way. Not a way that mattered to anybody else—'

'Apparently it does matter to someone else,' the local

newspaperman interrupted. 'Isn't it true that there've been threats against your life?'

Nina was sitting next to Augie on the couch. They took a moment to consult each other's eyes. They hadn't been able to decide in advance how public they would go, what, if anything, they'd refuse to divulge.

'Something about a poisoned bird?' pressed Arty Magnus. 'About an attempted hit-and-run?'

Peter Brandenburg dropped all pretense of hiding his restlessness. He squirmed, his face grew petulant and sour. 'Excuse me,' he said, 'but I thought we were here to talk about your work, not indulge in sordid gossip.'

The tone was meant to offend, but the sharpness of it was blunted by the humid air, heavy as wet wool, and Augie answered not with umbrage but with a languid irony. 'It would be nice to have the luxury to separate the two.'

There was an uneasy silence. Arty Magnus sipped coffee, Peter Brandenburg watched his tape recorder futilely turn. Nina tried not to sound like she was scolding. 'Peter, if Augie's in danger, that's more important than any—'

'Of course, of course,' said Brandenburg. He tried to sound conciliatory and almost managed. 'But in the meantime—'

'In the meantime you've got your story to do,' said Augie mildly. 'I understand. So let me say this about the work. I live in the tropics. Almost the tropics, if you want to be technical. And fact one about the tropics is that they are unbelievably fruitful. Everything grows here. Everything *over*grows here. And not all of it is beautiful.

Or gentle. Not by a long shot. You've got ugly choking vines, rubbery things with varicose veins. You've got soupy marshes that stink and reflect a putrid glare. You've got biting spiders, carnivorous plants, fish with spike teeth, shrubs with barbed thorns. And the lesson that goes with that? It doesn't so much matter if something is pretty, if it's benign; it matters that it's there, that it hangs on, that it produces—'

'So you're saying,' Brandenburg coaxed, 'you want to be as prolific as the tropics?'

Augie cocked his head and let that settle in his ear. 'That's impossible,' he said. 'But yeah, it'd be a worthy thing to shoot for. As prolific and as accepting.'

For the first time in the interview, Brandenburg wrote something in his leather notebook. But when he looked down to do so, Arty Magnus recaptured the initiative. He gestured toward the unfinished, unframed painting on its vast untidy easel. 'This picture,' he said, 'this bird here. This the bird that ate the poison?'

Brandenburg stiffened. He'd finally worked the conversation around to art, and now it was being dragged down again to gutter level. He slapped his pen against his notes and lectured: 'It's obviously a universal—'

'No,' said Augie, 'it's not a universal. As a matter of fact, it's Fred.'

Stung at being contradicted, the critic fell instantly into a sulk. Nina saw the narrowed eyes, the tightened lips, and flashed a look of mute advice to her husband.

Augie backpedaled. 'It's both, of course,' he said. 'I mean, it started as Fred, but then . . . Look, if you only paint what you already know, you're in a rut. Why

289

bother? You paint to find out what you know. You see what I'm saying? I painted this to find out what I knew about Fred. What I know about parrots. What I know about feathers. What I know about green.'

The New York reviewer rallied somewhat and started taking notes again. Arty Magnus held his stub of pencil against his lower lip and waited for the pendulum to swing back his way. Augie paused for breath, then went on with the untrammeled directness of a man thinking out loud.

'You paint to find out what you know, but then the painting outsmarts you, ends up knowing more than you do.' He gestured toward the monumental canvas, toward the parrot's downturned beak and frozen gaze. 'Look at those eyes, that stare. Is it accusing? Resigned? Is it serene or is it mocking? For the life of me, I can't tell. But I know, without a doubt, that bird knows something I don't know.'

For a moment everybody stared at Fred. In the thick and shimmering light, the parrot's plumage was velvety, its unsettling red eyes appeared to pulse.

Then a soft voice was heard from an unexpected direction. It was Reuben. He'd kept a discreet distance from the guests and was leaning over the kitchen counter. 'Maybe he knows who is trying to hurt you.'

Augie twisted and looked at his friend across the back of the settee. 'Maybe. Maybe he does. And maybe someday he'll tell us.'

CHAPTER FORTY-ONE

DETECTIVE SERGEANT JOE MULVANE had seen
countless crime scenes in his life, and they never failed
to depress him. The scenes of homicides, of course, were
especially appalling: the oddly metallic smell of blood,
the ghastly chalk-drawn silhouette showing where and in
what posture the dead guy had fallen. So often they fell
with one hand reaching out. Probably they were just
trying to hit the bastard that killed them, but it didn't
look that way when they chalked it on the floor, it always
looked like the victim was making one final grab at
something good and beautiful, something he would
never capture, never touch.

But even when nobody got hurt, when the crime was
just some dipshit burglary or apparently aimless B-and-
E, there was something bleak about the scene, something
that made Mulvane feel gloomy. It had to do, he figured,
with waste. Waste and stupidity. Shattered windows;
smashed crockery; clothing pulled from ransacked
dresser drawers and either torn or stretched all out of
shape – these morons destroyed more than they stole.
And there was something that never stopped seeming
pathetic about a broken thing: a trashed room, a cracked
mirror, even a busted coffee cup. You couldn't say those

things had ever been alive, but still, when they were broken they were as full of death as any corpse.

Mulvane was feeling the crime-scene gloom at first light Thursday morning as he stood on Ray Yates's gangplank on Houseboat Row and saw what had been done to the radio host's floating home.

The louvered front door had been wrenched out of alignment; it hung limp and useless on a single mangled hinge. Inside, all was havoc. The living-room upholstery had been slashed with knives, white fiber stuffing poked out of it like hair from an old man's ears. The drawers from a file cabinet had been yanked out, the files dumped in a chaos of paper. Liquor bottles lay smashed on the floor, brandy fumes wafted from shards of green glass. In the bedroom, the closet had been decimated, the palm-tree shirts thrown in a pile and stomped with dirty shoes. The medicine chest was torn off the bathroom wall, the shower curtain ripped from its rod. In the tiny kitchen, a rotting fish had been left on the counter near the sink; flies clustered on its clouded eye. Above the fish, a terse note had been scrawled on the wall in red magic marker. It said No Deal, Ray. Clean Up Your Own Mess.

Mulvane looked at the fish, the note, and the beat cop who had called in the crime. 'Probably Ponte,' he said.

'Dust for prints?' asked the cop.

'If you enjoy that sort of thing,' said Mulvane. 'You won't find any.'

Later that morning he drove to Olivia Street. Feeling grim himself, he expected others to be feeling grim, and he was faintly put out to find the members of the Silver household positively chipper. Reuben answered the door in a crisp new apron, candy-striped. Smiling, he led the detective through the house and out toward the pool. Nina was swimming laps. Her legs scissored evenly and powerfully, her hair streamed sleekly back behind her, and when she lifted her face from the water, the tension seemed to have washed out of it, eased by exercise and chlorine. Augie was sitting at a shady table. He had a cup of coffee in front of him and a sketch pad on his lap. He wore a straw hat and was chewing on a toothpick.

'Ah, Joe,' he said. 'Beautiful morning. Cup of coffee? Muffin maybe?'

'Just coffee,' said Mulvane. He lifted a chair and turned it backwards, then straddled the seat with his beefy thighs and rested his forearms on the back.

'Did that interview yesterday,' Augie said. 'With your friend Magnus and this big-deal critic from New York. Got a big kick out of it, I have to tell you.'

'That's nice,' Mulvane said.

If Augie caught the lack of enthusiasm, he didn't let it daunt him. 'It's a game, talking to press. I'd almost forgotten how amusing it is. They ask you questions about what you do, and you're supposed to pretend you can explain it. Then *they* pretend *they* can explain—'

'Augie,' Mulvane interrupted, 'listen, I'm sorry to rain on your parade here, but Ray Yates – how close a friend is he?'

The words, the tone – they killed the mood sure as turning the lights up in a bar. Nina was standing at the edge of the pool, her elbows on the wet tiles; her face socked in again, you could see flesh moving, tightening around her jaw. Augie slapped his sketch pad onto the table and threw the jaunty toothpick on his saucer.

'Joe,' he said, 'that's exactly the kind of question I don't know how to answer anymore.'

'His place was trashed last night. Not a burglary. Whoever did it left a fish on the counter.'

'A fish?' said Nina.

'Quaint Mafia calling card,' said Mulvane. 'There was also a note about a deal.'

Reuben came out with the detective's coffee. It took him no time at all to see that his friends were unhappy again. The spring went out of his step, his face took on a remorseful look, as if he were somehow to blame for the morning's high spirits being dashed.

'What kind of deal?' asked Augie.

Mulvane shrugged. 'Loan sharks kill people who welsh on big debts. Yates owns paintings which, if you're dead, are worth enough to bail him—'

'Are you suggesting,' Nina said, 'that Ray Yates got the Mafia—'

'No,' Mulvane said. 'If he'd got the Mafia, Augie would be dead by now.'

'Is that supposed to be comforting?' she asked.

'Well,' said Mulvane, 'yeah. Sort of. But what I'm suggesting is he might have *tried* to get the Mafia. So I'm asking how well do you know him? Is he someone who could do that to a friend?'

Augie and Nina looked at each other and riffled through their impressions of Ray Yates. Plump, easy-going good-time Ray, Ray who'd always have a drink, another drink, a conversation. Ray with his mellow voice, his flattering talk-show way of asking everybody questions and showing a practiced interest in their answers. Ray who always tagged along. Ray who tried to out-local the locals. Ray who went from place to place and thing to easy, temporary thing, and was a different person in every setting: Ray who was soft and scared and soulless in the middle.

'Poor bastard,' was all that Augie said.

'So you think that means—' said Nina.

'It means nothing,' said Mulvane, 'except that he's a crumb.' He put his untouched coffee on the table and stood up from his backwards chair. 'Good news is, the police are now officially looking for him. Just to tell him he's been the victim of a crime.'

The cop left. Nina shivered, not from cold but from a spasm of disgust. Her skin felt itchy, oily, soiled with the guilt of others. She dropped underwater, kicked out to the middle of the pool, and stayed down as long as she could, cleansing herself, fending off the bright and scorching surface, hiding.

Mood swings are tiring, and the morning's ups and downs left Augie feeling mopey.

He tried to put some finishing touches on the portrait of Fred, but not one brush stroke pleased him, he felt himself dangerously pulled toward muddying up his sprightly greens with brown, and rather than give in to that he put his paints aside.

After that, time dragged. It was four days before the summer solstice, the heavy sun struggled up the highest part of the sky like a fat man climbing stairs, and when it reached the zenith it seemed to pause a long time, panting, and the earth panted underneath it. Fronds drooped; flowers wilted; the blades of ceiling fans labored through the viscous air as though through pancake batter.

Around three o'clock there was a downpour which by rights should have ended the day. But it didn't. The sun was back in twenty minutes, as punishing as before. Steam rose from pavements, from the crowns of shrubs, and in the Silver house a small sin was committed: Everyone gave up on the endless afternoon and waited dully for the release of night and sleep.

After a cold dinner Nina went to bed to read. Reuben cleared the table, did the dishes. Augie stayed up just long enough to watch the early stars come out, and then he too retired.

He was going to his room when he saw something that redeemed the day. He saw Reuben praying.

The young man's bedroom door was open slightly, and behind it Reuben was at his bedside, on his knees. His hands were crossed on the cotton blanket, his forehead lay against them, a lamp on his nightstand threw a soft gleam on his dark and curly hair. He was wearing pajama bottoms and a sleeveless undershirt that showed his delicate shoulders and skinny chest, and he looked like a little boy. His lips moved, his head bobbed slightly as he prayed. After a moment he seemed to feel Augie's eyes on him. He looked up with a small shy smile.

Augie was nonplussed, embarrassed to be caught

watching. 'Reuben,' he said. 'I ... I'm sorry. I didn't mean to disturb you.'

'You do not disturb me,' Reuben said. His hands were still crossed in front of him; he still smiled.

'I didn't know you prayed,' Augie fumbled. 'You told me once you'd stopped believing.'

Reuben nodded solemnly. 'Yes,' he said. 'I stopped. I start again.'

'Ah,' said Augie.

'I start again,' said Reuben, 'because I am here. In this house. I have never known a house like this. There is much life here, much kindness. I must believe God smiles on this house.'

Reuben didn't stand but he lifted his back, twisted his slender shoulders, and turned his head straight on toward Augie. His torso was traced by the lamp's yellow glow, one side of his face shone as if in firelight, the other side was shadowed. It was an image Augie would remember.

'I hope He does,' said Augie. 'Good night, Reuben.'

'Good night, Augie. Sleep well.'

CHAPTER FORTY-TWO

Roberto Natchez dropped Friday morning's paper on his dim disheveled desk and coaxed the top off his Styrofoam cup of *café con leche*. With the usual snarls and sneers he read the dismal unreal news briefs from the outside world, terse by-the-way accounts of coups and famines, scandals and indictments, riots and revolutions. In everything he read he saw confirmation of what he knew: that the truth was everywhere suppressed, fakery in gross but temporary triumph. In Africa as in Russia, in politics as in culture, the appalling pattern held: Lying mediocrity prospered while deep honesty could only fume and seethe and starve, and so it would continue until there was a Liberator clear-eyed enough to show the world its vileness, and strong and cruel enough to root the vileness out.

Approvingly, he examined his scowl in the alcove mirror, sipped some coffee, then turned to the second section and saw the big lead article, its headline sprawled across the whole front page: *Augie Silver – Key West's Greatest (Twice-) Living Artist.*

This sent Natchez briefly back to his looking glass. He did a double take, snapped the paper in what he intended as a gesture of mocking disbelief. Then, with a throbbing pulse in his temple and a quickly tightening knot in his stomach, he began to read.

'Our town,' went Arty Magnus's opening, 'is a cultural mecca with many pilgrims and very few prophets.'

Already Natchez was so affronted that he laughed out loud, erupted in a demonic cackle that hurt his throat. Was it conceivable that this cipher of a local reporter was going to call Augie Silver – a dauber, a decorator – a *prophet*? No, it was too ridiculous, too grotesque.

'Artists come here,' the article went on, 'expecting – what? To be magically, effortlessly infused with the island's atmosphere? To absorb talent by some sort of painless tropical osmosis? Well, it doesn't work that way, as longtime Key West resident Augie Silver can testify. To understand the allure, the resonance, and the dangerous beauty of our corner of the world is a difficult, harrowing – and potentially fatal – experience.'

There followed what Roberto Natchez considered a strained transition to an unctuous, overblown account of Augie's misadventure at sea – and this evoked another derisive chortle from the poet: The man has a trivial mishap in a sailboat, a rich child's toy, and this is evidence of his profundity, this marks him as a seer?

Absurdity followed absurdity in the article. Augie Silver's bland commercial work was described as 'haunting and uncompromising.' His prissy bourgeois house was characterized as 'cozy and devoid of ostentation.' Augie himself – sloppy, haphazard, careless Augie – was passed off as 'a man of unpretentious dignity, who wears his great gift with modesty and humor.'

Great gift? thought Natchez. Ha! A gift for public relations maybe, a gift for facile showmanship . . .

But then the profile took a darker turn. Fame also had its perils, and there had recently been threats, the piece revealed, against the artist's life. The details were withheld, though Arty Magnus allowed himself to observe that Key West had no shortage of crackpots to whom any outrage, from the sickest prank all the way to murder, might conceivably seem justified. 'Indeed' – and here the journalist ended with a flourish – 'such twisted and deluded souls are symptomatic of the untamed hothouse life of the tropics – the life that Augie Silver so powerfully and unsparingly portrays.'

Natchez let the paper fall flat against his desk. He glanced at the mirror and attempted a supercilious smile, but his face was too tense for that, his upper lip did a mad-dog twitch against his eyeteeth. '*Crackpots*.' He said the word aloud, then he gave a bitter laugh that curdled in his windpipe and closed his throat like the taste of sour milk. Crackpots. Wasn't that just too typical? Anyone who took a stand against a fraud like Augie Silver must by definition be a crackpot. What simpler, more insidious way for the mendacious, mediocre status quo to maintain its death grip on the imagination than by pinning the label *crackpot* on anyone who saw beyond its narrow, constipated limits?

The poet did not remember rising from his chair, but he found himself pacing the confines of his small apartment. He paced, he wheeled – and then he saw the Augie Silver canvas still hanging on his wall. Why in God's name did he keep that wretched thing? He wouldn't stoop to sell it – never! – but why did he allow it to sully his workplace? Maybe, long before, he'd kept it as a kind of private joke, a goad, but that was in a less ripe phase of his development. Such frivolity, such an invasion of marketplace crassness, could no longer be abided.

Roberto Natchez had a silver-plated letter opener. He'd bought it many years before; it had struck him as a necessary accoutrement for a budding literary man, though the implement, weighty and portentous, seemed designed for the unsealing of more important mail than the poet ever got. He grabbed it now and stood before the painting Augie Silver had given him in friendship. His face contorted, he raised the blade and let the point of it rest lightly near the center of the canvas, poking at a swath of sunshot sky. He breathed deeply, gripped his weapon as tightly as though he were about to plunge it into flesh, and he slashed. He slashed again and again, the canvas made a rasping, screaming sound as it was rent, flecks of brightly colored paint floated off the sundered cloth like tinsel glitter. He slashed until the picture was in shreds too narrow to hold the knife, and then he stepped back, breathless and sweating, to see what he had done.

The frame had been knocked askew, ribbons of canvas hung down at random angles over the bottom of it. Natchez smiled. He examined the ghastly smile in the mirror, then turned to the painting again. He moved toward it, intending to take it off the wall, smash it, and put it in the garbage. Then he had a different idea. He'd leave it where it was and as it was. Let it hang there in tatters. Let it hang there dead. It struck him as somehow more authentic that way, more in the spirit of the crackpot tropics.

Clayton Phipps had not left his house in four days and was turning a sickly shade of yellowish gray. He hadn't shaved, he'd slept only for brief intervals at odd hours. His scalp seemed to have stretched from the weight of fatigue; a roll of loose skin gathered at the base of his skull, another formed a curving ledge above his eyebrows. When he finally ventured out late on Friday afternoon, the damp white light stung his eyes, and the concrete sidewalks felt bruisingly hard against his feet.

He walked to Augie Silver's house and knocked softly, tentatively, on the door.

Reuben opened it. 'Meester Pheeps,' he said. There was surprise in his voice, though it was unclear whether it had to do with the visit itself or the neat man's slovenly condition.

'Is Augie home?'

Reuben recognized suffering; he recognized repentance. He answered gently. 'He is home. I do not know if he likes to see you.'

Phipps gave a resigned and tired nod. 'Would you ask him, please?'

Reuben left the visitor standing at the door; in deference to his unhappiness, he did not close it in his face. Augie was in the backyard sketching Nina as she swam. He put his pencil down at Reuben's news, and hesitated only for an instant. 'Yes,' he said, 'of course I'll see him.'

There is a kind of fondness that can co-exist with

302

disappointment and that persists even in the absence of forgiveness – a fondness that itself becomes an unexalted but tolerable species of forgiveness – and this is what Augie Silver felt as his old friend came through the French doors and approached him. He looked at the white stubble on Phipps's jowls, the black bags under his sagging eyes, and he found it unexpectedly easy to muster a wry affection. 'Clay,' he said, 'you look like hell.'

The other man managed something like a smile. 'Thank you.'

'Whisky?'

Phipps's shirt was damp, he was itchy behind the knees. 'Awfully hot for whisky,' he said.

'That's obvious,' said Augie. 'Let's have whisky anyway.'

Reuben went for drinks. Nina, dimly aware of muffled voices, peeked above the water just long enough to identify their guest; she decided she would keep on swimming. For a few moments no one spoke; Phipps seemed to be recharging, taking nourishment from the fact that he had been invited in, that he had not been turned away forever. Not until the Scotch and ice arrived and the two men had clinked glasses did he say another word. 'Augie, those paintings. I was thinking. Maybe it's not too late to withdraw—'

'I don't ever want to see those pictures again, Clay.' The artist's voice was soft but it was definite. 'I don't imagine you do either. It's history. Cheers.'

The chilled whisky was both cold and hot; it tickled first and then it burned.

Phipps looked into his glass. The ice was melting so

fast he could see water streaming off the cubes, shimmering pale currents snaking through the brown liquor. 'What happened to us, Augie? To our hale little group of buddies?'

'I know what happened to me,' Augie said. 'Damned if I know what's going on with you guys.' He watched his wife swim. He loved the way she turned, reaching for the wall then becoming a liquid J as she reversed direction underwater. After a moment he said, 'You going to the auction?'

Phipps listened hard for a note of rancor, but he heard no blame. 'I was going to,' he said. 'Now I just don't know.'

'You might want to decide,' Augie said. 'It's three days from now.'

Phipps shrugged absently. 'There's a fellow does charters in a Learjet. Dies in the off-season. Said he'd take me anywhere, anytime for a mention in the newsletter.'

Augie could not help smiling. Incorrigibility might not be the loftiest of human traits, but there is always comfort in consistency. 'Same old Clay,' he said, 'the freeloader's freeloader.'

By way of answer, Phipps raised his glass. But the twinkle in his eye lasted only for an instant. Then his face caved in, his gray cheeks went slack, his voice turned shrill and maudlin. 'Isn't there anything I can do? I feel like such a shit.'

'Don't feel like a shit,' said Augie. 'And no, there's nothing you can do.'

With effort, Phipps leaned forward, put his elbows on

his knees. There was a creaking sound, it was unclear whether it was the furniture or his disused joints. 'Augie, these threats, are you really in danger?'

'D'you think I was grandstanding the other night?'

'Maybe I can help,' said Phipps. 'There has to be some way I can help.'

The painter regarded him. He was fat, he was old, he was bald, he was slow, he was searching desperately for some shred of grandeur within himself. Augie patted his knee and with his other hand poured him half a glass of Scotch. 'Maybe there will be, Clay,' he said. 'In the meantime, drink up, go home, and get some sleep.'

CHAPTER FORTY-THREE

THAT WEEKEND was the hottest of the year.

People woke up sweating, tangled sheets kicked down near their ankles; pillows took on a sour smell, a smell like something from an overcrowded hospital. The wind went dead calm and the clouds melted into a shroud of rainless haze. Asphalt softened; houses swelled; window sashes seized like rusted pistons. The ocean went improbably flat and soupy green; there seemed to be a cushion of milky white between the water and the air, a zone reserved for the vapor that was constantly rising as from a pot about to boil.

At the Silver house a kind of equatorial stupor had set in. The stupor did not undo anxiety but gave a giddy, unreal cast to it. It seemed impossible that someone was trying to murder Augie; it seemed impossible to prevent it. His killing was so inconceivable that it seemed at moments almost not to matter; then the enormity of imagining it did not matter broke through the haze, and another wave of panic surged over the household. The panic gradually subsided into temporary exhaustion; then, after a nap, a swim, the debilitating march of moods replayed itself.

On Saturday night, in bed, naked, uncovered and not touching, Nina said to Augie, 'I so want to believe that somehow, after Monday, this will all be over.'

Augie, depressed and sulky from the heat and the fear, perversely made a joke he realized would not be funny. 'No way,' he said, 'the summer is just starting.'

He turned over on the soggy sheets and tried to go to sleep.

A lot of guys didn't like to work on Saturdays and didn't like the four-to-midnight shift. They had wives, families, girlfriends, boyfriends. They had dinner dates, poker games, softball leagues to get to. Which was fine with Jimmy Gibbs. To him, a day was a day and the evening shift had certain advantages.

For one thing, it was cooler, sort of. As the sun got lower, the steel roof of the washing shed stopped groaning against its rivets. The steam was still as suffocating, Gibbs's short gray ponytail still got glued with sweat against his neck, but at least in the short breaks between spotless rented ragtops a man could drop his chamois and draw a breath or two that didn't scorch his lungs.

Then too the lighting, or the lack of it, was better after dark. Inside the shed, orangy spotlights gave a fittingly hellish cast to the dancing sheets of vapor. Out in the yard, purplish floods, rather feeble and spaced too far apart, cast a weak gleam on the fleet of convertibles that stretched away a hundred yards or so to a perimeter of chainlink fence. Beyond the fence, through a broad gate to which most workers had a key, was an employee parking lot that was barely lit at all.

That was the lot where Jimmy Gibbs parked his truck. Except today he didn't have his truck. Nobody knew it, but he'd walked to work, three miles maybe from Stock Island, carrying two empty five-gallon gas cans. He didn't try to hide them. What was unusual about gas cans in a place where people were always fiddling with cars? He stashed the containers in the washing shed, and when the guy who worked the pump went on break, he casually strolled over and filled them up. Sometime later, after dark, he tucked the cans into the trunk of an anonymous lease-tagged ragtop as it clattered by on the conveyor. He drove the washed car out of the shed and parked it near the others, only a little farther from the purple floodlights, a little closer to the gate. He put the key into his pocket.

At midnight, when the shifts were changing, Jimmy Gibbs went to the employee men's room, slipped into a toilet stall, and sat there till his shift mates had gone home and the new group had settled in. He felt good. Things were going smoothly.

Talking to no one, he walked past the washing shed and through the yard. He opened the gate, strolled back to the car with the gas cans in the trunk, drove it through, got out and unhurriedly locked up behind himself. He felt so calm he even took a moment to find a good station on the radio before he motored away. There was nothing to worry about. Tomorrow he was off, and by Monday he'd be back at work, scrubbing coral dust off fenders and scratching birdshit off windshields, a little tired maybe but neither surlier nor friendlier than tonight, acting like nothing at all had happened.

On Sunday morning Joe Mulvane stopped by the Silver house. His blue shirt was translucent with sweat, you could see the whorls of stomach hair. Ray Yates had not been found; the detective had no news for them; they had none for him. He gulped a glass of ice water and he left.

The white sun climbed the sky, and even Reuben seemed knocked off balance by the pulsing force of it. His movements, like those of a distracted cat, were less lithe and weightless than usual, his relative awkwardness resulted now and then in a small sound – a brushing against furniture, the clatter of a plate – that seemed loud because of its unexpectedness. At moments he was gripped by an antsy drive for projects; he rearranged cabinets, folded and refolded linens. Between spurts of ambition he slipped into a kind of trance, a waking siesta in which his eyes stayed open; he would answer normally if spoken to, yet seemed to be asleep and dreaming. He fell into long gazes at the picture of Fred the martyred parrot, met the bird's red stare and communed with it somehow, seemed to plumb the mysterious space behind the paint in a way that not even the painter had done.

Afternoon came, shadows lengthened. But the sun stayed and stayed, stayed like a draining and obnoxious guest who moved tantalizingly to the threshold but would not go home.

The heat killed appetites, digestion seemed a gross and thankless exercise. Not till evening did anyone think about food. Then Reuben tossed a salad, sliced some fruits. When the three of them sat down at the poolside table, the sky was still flame-red in the west and it was nearly 10 P.M.

The phone rang. Reuben jogged into the living room and answered it. A harsh thick voice said, 'This is Claire Steiger. I need to speak with Augie.'

'Meester and Meesus Silber,' Reuben said, 'they just sit down to dinner.'

'Get him, Chico,' said the agent. 'It's important.'

Reuben paused. He'd gotten unaccustomed to being insulted and realized quite suddenly that he didn't have to take it. 'What you say is very stupid. I will tell Meester Silber you are on the line.'

Augie dabbed his lips and went toward the phone. Nina strode ahead of him and switched the speaker on. 'Hello, Claire,' the painter said.

The agent took no time for pleasantries. 'That little prick,' she said. 'That clever vile sneaky little prick.' She sounded like she'd been drinking, and this was unusual – not for her to have a glass too much, but to let it show, to lose control of her measured tone, her polished diction.

'Who?' said Augie.

'Brandenburg,' Claire spat out. 'The sexless little creep bastard.'

Half an hour before, the agent had come into the city from Sagaponack to find that an early copy of *Manhattan* magazine had been brought by courier to her building on Fifth Avenue. She'd read the piece on Augie and started swilling vodka. It had been such a perfect weekend, that was the bitch of it. Kip was away, off finagling with his bankruptcy attorneys; she'd had her beloved beach house to herself. She'd slept with a south breeze bringing her the sound of surf; she'd wakened to a soft damp mystic light pouring serenely through her gauzy curtains. Two days' peace had been enough to soften her, albeit briefly, to trick her into imagining that things might yet turn out all right, that somehow she could buy back her mortgaged life. 'He's ruined us. The little eunuch has ruined us.'

More than anything, Augie Silver was confused. 'Claire, it wasn't even a review. What could he possibly have said—'

'Nothing bad,' she cut in bitterly. 'Not one disparaging word. That would be too direct for Peter. Too honest. He took a much wormier approach. Here, I'll read you some choice bits.'

There was a pause in which was heard the rustle of glossy pages. Augie and Nina could almost see the clumsy workings of Claire Steiger's drunk and trembling fingers.

'Here, how's this?' she said. '"Augie Silver, a mercurial artist whose each new phase seems almost to undo the work that's come before" . . . Or this: "With a candor that more careerist painters might gasp at," blah, blah, blah . . . Oh, and here's the capper: "After a three-year retirement that saw his earlier canvases become sought-after rarities, he seems bursting with creative drive and has set himself the daunting goal of being "as prolific as the tropics."'

She fell silent. Through the speakerphone it sounded almost as though she was panting, not out of breath but waiting avidly, hungrily, for someone to join in and fortify her pique. No one did. Augie and Nina looked at each other. Reuben had moved away and was staring at the picture of Fred.

'Don'tcha see?' Claire resumed, though of course Augie and Nina did see. The distraught agent raved on anyway. 'It's all in code, and every fucking word of it is telling buyers not to buy, to wait. The older work might turn out to be considered minor, just a warm-up. Then again, you don't think about your career, you could shoot your mouth off and blow the whole thing any minute. And now you're gonna flood the market—'

She broke off finally, blowing air between her teeth, and it was a mercy she could not see Augie at that moment, because Augie was smiling. The smile had appeared gradually, had taken the painter unawares, starting small and then spreading almost to a grin.

'Damnit, Augie,' said his agent, 'say something.'

'Claire,' he said, 'it's only one auction.'

'Only one auction,' she mimicked. 'Only one auction. Goddamn you, Augie, you're impossible.'

She hung up, the speakerphone squawked static at the loud bang of the receiver, and as soon as the connection had been broken the house seemed cooler. A faint breeze slid through the French doors, it carried a whiff of jasmine and chlorine.

Nina waited a moment, then said, 'Augie, why the smile?'

He reached for her, took her forearm in his hand. 'I feel like I've been reprieved,' he said.

His wife just looked at him.

'If someone's trying to kill me,' he went on, 'they'd wait at least until my price goes up again. Don'tcha think?'

Nina smiled wanly. Outside, dry foliage rattled; it sounded not like living leaves but like beans and pebbles trapped inside of pods. Reuben also tried to smile. But he was still staring at the painted parrot, and the bird's red eyes seemed to be saying something different from what Augie said. The young man turned his face away.

CHAPTER FORTY-FOUR

CLAY PHIPPS HAD TAKEN Augie's advice. He'd gone to bed on Friday afternoon and slept through till 4 A.M. on Saturday. He read till dawn, then, groggy and disoriented, puttered in his house and fiddled in his garden before straggling back to bed around five that afternoon. Sunday he again woke up in darkness and went to sleep in daylight. By 2 A.M. on Monday he was all slept out.

His eyes snapped open as they sometimes did when he was in the deepest throes of jet lag. He felt a similar sort of edgy alertness, an energy more delicious because it could not last, a refreshing dislocation; though he was in his own bed in his own house, he felt a freedom that usually came with being far away: He felt he could, if he dared, afford to be a different person, a bolder person.

But bold how? For what? He scratched his belly, looked up at the ceiling, and wondered what was still worth being bold about. His writing? No, he'd blown it forever on that front. His love life? Well, maybe, if a fitting partner ever came his way. But in the meantime he came up with just one answer, and the simplicity of it surprised and pleased him: his friends. It was worth it to be bold and vigilant and insistent upon frankness with his chums. Wasn't it just exactly that sort of boldness that had brought Augie to his door in the middle of the night? That had cleared the air, got them talking again? There was a lesson there, Phipps thought. He had other friendships that were in trouble. What had happened to Yates, to Natchez, to their close if barbed camaraderie? Yates had left town without a word; Clay Phipps knew it only by his absence from the airwaves. Between good friends, it had come to that. But Natchez was here, a mere four blocks away. Why not go to him? Why not hammer on his door, wake him up, grab him by the shoulders, and force upon the poet the kind of cleansing confrontation that Augie had initiated with *him*?

Excited by his own resolve, he dressed by the light of a bedside lamp and went out into the night.

It was close to three now and the moon had set. A filmy canopy of mist slid along the sky, it was visible only by the way it dimmed the stars then thinned to let them shine more brightly. The heavy air carried reminders of the ocean, a hint of fish and seaweed. A stray and unkempt dog lolled by, its tongue hanging, its paws making dry clicks on the pavement, its head down in the shameless skulking posture of the scavenger.

Clay Phipps felt brave and young in the empty streets, he almost strutted. But his knees were not good at stairs, and as he labored up to Roberto Natchez's garret, he used his arms as much as he could to haul himself along the banister. By the time he stood on the third-floor landing, he was sweating and winded. He looked through the skylight at the flickering stars, took a moment to compose himself.

His newfound boldness was a tenuous thing, and his

first knock was a soft one. But no matter – the poet's door, which was not locked or even closed securely, swung open under his light touch. Phipps, nonplussed, fell back half a step, then peered into the dark apartment. 'Natch?' he said.

There was no answer, and something in the way his own voice was swallowed by the darkness told him with certainty that no one was at home. He stepped into the corridor and switched on its dim light. The first thing he saw was a small reddish feather on the floor, the first thing he heard was the erratic whirring whine of an out-of-balance ceiling fan. He inhaled and caught a strange bad smell, a smell from the bottom of a forgotten garbage can.

One small step more brought him to the living room. He switched on the ceiling light and his jaw fell slack. On Natchez's desk was a strangled chicken, its yellow feet clenched and brittle; the bird's narrow head faced back along its spine, a single drop of blood had spilled from its beak and dried on the poet's blotter. Swinging slowly from a blade of the ceiling fan, slightly stretched from the outward force of turning, was a hanged gray cat. It had been hanged with an old necktie, its fur overlay the knot like the loose flesh on an old man's throat; its open eyes were glazed and bulging, its claws were out and just barely whistled as they sliced the air.

Rapt by this dead menagerie, Clay Phipps did not for a moment notice the Augie Silver painting murdered on the wall. When he saw it he could not believe it. He moved closer; the dead cat's tail brushed against his ear as it swung by and he shuddered. He lifted a tatter of canvas; he felt the flaking paint and felt, as well, the rage, the hate. 'Good Christ,' he said aloud. 'It's Natch.'

Dizzy, reeling, sickened, he bolted the apartment and trundled down the stairs. Sweating in the silent street, he turned toward Augie Silver's house and begged his flaccid legs and burning lungs to take him faster than they could.

He was still five blocks away when he started hearing sirens.

CHAPTER FORTY-FIVE

DADE COUNTY PINE is rich in resin and makes good kindling. Houses built from it burn very fast and very hot, with blue and yellow flames that lick their way from board to board and make popping crackling sounds as they sear into the deep hollows of captured sap.

The fire at the Silver house did not seem to have a beginning in either space or time. It sprang up everywhere at once, and there was about it an awful aspect of fulfillment, as though embers had been smoldering forever, waiting with a patient malice to burst forth and consume. Flames crawled up the porch steps and lapped at the front door. In the side yards, sparks shot from knotholes and ignited shrubs and palms; green things hissed away their moisture in the instant before they caught and blackened. A ring of fire framed the backyard like something from an infernal circus; oleanders burned like pinwheels and gave off poison fumes, the great umbrella of the poinciana began to flame, its dainty leaves tore off and flew away like fireflies.

In the same horrifying instant everyone woke up. Augie and Nina, naked, feeling their skin begin to bake and coughing in the strangling smoke, ran into the hallway. Reuben, in his innocent pajamas, was already on his way to fetch them. United now, they staggered into the hell of the living room. Sheets of yellow flame were flapping like ghosts in the windows; here and there panes exploded from the heat. The picture of Fred the parrot turned incandescent in the ungodly light; the bird's red eyes absorbed flame and flashed back blood. There was a low whistling roar as the fire greedily sucked air into itself, leaving less and less to breathe.

Bent low, their hands cupped over their mouths and noses, the three of them moved toward the front door just as the door crackled and began to blaze. They wheeled through the thickening smoke, coughing, choking, eyes tearing and the tears instantly simmering to nothing. Reuben led them over the steaming floor to the back of the house, he picked up a chair and smashed the glass panels of the French doors. Fire was converging on the portal, it was becoming an unbroken archway of flame. Reuben went through first then grabbed Nina by the wrist, then Augie, and pulled them after. There was no way out of the backyard, all its borders were made of fire, black smoke billowed up, rained down, spread its toxins everywhere. Reuben pushed his friends toward the swimming pool, urged them toward the flashing water, the only thing that was not burning.

Weakly, desperately, Nina and Augie dragged themselves across the patch of lawn and tumbled in. The splash of their landing was lost in the sputter and whoosh of the fire, the mild water felt like dry ice against their reddened flesh. For a moment they did not realize that Reuben was not with them.

Then they turned back toward the blazing skeleton of

their home. The tin roof had buckled, entire walls had burned away, the house was ceasing to exist. Against the wreckage of what was left, moving through the indigo smoke sparked with orange flame, they saw a slender form. Reuben was going back in; he was going to rescue Augie's canvas.

'My God,' the painter said. He screamed out Reuben's name to call him back; the sound was swallowed by the fire and the futile whine of approaching sirens, for all its anguish it went no farther than an unfelt prayer.

The young man vanished in the black and choking fog. When he appeared again, the huge prophetic picture of the parrot was on his shoulders and he was struggling toward the doors. But the flames were beyond all boundaries now, there was no inside and no outside, there was only fire everywhere. The fire caught up with Reuben, and when he staggered through the blazing archway, he himself was burning. Yellow flame crawled up his legs; pathetically he tried to run and the flames streamed back behind him; a blue gleam came off his burning hair. He struggled forward then pitched down on the patch of grass; with supreme effort he tried to throw the monumental painting clear of the inferno; it landed very near him, singed but not destroyed.

Augie, dazed, acting without the need of thought, pulled himself from the water and crawled beneath the waves of smoke to the unconscious Reuben. An acrid smell came from the young man's scalp, flames still licked at his back and legs; Augie smothered them with his own wet body, choked back nausea at the unspeakable feel of his friend's oozing skinless flesh. He pulled and rolled the ravaged form toward the coolness of the pool; it left a trail of ash and blood. Nina helped him lower the unmoving body into the water, then cradled it against herself as Augie, weeping, worked desperately to breathe life back into Reuben's slack mouth.

CHAPTER FORTY-SIX

CHARLES EFFINGHAM, the white-maned chairman of Sotheby's, had been in the business forty years and could predict the success or failure of a given sale by the presence or absence of a certain smell in the auction room. This smell needed to be ferreted out behind the aromas that always pertained in gatherings of the wealthy – the round spiced scents of expensive perfumes, the creamy leather musk of the finest shoes and handbags. The odor Effingham sought out was rather less refined. It was a lusty, avid smell; nervous and glandular, it was a grown-up, toned-down version of the soupy stink of prep school dances. It was a smell that happened when people wanted something badly and were willing to be as stupid as necessary to get it.

In the minutes before the opening of bidding at the Solstice Show, the chairman worked the room. He greeted, he joked, he sniffed; he didn't smell much lust.

'I think I'll sit in the back,' he said to Campbell Epstein, the head of Paintings. Epstein got the message; it made his stomach burn and caused the scallop-pattern furrows in his forehead to etch themselves a trifle deeper.

And yet the turnout wasn't bad at all. Perhaps a hundred fifty people were treading the huge Bokhara carpet in the auction room, chatting softly under the Venetian crystal chandeliers. The heavy critics, the important dealers, the big collectors were there in force. Claire Steiger was there, hiding her hangover and her despair. She talked with Avi Klein and several other of her clients, clients to whom she had refused to sell Augie Silvers back when the price was skyrocketing; she felt them gloating now, she smiled but her face hurt. She made a point of keeping far away from Peter Brandenburg, whose calamitous article had already been read by nearly everyone and was the subject of half a dozen conversations in that room. Dressed in perfect linen, distant and impregnable, he stood by himself and made notes in his well-thumbed copy of the auction catalogue.

Among the debonair crowd were a few people who were less so. One of these was Ray Yates. Bearded, wearing sunglasses and an ill-fitting jacket over a palm-tree shirt, he skulked in a corner and avoided the insulting glances of the security guards. He'd been running for his life for almost two weeks now; the habit of furtiveness did in fact make him look decidedly suspicious. And lonely, desperately lonely. So much so that when, just at ten o'clock, Clay Phipps, looking frazzled but not inelegant in a pale yellow suit, swept into the room, Yates almost threw himself against his chest.

The new arrival barely had time to drop a mention of his Learjet ride before the auctioneer pounded the gavel and people were asked to take seats.

The auction began, and it went badly from the start. Works by Larry Rivers and Jim Dine sold for disappointing prices after languid bidding; a Helen Frankenthaler was practically stolen. Campbell Epstein, sitting near the auctioneer at a table manned by unbusy spotters, looked slightly jaundiced. A Jasper Johns was carried for display through a door at the auctioneer's left; no one ante'd up the work's lofty minimum, and the spurned canvas was ignominiously carted back to storage.

After twenty minutes a young assistant approached Charles Effingham and whispered in his ear. The head of Paintings, his yellow tie dancing against his throbbing Adam's apple, watched the chairman rise and leave, and wondered if the sly old boy had arranged to be called away from the debacle.

The sale dragged on; people started looking out the windows. 'The next lots,' droned the auctioneer, 'numbers C-forty-seven through C-seventy-four, are by the contemporary American Augie Silver.'

There was a stirring at the mention of the name, but it was perverse. Heads turned toward Peter Brandenburg; heads turned toward Claire Steiger. As during a streak of lousy weather, people perked up not in hopes of improvement but with a morbid curiosity as to how bad things could get.

'What am I bid,' the auctioneer continued, 'for lot C-forty-seven, an early work, a lovely seascape, eighteen by twenty-four inches? The medium is oils, the estimated value is twenty thousand dollars.'

'Three dollars,' someone said. 'Same as an issue of *Manhattan* magazine.'

An edgy titter went through the room; the auctioneer squelched it with the gavel. 'Serious bids only, please.

324

Do I hear an opening of five thousand dollars for the Augie Silver seascape?'

Silence spread like a fissure in the earth. Ray Yates and Clay Phipps, sitting side by side, looked between their feet and saw their hopes of a windfall slipping down into some black and bottomless chasm.

Finally a plump hand went up. It belonged to Avi Klein. He had a wry look on his face, as if it were intrinsically droll to buy something, anything, for a mere five thousand dollars. No one topped his paltry bid.

The next two works, whose estimates had been thirty-five and fifty thousand dollars, were sold for seven and nine respectively, to another longtime customer of Claire Steiger's, another high roller turned bargain hunter.

Had Charles Effingham still been seated in the auction room, his keen nose would have by now detected a smell of something funky, something feral. It was not the reek of acquisition, however, but the meaner stink of scandal, the nasty excitement of being witness to a disaster, seeing the undoing of a career in art. A fourth Augie Silver was gaveled at less than a quarter of its estimate; a fifth picture did no better. Moment by moment, bid by grudging bid, Augie was being pulled down from the ranks of painters who mattered, was being flayed, shrunk, expunged from fashion, chipped away at like a toppled monument.

Claire Steiger mustered her composure but could not keep her lower lip from quivering.

Then an unexpected thing occurred. As the auction moved on to the later, larger, presumably more significant Augie Silvers, Peter Brandenburg began to bid.

With a gesture so refined as to be nearly invisible, he raised his neat hand inside his immaculate linen sleeve. A spotter zeroed in on his impassive face; after that, nothing more ardent than a slightly lifted eyebrow was required to confirm his willingness to top. Almost before his fellow bidders realized it, he'd bought Jimmy Gibbs's painting for sixteen thousand dollars and one of Ray Yates's for twenty-two.

A quick-fermenting exhilaration mingled with confusion filtered through the room. It was not unheard of for a critic to buy pictures, but it was rare. Critics had power, not money, and while Sotheby's lived on prestige it did not accept prestige as payment. Then too there was the ethics of the thing; it had been, after all, Brandenburg's article that had cast such a pall on the proceedings. But now that the famous critic was bidding, people thought back on what they'd read, and reconsidered. What had he really said that was so terrible, so damaging? He'd said that Augie Silver, an artist who was always growing, changing, was embarked upon a new phase of his work, a phase that promised to be extremely bold, ambitious, risky, and productive. Clearly, Brandenburg was gambling that this new phase would carry the artist to the next level of fame and reputation, the level at which everything the painter had ever touched would be assured of holding value.

While other bidders were reasoning this out, Peter Brandenburg bought Ray Yates's other canvas for twenty-eight thousand dollars, and two of Clay Phipps's pictures, one for thirty-seven thousand, the other for forty-four. The prices were still well below pre-auction estimates, but the gap was narrowing, the numbers were becoming respectable.

And now the bidding livened. The paintings that were left were the prizes: the artist's personal favorites that he'd given to his closest friends, the canvases of special merit that Claire Steiger had been stockpiling. Avi Klein jumped back into the fray; other top-tier collectors joined him. Brandenburg copped two more pictures, but they cost him – the six-figure plateau loomed very close.

It was reached in a phone bid from Japan, and once that magic divider had been crossed, the floodgates opened and it became a different kind of auction. Gone was any thought of bargain seeking; archaic was any notion of buying pictures for less than estimated price. Bidding went from thousand-dollar increments, to five, to ten, to twenty-five. Buyers sweated in their gorgeous suits; the profitable stink of art lust wafted forth. Spotters danced out of their chairs, the auctioneer cranked up the volume, put some syncopated jazz into his patter. A canvas went to Brandenburg for a hundred and twenty-five; the next was bought by Klein for one fifty; the following picture was scarfed up by the absent Japanese for an even two hundred thousand. Around this time Peter Brandenburg dropped out, and the big boys took it as a token of their prowess that they'd subdued him. By some mysterious buoyancy, the price fluttered higher till it transcended the niggardly custom of being reckoned in thousands and entered the quarter-million range. People leaned forward in their chairs, fanned themselves with catalogues, and barely breathed as the bidding on the final Silver canvas climbed ever upward and ended at last at the lofty level of three seventy-five.

When it was all over, the auctioneer pounded his gavel and pounded some more, but the buzz in the room only mounted, a kind of rarefied bedlam had set in, it was a frenzied letting go poised tipsily between catharsis and exhaustion. Everyone, it seemed, was winded, wilted, fidgety – everyone but Peter Brandenburg, whose linen suit was crisp, whose forehead was unlined and dry. He'd bought fourteen paintings in all and spent just slightly over a million dollars that no one knew he had. He'd led the bidding for so long that no one really noticed that all but his last two purchases were bargains. He'd jump-started the auction, then he'd gotten out. He was very pleased. A whole new scale of value had been established for Augie Silvers, and Brandenburg and his partner now had the biggest holdings. The imminent leap in prices would allow them to live very comfortably indeed.

The auctioneer continued to call for quiet; the audience continued to ignore him. Then quite suddenly the door to the left of the auction lectern opened and Charles Effingham, his white hair resplendent, stepped spryly through it. He raised both hands like a politician at a rally to ask for order. The buzz thinned to a hiss of flattered surprise – to be addressed by the chairman of Sotheby's was a rare event – then it gradually subsided. Effingham pushed aside the auctioneer's microphone. With his leonine growl of a voice and his precise clipped consonants he didn't need it.

'Ladies and gentlemen,' he began, 'those of you who deal with us regularly are aware of Sotheby's deep regard for tradition. But we believe, as well, in being responsive to extraordinary circumstances. And in light of what I must say is the exceptional interest occasioned by these Augie Silver paintings, I would like now to do something most unusual: I would like to offer for sale a work not listed in the catalogue – a work, indeed, of which I myself was not aware until a few short moments ago. The work is unframed and off its stretcher. It in no way conforms to our general standards of presentation, yet I am confident you will agree it is in every way a remarkable picture. The house has placed on it a reserve price of one million dollars.'

The chairman nodded toward the open door. Two assistants came through lugging chairs, which they placed some six feet apart near the lectern. Two more employees followed, carrying between them a large furled canvas. They stepped up onto the chairs, signaled with their eyes, and let the picture unfold. The heavy scroll dropped open with a muffled snap.

A huge parrot in biting green looked out red-eyed and all-seeing from a prodigious wanton jungle. The edges of the canvas were singed and frayed, here and there the foliage and plumage were smudged with soot and dulled with ash; yet, like the flaws and cracks of ancient statues, these imperfections somehow increased the work's unsettling power, bore witness to the ravages and dangers of existence and asserted the reckless and undaunted determination to endure.

No one had ever seen a picture quite like this, and there was a kind of nervousness, shame almost, in the rumbling inchoate murmur that greeted it. The painting somehow showed too much, cut too deep, was at once absurd and wise, sacred and wildly uncouth. People wanted to tear their eyes away and could not; the parrot's seared and searing gaze locked on like a strangling hand and would not let go. The murmur mounted, took on something of the character of keening. Then a voice, calm and certain, cut through it.

'It's a fake.'

All eyes turned toward the speaker, who appeared just the slightest bit surprised that he had spoken. With the room's attention pulled away, no one at first noticed the two people who now slipped through the door.

'Why a fake, Peter?' said Augie Silver. His scorched red skin made his dark blue eyes look purple, he was wearing big clothes borrowed from Clay Phipps and they added pathos to his haggard frailty. 'A fake because the real one was destroyed in a fire early this morning?'

'Fire?' said Brandenburg. 'I know nothing about a fire.'

'Yes you do,' said Nina Silver. Her face was taut and scarlet, her legs were blistered beneath the man's shirt she was wearing as a dress. She looked up at the parrot's red and flashing eyes; Brandenburg's gaze ineluctably followed hers. 'Who set it, Peter?' she went on. 'Did you hire someone?'

The room was silent, it was as if the air had changed its character and would no longer carry sound. Time too became something other than itself, it congealed like stanched blood and ceased to flow. Eyes flicked back and forth from Brandenburg to Augie, from Nina to the painting. And in that long suspended moment a sick certainty was growing like a cancer in Claire Steiger. Secretly she glanced to her left and to her right; there were strangers there. There were strangers everywhere, and she was sitting here without her husband. Her hand rose slowly to her mouth as if to hold her insides in. She spoke softly and she looked in no particular direction. 'Kip,' she said. 'It was Kip, wasn't it?'

Peter Brandenburg stood up slowly. His eyes were riveted straight ahead, still locked in a futile stare-down with the painted parrot. He didn't raise his voice. 'He said everything was taken care of. He said everything was just as it should be.'

The security guards moved unhurriedly toward the critic, and the critic made no move to elude them. But he didn't like to be touched, he pulled his elbows back and made it clear he would go without resisting.

The auctioneer pounded the gavel and pounded some more, but it was a long time before order was restored.

CHAPTER FORTY-SEVEN

'IT WAS NINA who figured it out,' said Augie Silver.

They were sitting at Clay Phipps's – their home while their own house was being rebuilt. It was a steamy evening at the beginning of July, the air smelled of closed, defeated flowers, and the ceiling fans turned lazily, heavily, seemed at every moment to be winding down. Joe Mulvane, his blue shirt splotched with sweat, leaned forward in his chair with his elbows on his knees. Claire Steiger sat on the sofa with her legs tucked under her; her dandelion hair was round, her face was round, her curled body was relaxed in comfy circles. She was vacationing at the Flagler House, recovering from many disappointments, and yet she seemed serene. Clay Phipps had had his living room painted; gone were the lewd, accusing rectangles where Augie's pictures had been hung; gone with them seemed to be Phipps's penchant for self-blame, the nagging self-disenchantment that led him to do things that were blameworthy.

'Really it was Reuben who figured it out,' Nina said. 'The way he seemed to know it would come down to that painting.'

Augie nodded. There was wonder in his face like the wonder of seeing the full moon lift red and mottled from the Florida Straits. 'Yes, that was remarkable,' he said. 'But the real breakthrough – that was yours.'

Joe Mulvane leaned forward a notch farther. 'Excuse me,' he said, 'but I guess the detective's always the last to know: What was the breakthrough?'

Nina paused, savored the moment. She'd gotten younger in the last couple of weeks. Her skin had healed, her husband and her life were safe; she'd been swimming every day and she was full of joy. 'You know how it is,' she said, 'when you lock yourself into a certain way of looking at a problem? The way, after a while, you're stuck with that approach, whether it gets you anywhere or not? Well, we'd been assuming all along that whoever wanted to hurt Augie was trying to drive the prices up, so they could sell. Then, the night of the fire, the timing of Brandenburg's article, it suddenly dawned on me that the plan was to drive the prices *down*, so they could *buy*.'

'*Then* sell,' put in Clay Phipps.

'At a vast profit,' Augie added. 'And very soon, so Kip could meet his July first obligations. The choreography had to be quite precise. When Kip set the fire, he timed it so the auction would happen before the news of my death had reached New York. Peter buys low, then I'm dead, and boom, prices go crazy. They turn the pictures over almost immediately.'

Mulvane considered. 'But at the beginning, with the poison tart—'

'At that point,' Augie said, 'things were simpler. Kip was working alone then. His plan A was to kill me far enough ahead of the auction so he'd make his money on the pictures Claire had.'

The dealer shook her head in self-reproach. 'I encouraged him. I'm the one who planted the idea that, handled right, the auction could bring in enough—'

Augie reached over and patted her knee. 'Claire, Claire, you're my agent, don't ever blame yourself for jacking up my price ... But anyway, when the tart killed Fred instead of me, Kip started getting worried that he was running out of time, that he needed a different strategy. That's when he persuaded Brandenburg to come aboard.'

Claire Steiger frowned. 'Another thing I did,' she said. 'Threw the two of them together.'

The others let that pass.

'The turquoise ragtop,' Nina said. 'Kip drove it, but it was rented with Brandenburg's ID. Brandenburg didn't own paintings, we had no reason to put him on the list of names to check.'

'And the picture on the license?' Mulvane said.

'When someone looks as rich as Kip, clerks don't check things very closely,' said Claire Steiger. 'Besides, there's a more than passing resemblance between them – that same kind of constipated preppy handsomeness. Probably that was part of the attraction.'

'Attraction?' said Clay Phipps. 'Don't tell me they were an item.'

'Oh, God no,' said the agent. 'Nothing so straightforward as that. But I think there's no question that Kip had him in some crazy kind of thrall. Maybe it was in some way sexual. Probably it was. But who knows what that means between a straight, stiff, married man and a cold-fish eunuch who can't even bear to have a friend pat him on the wrist?'

There was a pause. The ceiling fan turned slowly, heavy air seemed to spiral down from it like something solid. Outside, sagging fronds scratched sleepily against tin roofs.

'I can see it,' Claire went on. 'Long close talks in the locker room after a good hard game of squash. Kip starts talking about business, about deals – he makes it sound extremely exciting and adventurous, amoral, heroic. I can see Peter being totally mesmerized, aroused in his way, at the idea of dealing with deeds rather than words for a change.'

'Not to mention,' Augie said, 'having Kip bankroll him with borrowed funds so he could finally make some money to go with his clout.'

'Yes,' said Claire. 'I imagine the thrill wears off having one without the other. And if you think about it, Peter and Kip made a formidable team: a critic with an incredible ability to manipulate the market, a wheeler-dealer with an incredible ability to manipulate the critic.'

'So say they'd pulled it off,' said Joe Mulvane. 'What then?'

Claire shrugged. 'Peter – who knows? Maybe he'd have run off to Tahiti, the south of France—'

'Maybe he thought,' Clay Phipps put in, 'that Kip would run off with him.'

'He might have thought that,' said the agent. 'Kip wouldn't be above leading him to think it. But I can't imagine it would've happened. They would've had to hide the partnership, of course. And if Kip had raised enough to buy his way out of bankruptcy, he probably would have had some new stationery printed up and gone back into business.'

The mention of bankruptcy made Claire think about her beach house. Her eyes went vague and she stopped talking. But the sadness seemed to pass right through her, she held it no tighter than the sun holds clouds. She'd put herself through this a thousand times and had finally realized, what the hell, it was a wonderful house but it was just a house. She began chatting again as though someone had asked her a question, though no one had.

'And me, I'm starting over. Fresh. The big apartment – gone. The Sagaponack house – gone. I'm moving the gallery to a smaller space, I'm getting rid of all the debt that asshole got me into—'

'But you know, Claire,' said Clay Phipps, 'some of that debt went for very worthy causes.'

'Like?'

The host decided not to mention how much of it had gone toward his own quite affluent retirement. 'Like fifty grand of it,' he said, 'saved Ray Yates's life.'

'He paid off Ponte?' asked Joe Mulvane.

Phipps nodded. 'After commissions, he came away with forty-five thousand. He paid back the forty he owed – and I think he's already thrown away the extra five. Some people just don't learn.'

'Yeah,' said Joe Mulvane, 'but other people do. Jimmy Gibbs, for one. Maybe I'm a jerk for thinking this, but I think he's really got a shot.'

'The deal's done?' Augie asked. 'He bought the boat?'

'Made the down payment,' said the cop. 'Now all he's gotta do is find customers and stay on the wagon.'

'Will he?' Nina asked.

'He loves that boat,' said Mulvane. 'And besides, it's part of the deal that was cut with the car company. He stays sober a year, they'll drop all charges.'

Augie shook his head, and said, not without affection, 'I never figured Jimmy for a car thief.'

'He wasn't one,' said Joe Mulvane, 'till he gave up believing he'd ever see any money from your painting. Then he got it in his head he owed himself a bunch of cash. Heard about the stolen rent-a-car racket and liked the arithmetic: five grand a car at the loading docks in Jacksonville, a pat on the back and no questions asked.'

'How close did he come to going through with it?' asked Clayton Phipps.

'Got about as far as Boca,' said Mulvane. 'Then he stopped at roadside to pour in some of the extra gas he'd brought – he didn't want to pull into a station and take a chance on getting the tag spotted. That's when he decided he was too old to become a thief. He drove back and confessed.'

Augie rubbed his jaw. 'Solstice weekend,' he said. 'The weekend everyone went crazy.'

'The weekend Natch went crazy,' said Clay Phipps.

'Better crazy than killed,' said Joe Mulvane. 'To go to Cuban bars in the middle of the night and try to rabble-rouse . . . Was this guy the last person in the world to figure out there's no more gung-ho American on earth than a refugee Cuban? He comes in and starts sounding like a Communist, like Fidel . . . He's damn lucky to have landed in a nice cushy private nuthouse and not the morgue.' He paused, then added, 'But something I don't understand. Supposedly this guy was a struggling poet. How does he end up in such a pricey nuthouse?'

Nina looked at Augie. But Augie didn't want it known that he was funding his deranged friend's treatment. He just said, 'Natch isn't a bad person. Just frustrated. Misguided.'

'Misguided,' hissed Joe Mulvane. He was a homicide cop, he didn't have much use for words that were excuses. 'Some are misguided. Some are weak. Or jealous. Or downright evil. You can say some are worse than others, but they kill somebody, dead is dead.'

'Fair enough,' said Augie. 'But I'll tell you something – I'm very grateful for two things. I'm very grateful to be alive, and I'm very grateful it wasn't one of my good friends that was trying to kill me.'

'Amen to that,' said Clay Phipps.

'And Joe,' Nina added, 'we're very grateful to you. I'm not sure we've ever thanked you properly for all you did for us.'

Joe Mulvane was not especially good at accepting thanks; it was also true that in this instance he believed in his heart that he had utterly failed. 'I did nothing for you,' he said. 'I couldn't prevent an arson, a tragedy . . .'

The words pushed air out of the room. Eyes stung and for a long moment there was nothing left to breathe. When Augie finally filled his hollow chest it was with the rapture of some great hunger sated, some great gift acknowledged and given thanks for. The air had come to smell of jasmine and dry shells.

'Reuben,' Augie said. He said it softly, he shook his head in awe. 'What a remarkable person. The only truly unselfish person I have known in all my life.'

The remark was aimed at no one, but it made the others squirm.

'He'll be all right?' Claire Steiger asked.

'He'll be all right,' said Nina. 'He'll have a long recovery, a hard adjustment. But he'll be all right.'

There was a silence, a long moment of reflection and regret that could only end in fidgeting and thirst. Clay Phipps cleared his throat and rose. 'What say we have some old Bordeaux?'

Augie Silver had remembered how to sweat. He mopped his forehead. 'Awfully hot for Bordeaux,' he said.

'Awfully damn hot for anything,' said Joe Mulvane.

'It is,' said Clay Phipps, moving toward the kitchen, 'but goddamnit, let's have Bordeaux anyway.'